STOLEN ⌐ı THE SHADOW KING

Kingdoms of Lore: Underworld

ALISHA KLAPHEKE

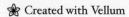

For all the women who don't yet realize they are the most powerful one in the room

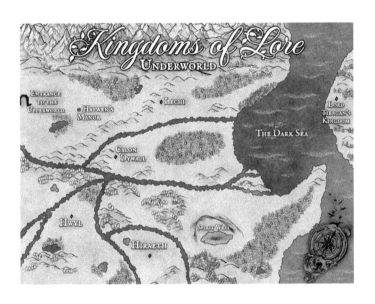

CHAPTER 1

T his was a terrible idea. Maren was doing it anyway.

She gripped her oaken wand—the deep grain familiar against her skin—and stared into the Between's billowing fog. A cool breeze touched her cheeks and forehead, and she gasped at the biting chill. All scents disappeared. The misty clouds shifted with the shapes of spirits. The spirits looked just as they had in life, though now they were almost colorless, and their bodies emitted a pale, blue-white glow, the details of lips and eyelashes a shade darker. They talked quietly to one another and walked in clusters, some disappearing at the borders of the Between as new ones grew visible. This place existed between the Underworld and the land of the living.

Maren cleared her throat. "I call the Shadow King, Ruler of the Underworld."

Every spirit rotated to face her, and a chill scrambled down her back. She couldn't see them clearly, but she imagined their looks of shock from the way they whispered in quick bursts.

Maren nodded. "I know. I'm a bit mad. But I'm sincere. I call the Shadow King." She clicked her tongue and searched the churning mists of white and gray. "Any time now..."

Her bones shivered inside her clammy skin, and she sighed. She wished he would show up. She wasn't standing here in this deep and dead cold howling his name for the joy of it. The entire fate of the world depended on finding out what Aury's vision from yesterday had meant, and only the Shadow King could answer such a question.

But it seemed he didn't care to help out this day.

She moved her wand across the space in front of her. "Return."

With a jarring slam, her spirit returned to her body in the land of the living. She blinked and looked up into the branches of the Sacred Oak. Clothed in autumn's gold and brown, the Oak hummed, its power permeating the air and reverberating lightly through the ground under Maren's boots. Aside from the hum, a woodpigeon's coo and the shuffle of the turning leaves overhead were the only sounds in the Forest of Illumahrah.

Maren walked to the Oak and set her hand on the trunk. Her wand shivered in her grip, knowing its mother. All wands came from the Sacred Oak, given magically to witches in this kingdom and, sometimes, beyond. The Source, the High Power, had set this tree into the world to serve as a conduit for all magic.

Breathing deeply, Maren enjoyed the flow of magic simmering through her human witch blood. The power was warm and soft, tingling along her skin and sparking lightly over her palms and between her eyebrows. She was trying very hard not to panic about the vision, about the reason she'd visited the Between, and the magic helped a good bit. Maybe the vision was wrong. Maybe it was nothing. Maybe the world wasn't actually going to end suddenly and horribly.

She returned to the dusky-hued pony she'd borrowed from the fae court. With a flick of her wand and a sharply focused imagining of a ripe apple, Maren magicked a treat for the creature. Her palms and the spot between her eyes warmed with the flow of power. Once the pony had gobbled it down with her soft lips, Maren sheathed her wand at her belt, mounted up, and began the short ride back to her found family.

At the Agate Court stables, two fae lads not much younger than Maren—who was just eighteen—were mucking stalls, their horns and pointed ears showing through their tied-back hair. Maren tried not to stare. She was still getting used to seeing non-human beings. She'd always known they were around, but none lived in her home kingdom of Wylfenden. Here in the kingdom of Lore, humans with no power, human witches like her, elves, and fae all lived in relative harmony. A smile pulled at her lips. It was fascinating, and it was downright impressive that even with all their cultural differences, they didn't explode into violence.

The pony's shoes clomped over the cobblestones as Maren led her under the archway's green-painted runes of safety and healing. The cobblestones had been set into patterns that showed the elemental magics—air, water, fire, and earth.

Swirls of lighter stone within the shiny black rock represented air. Air could help one leap higher or sense current or future events.

Water and fire appeared to fight one another, carved stones as sharp as the tips of flames intermingling with rounded blue-tinted rock laid out in whirls. Their powers were best for fighting, but water also helped some scry.

To display earth, brown and dark gray stones formed oak leaves and a single branch that circled the entirety of the design. Earth power took a different form with each person. It varied rather alarmingly from simple weavings for making clothing to wielding legendary wooden swords for shifting the very ground like the goddess Vahly did once upon a time.

Witches like Maren touched all magics but found that certain affinities were stronger than others. Maren had always been a little air and a little fire. Air helped her speak to and see the spirits. Fire had been of help during the battle they'd recently fought, though her power in that regard was nothing outstanding.

In the grooming stall, Maren took a wide brush from the rack on the wall and began brushing the pony down, a pleasant chore. Her magic couldn't manage such specific, little spells as tidying a horse, but she didn't mind the work.

The stable hands glanced her way and whispered something in the fae tongue. She couldn't speak their language, but their narrowed eyes told her enough. No one really liked to be around the Deadspeaker. Maren wasn't clear on why exactly. Perhaps they were afraid she would hear something they didn't want her to know, or maybe it was just that she was close to death and her presence reminded them of their mortality. Fae lived a long, long time though, so one would think they'd be at ease. It could be that the longer one lived, the more precious every day became.

"Careful how you look at me, lads," Maren said. "I might just summon up your great-grannies, who, I'm certain, taught you better manners."

Their mouths popped open in shock. They turned away and began filling buckets with feed, all muttering silenced.

Maren went back to her brushing.

"Thanks for not taking off while I was working today, Pony." She couldn't remember the animal's name, but the pony didn't seem to care. "I know it had to be incredibly off-putting to see a lifeless body just standing there." When she visited the Between, her body was nearly dead with just enough spirit left in it to keep her alive and able to return.

The pony snorted, and Maren set to combing a cluster of dark burrs from her mane.

"Your Highness!" One of the stable lads had stopped his mucking and bowed at the waist. He straightened, eyes shining with awe.

Princess Brielle of Wylfenden and Balaur, Maren's best friend, walked in, her red hair lifting in the morning breeze. "How is the new foal doing? I didn't realize I'd be here long enough to see him born."

"Meetings upon meetings still, eh?" Maren peeked her head around the corner of the cleaning stall. She hadn't told Brielle about the vision yet, so the princess was blessedly ignorant.

"Maren!" Brielle hefted her skirts, ran over the cobblestoned ground, and enveloped Maren in a vicious hug.

Brielle had rescued Maren from the Wylfenden king's dungeon—from Brielle's own father—and Maren had befriended the amazing woman right away, loving the way she wasn't like any other princess. Brielle might have been wearing a fine gown of emerald, decorated in fox fur, as befit the soon-to-be queen of Balaur, but Maren knew well Brielle wished to be in trousers and digging up ancient artifacts high in the mountains.

"Why are you brushing out your pony?" Brielle's face turned stormy, and she whirled on the bug-eyed stable hands. "Do you dare to insult my dearest friend, the Deadspeaker? Show some respect and take care of her mount immediately."

"Apologies, Your Highness," the lads mumbled as they tried to take the brush from Maren.

"Eh!" Maren held the brush up high even though she was shortest of them all and it made little difference. "I'm taking care of this pony. I'm fine, Princess," she said to Brielle. "I enjoy this kind of thing."

Brielle smiled warmly, took a second brush from one of the stable lads, and joined Maren in the chore. When they finished and handed the pony over, Maren followed Brielle out of the stables and toward the side entrance to the Agate Palace, home to the fae court.

"So many discussions today at court," Brielle said. "If I hear one more old man say the word *negotiation*, I might die."

Maren wasn't envious of the meetings that Brielle had to endure, but sometimes she secretly wished she could pipe up with an idea or two. Right now, though, she just wanted to get back inside without Brielle asking what she'd been up to.

"Why were you riding alone? I would have come with you had you waited an hour."

Blowing out a breath, Maren decided not to lie, exactly, but to keep some of the truth back until she had more answers. "I needed some quiet time to myself with the Sacred Oak."

Brielle nodded. "It's amazing to be so close to the center of the worlds."

The Sacred Oak held everything in place with threads of magic that reached through the earth and sky and sea. It was the keystone of existence.

"I'll miss it when we go back to Balaur." Maren lived in the mountain elf kingdom of Balaur with Brielle, who had married the High Prince there.

Maren popped her knuckles, her head aching. If yesterday's vision was right, was there any point to returning to Balaur?

CHAPTER 2

With a tray of her freshly baked cinnamon rolls in hand, Maren walked into the great hall. Banners in obsidian and deep emerald stretched along the ceiling's wooden beams. Below, by a snapping fire, a group gathered around a chess board at one of the round tables. She'd normally be excited about a lovely afternoon by a fire with friends, but Aury's vision—and the fact that Maren had tried to summon the Shadow King and had no idea what effects that might have—threw a black cloak over the whole day.

It was definitely a time for baked goods.

She snagged one from her tray and chewed it greedily, savoring the spicy black cinnamon and the rich butter. The texture was perfect too—chewy but not overly so. She wasn't amazing at archery or chess, but she could bake cinnamon rolls good enough to die for. Her time in the palace's kitchen had been helpful in clearing her mind, as it always was. When she rolled dough and measured ingredients, her mind calmed, and she could think.

Aury—Princess Aurora of Lore, the one who had seen the terrible vision—stood, tucked her water mage staff against her chair, and made a beeline for Maren. Her staff was also a gift of the Sacred Oak, Mother of all Trees and the Source's Conduit. Everything was tied to the Oak.

Goddess Vahly, Maren prayed silently to the earth goddess, *if you can hear me, please help us…*

Maren didn't pray often, but when she did, she wholly meant it.

Aury's blue eyes said she wanted to know what had happened at the Oak today, and she wanted to know immediately. Though Aury was a friend, Maren still did her best to make the silver-haired princess happy. Water mages, though human like Maren and Brielle, were known for their insistence on being in charge, and Aury was far more demanding than any of them.

"Not here," Maren whispered. "Later."

Aury took a cinnamon roll and gobbled it down, rolling her eyes with pleasure. Once the bite was swallowed, she bumped Maren with a sticky hand. "So you don't know any more?" Her lips pursed, and she glanced from Maren to Brielle, who was talking to the group animatedly. "We can't tell them about the vision?"

Maren veritably dragged Aury to the table, which wasn't easy considering the tray of sweets. "No. Not yet. Let's wait." She really didn't want everyone panicking about the end of the world before she and Aury had more time to find out if it was worth the agony.

Aury huffed and took the tray from Maren to set it on the table. "Fine. But—"

A fae servant ignored Maren to refill Aury's goblet with wine that smelled like roses and dangerous choices. Brielle—seeming to notice the fae servant's impolite behavior toward Maren—grabbed the goblet sitting beside her husband's elbow and handed it to Maren with a tight smile.

"Thank you." Maren took a swallow and let the warmth of the drink chase away the last of the Between's chill. Visiting that place was like taking a swim at Frostlight. "Eh," she said, tugging the servant's sleeve, "stop acting like my uncle George."

The fae servant wrinkled his nose. "I am sorry. What did I do?"

"You acted like a horse's arse." Maren gave him a withering look. "I don't care if you think I should or shouldn't be here, but I do care if you don't give me wine. And some of my friends breathe fire, so..."

Swallowing, the servant glanced at Dorin, High Prince of Balaur and Brielle's husband. His ferocious look was pretty handy sometimes.

The servant bowed and apologized quickly before scurrying away.

Lifting her wine to Dorin, Maren tsked the fae court at large, then took another sip.

Dorin studied the servant who was leaving the hall, his light hair golden in the firelight. "I'll talk to the fae council about the staff's behavior, Lady Maren."

He shuffled his dragon wings and settled back into his chair beside Brielle. The fair-haired and slightly scaled Dorin was not only a mountain elf but an elven dragon shifter, the blood of the ancient dragon clans active in him like in no other. He'd spent years in the highest altitudes studying the creatures closely, so closely, in fact, that his proximity had somehow ignited the sleeping magic inside him.

"Oh, I'm sure that'll work. The fae are so compliant," Maren joked.

The group chuckled as they devoured her cinnamon rolls and moaned with pleasure.

After eating two, Filip moved a knight on the chessboard. His opponent, Brielle, growled and stared at the pieces. Prince Filip was Dorin's brother and Aury's husband. His pointed elven ears moved slightly under three rows of tightly braided hair, and his sharp elven teeth showed as he grinned. The warrior prince was winning.

Dorin had switched to studying Maren now, as many often did. Though she could never say the elven dragon prince was afraid of her—or of anything, really—he did seem to view her as other, for lack of a better term.

Of course, none of them truly understood the connection Maren had to the spirits. They didn't even ask her about it.

Aury could have asked what exactly the Between was when they'd first discussed Maren's plan, but no, Aury had simply gone along with it and refrained from digging into what Maren's magic was. Maren knew Aury, just as the rest of them—except Brielle—kept a sliver of emotional distance because of the power Maren had to communicate with the spirits.

"Are you just waiting on the next meeting?" Maren teased, knowing all of them preferred other activities to long, drawn-out negotiations.

Her friends were not simply going through the motions of royal work though. They were embarking on a true and lasting peace between Wylfenden and Lore. Their work to develop farm shares and trade between foreign guilds had thus far saved many from starvation and decreased the death rate in the lower and middle classes across the continent.

Not only had they helped Maren escape in the spring, they'd also brought down the tyrant who had been Brielle's father.

These were heroes here.

Was Aury's vision a chance for Maren to be a hero? Or was she being arrogant even thinking that?

Maybe she and Aury should tell the others the truth now.

They'd have ideas on what to do, surely. But not all of the events Aury saw when she scried came true. Or at least, the events could be altered somewhat by action or circumstance. She was a powerful water mage, but the future wasn't set in stone, as Aury always said.

Nonetheless, the vision Aury had described had sent a plague of nightmares to Maren every single evening since then. Maren gripped the cool stem of her goblet and fought off a shiver. How much time did they have? Aury hadn't even told Filip about the vision yet. She'd gone straight to Maren because of the details.

"Lady Maren," Filip said, his gray eyes bright, "what

move should I make next?" Filip was a warrior first and a prince second. He never stopped chatting strategy.

Setting her goblet down, Maren went around the table and put a hand on Filip's chair. She leaned over the board and winked at Brielle across the pieces. With one hand behind her back on her sheathed wand, she touched the board with a fingertip like she was simply bracing herself a bit. The black and white squares blinked in and out, faster than most would notice, and the pieces shifted here and there. Suddenly, Brielle was a move away from checkmate.

"Take down her sacred man," Maren said to Filip, pointing to the piece with the slanted cut along its tapered top.

"Interesting choice." Filip tapped his chin and did as she suggested.

Brielle swooped in and moved her pawn into place. "Checkmate!"

Filip chuckled good-naturedly. "Of course. Why did I think you two would ever be on opposite sides?" He stood and smiled. "Anyone in the mood to wrestle? Or swords? Dorin?"

"I could be persuaded." Dorin dusted crumbs from his hands, gave Brielle a quick kiss, then tucked his wings and moved away from the table.

Dorin and Filip decided on a small boundary for movement, then locked arms and began the Balaur art of wrestling. Maren had to laugh. If the fae queen came in now...

As Dorin's wings spread wide and Filip hooked a leg around his brother's knee, Aury pulled Maren aside.

"We have to talk to everyone," Aury said.

"Something else happened. What are you not telling me?" Maren cracked her knuckles as a cold sweat bloomed along her back. This was definitely getting out of hand.

CHAPTER 3

Maren focused on Aury's face. Dark circles ringed Aury's eyes, and her cheeks had lost their usual pink.

"I saw the vision again," Aury said.

"Was it the same?" Maren asked.

Aury nodded, fear lancing through her eyes. "And it was clearer. That tends to mean the event is more likely to occur and is closer to being painfully true."

An imaginary dagger pierced Maren's chest. She reached for Aury's hand, wanting the comfort of her new friend's touch.

The vision Aury had seen in the water had shown the Sacred Oak collapsing into the earth, the world turning to gray ice, and the Shadow King cursing his ringless left hand.

Aury had viewed magic turning to lifeless cold and the very end of existence.

Now, Aury gripped Maren's fingers tightly and gave her an encouraging smile.

Dorin and Filip were at an impasse, one with a foot at the throat and the other with talons set to cut through the inner thigh. Both brothers were laughing about it, joking in their quick Balaur tongue. Usually, they spoke Lore—the common language.

Maren cleared her throat and addressed the small group. "We need to talk. Can you clear out the staff?" She jerked her head at the two servants standing at the doors to the hall.

Dorin untangled himself from Filip and waved them off. They bowed and scurried away as fast as their feet could carry them.

Aury spread her arms and began to detail what she'd seen in her scrying bowl. "Gray ice was devouring the world. Every tree. The land. The people." A shudder went through Aury, and her jaw muscles tensed and moved. "The Sacred Oak fell, dead, I think." Several people whispered oaths, shock threading through the room. "And the Shadow King was there. It was... It was the end of the world."

It sounded even worse now, hearing it like this, in front of everyone. Brielle, Dorin, and Filip were bristling, looking more than ready to start another war.

"That is..." Brielle's mouth moved, but it took a moment for her to speak. "That is not good."

"Spot-on observation, my friend," Maren said. "But do you have any ideas on what to do about it?"

Brielle seemed to shake off the shock. "How did you know it was the Shadow King?" she asked Aury. Her face had gone deathly pale. Everyone knew he was the king of the Underworld.

"I just know," Aury said. "The scrying told me, somehow. I don't always fully comprehend this area of my power."

Brielle nodded too quickly.

Dorin swallowed, looking ill, then leaned on the table, lacing his talon-tipped fingers. The firelight glowed through the thinner expanses in his wings. "You believe this vision you've had," he said to Aury, "that it means the end of everything. Of this realm and the Underworld."

"I do," Aury said, quieter than Maren had ever heard her speak.

Filip's head fell back, and he shut his eyes, his hands flexing into fists. "It can't be. This can't be the end." His eyes shot open, and he gazed at Aury with such passion and devotion that Maren had to look away. She could only imagine how it would feel to know the world was coming to an end and you only had a short time to spend with the love of your life.

Dorin, eyes glazed with deep thought, went to Brielle and stood by her, only their hands linking. Brielle bit her lip, unshed tears glistening on her eyelashes. Somehow, the more subtle show of care hit Maren more powerfully than a dramatic kiss would have. Just those fingers entwined... Maren's heart ached for them. Their relationship was so new.

Clearing his throat and swallowing again, Dorin set his gaze on Maren. "We know little about the Underworld. A few stories here and there, but..."

"Does anyone here know more about the Shadow King besides the fact that he is the king of the Underworld?"

Maren asked. "Even though I'm the Deadspeaker, I don't know much. Tell me anything. Everything. Even if you," she said to the room, "always thought what you heard or read was just a story. Even the tiniest detail might help."

"He's not human," Aury said, shrugging. "He's an elven man."

Like Filip and Dorin were. Maren, Aury, and Brielle were human, but they had plenty of experience with elves. Humans could be witches, water mages, or powerless. Elves generally had the ability to run faster, see farther, and were incredibly tough to kill. Fae were different entirely in that they had the ability to heal.

Aury exchanged a look with Filip. Maren secretly wished for someone to look at her that way.

Grabbing her goblet of wine, Aury began pacing. "I would bet all that the fellow is painfully handsome."

Filip barked a laugh. "Leave it to my wife to think of flirting when death is breathing down the backs of our necks."

Aury smiled sadly to herself and kept pacing. She was hiding her panic, but Maren could see it in the way she walked with her arms tense and her shoulders bunched.

Shaking his head, Filip raised his eyebrows and rubbed his chin. "I hate good-looking enemies. I'd much rather cut down a monster that looks fittingly grotesque."

Maren crossed her arms and tried to keep it together as fear slithered down her back and circled her ribcage tightly. She decided Aury's idea to joke was a good tactic to keep from screaming. "Just because the Shadow King is incredibly dangerous doesn't mean he has fine looks."

Aury raised a silver-blonde eyebrow.

"Fine." Maren shrugged. "Perhaps danger gives him a leg up."

Brielle's gaze went to Dorin's talons. "Danger ignites passion."

Maren steeled herself, attempting to breathe despite the grip fear had on her. "All right. Let's focus on the task at hand."

Filip stood beside the fire, looking down into the flames. His hatchet, the weapon he preferred in battle, hung from his belt and reflected the flickering light. "Costel read a scroll about the Underworld king's origin story once." Sir Costel was one of Filip's men. One couldn't keep the academic-turned-warrior out of the library.

"Of course he did," Maren said.

"Costel informed me," Filip said, "that the Shadow King and his folk are shadow elves."

"I've never heard of shadow elves." Maren took her wand from her belt and pretended to wipe it clean. She really just wanted to feel the comforting warmth of its magic.

Filip glanced at Maren. She liked the second prince of Balaur quite a bit. He was humble but brave and loved life like Maren did—always ready for a dance, a good drink, or a walk through the woods. He was a good friend. "Neither have I," Filip said. "Costel told me they're a race of elves with a magic unlike anything in the realm of the living."

"If they're elves," Maren said, "they're alive. But they're in the Underworld. I'm confused."

"Me too," Aury said. "And we'll ask the Shadow King when he shows up."

"When he what?" Brielle stood, her red hair falling from her loose braid.

Maren huffed a laugh. "You make it all sound so casual, Aury. I realize you are both a princess and the Magelord, but aren't you just a wee bit afraid of this fellow?"

"So you're going to summon the Shadow King with your power?" Dorin asked Maren, his gaze more dragon than elf at the moment.

Maren held her wand tightly in one sweaty hand. "I already tried once."

Nervous glances flew from person to person.

"I plan to try again," Maren said, "and I'd like you all to be at my side. I won't lie. I'm afraid. Very afraid." The way the spirits had stared and gone silent when she'd tried to call the Shadow King had put her on edge.

Aury grinned. "I like fear. Sharpens the senses."

Filip came up behind Aury and wrapped a protective arm around her.

Maren whistled. "We are very different. But I love your honesty, water mage."

"And I yours, witch." Aury smiled, but the serious nature of what they were dealing with seemed to dampen the light in her eyes. "We aren't that different. You bore easily."

"How does that play into fear?" Maren asked.

Aury glanced down at the scar on Maren's forearm before her attention shifted to Maren's face as if she were studying her. "You're willing to deal with some fear in exchange for a diverting adventure."

Maren snorted. "I'll give you a gold coin if you call the Shadow King diverting when he arrives."

"I'll do it for your cinnamon roll recipe," Aury said.

"You're going to bake?" Maren asked.

"I have cooks." Aury crossed her arms.

"Spoiled princess," Maren said, grinning.

Aury pinched Maren teasingly, then the moment flew away, leaving behind only their joined fear of what was to come.

Brielle pushed her hair behind her ears. "Well, what are we waiting for? Who knows how much time we have to figure this thing out? It might already be too late."

"To the Sacred Oak, then?" Aury asked.

"And the entrance to the Underworld," Maren said, hoping she wasn't about to get them all killed.

CHAPTER 4

The Sacred Oak's limbs reached far past the hallowed ground to the dark of the pines and green-black ferns. Beyond the Oak, emerald-colored moss cloaked a rocky hill. Most believed the hill marked the entrance to the Underworld.

Maren was trying quite hard not to run screaming while Aury and Filip were busy arguing about the Shadow King and whether or not he was generally a foul fellow.

"Why do we think he's dangerous though?" Filip stood a few feet back from Aury, his hatchet ready. "That's all I'm saying. He could just be a man doing his work. No more than that."

"Right," Maren said, taking Aury's side. "The King of the Underworld is probably a real sweetheart."

Filip laughed darkly, and Aury, staff in hand, shushed him as she walked closer to Maren. The rest of the group made a half circle around them but gave Maren and Aury a bit of space.

"You want me beside you, yes?" Aury asked, spinning her mage staff.

"Since you scried this problem," Maren said, "it might be good to have you at my elbow. I have no idea how this will progress. If he asks me something about your vision, I want you close by so I can pop back and discuss it with you quickly. Plus, I feel better having you watch my body while I'm in the Between. I didn't love being alone doing it yesterday. Not here, near the Oak and the Underworld's hill."

Aury nodded and glanced back at Goldheart, her horse.

"If anything happens, we have all of them at our backs," Maren said, jerking her chin at Filip, Brielle, and Dorin.

Aury raised her chin, her eyes blazing with that look of determination she always had before a fight. "You're running this campaign. I'm your second. But if this goes south, get on horseback fast. I want you able to flee if we end up in a fight. We have no idea what the Shadow King is capable of."

Maren exhaled. She could do this.

A shudder wrapped her in cold arms.

The Between welcomed Maren in quickly.

Spirits clustered at the edges of the Between, their whispers quick and full of fear.

"Hello," Maren said, trying to sound calm and confident. "Sorry to disturb, but..." Now or never. "I summon the Shadow King."

The spirits disappeared from view. Only the

billowing mist remained. Maren gripped her wand and returned to the land of the living.

"Nothing?" Aury asked, rubbing Maren's cold arm to bring back the blood flow.

"No, but the spirits disappeared." Sweat slicked Maren's hands. She couldn't stop shaking. "I don't know what—"

Thunder drummed through the ground and air, startling an unkindness of ravens from the Sacred Oak.

"What is that sound?" Brielle asked, raising her voice to be heard.

A strange wind howled, low and mournful, from the rocky hill beyond the great tree. Goldheart and the other horses bucked and reared, and Maren dropped her wand. She tried to move to retrieve it, but fear had her frozen in place.

Black shadows shaped like the roots of an ancient tree peeled away from the shady places in the wood and gathered as the wind rose and the howling grew louder.

"Maren!" Aury's silver hair lashed around her face in the sudden gusts while she raised her mage staff. "Go to Goldheart! Mount up!"

"But my wand!" Maren knelt and searched the leaf-strewn ground.

A voice like a storm shattered Maren's thoughts. "Halt, Awenydd."

The man's words, bladed and curt, were in sharp contrast to his melodious, strange accent. Ice slid down her spine. Who was Awenydd? Did he have her confused with someone else?

"You are mine to claim." Sitting atop an ebony steed

in a newly formed crack in the legendary hill, the owner of the voice had long night-black hair and dark eyes filled with a light like glowing coals. Obsidian-hued shadows twisted and tapered around him like massive, writhing roots.

Maren couldn't shout, but her mind whirred, one fact in particular rising to the surface.

He was the Shadow King.

Her heart frosted over and refused to beat.

He kicked the horse and galloped toward them.

Aury lashed out with her staff and threw a wall of ice around Maren. The clear material showed a blurry Filip, who shouted a battle cry. Horse hooves cracked and smashed the ice. The Shadow King looked down at Maren, his eyes glowing a ruby red. Filip wheeled his axe at the Shadow King as Maren dug in the leaves for her wand and swore with every foul word she'd ever heard in her entire life. The Shadow King raised a shimmering black sword, then cut into the hill of earth beside him.

The ground exploded.

Beyond the remnants of the ice wall, black dirt rose and threw down Filip, Dorin, and Brielle, shrouding them in earth. Only Aury and Maren remained free. Aury ran to Goldheart, mounted, and turned her horse toward Maren, who was chained by terror.

The Shadow King's sword, night-dark and glittering, held clumps of plant roots and mud. That sword had moved the ground, just like the goddess Vahly's oaken sword in the ancient stories. Maren could hardly believe what she was seeing.

"Maren! Here!" Aury thrust her staff upward, sending rippling blue magic toward a pine above the Shadow King's head. The water from the bark and needles and cones oozed from the tree to fly toward the Shadow King in the shape of a million tiny arrowheads.

Maren spun, scrambling and climbing up behind Aury on Goldheart, her wand forgotten. There was nothing to do but flee.

Dorin's dragon wing appeared through the churned dirt, and he broke free, breathing citrine fire at the Shadow King, who had thrown up a tangle of shadows that deflected Aury's ice arrows. The Shadow King drew his mount sideways in an expert move, evading the fire. Brielle and Filip struggled, then escaped. Brielle drew two knives from her sheath and threw them. The Shadow King's swirling magic pulled the knives from the air and tossed them down like they were nothing. With his ebony steed rearing and pawing the air, he drove his sword into a boulder. A boulder! The rock trembled, shattered, and spun in a storm toward Filip, Brielle, and Dorin.

Then the Shadow King was suddenly riding beside Maren and Aury. Rough hands seized Maren by the waist, and Goldheart reared as the Shadow King pulled her from the mare. Maren bucked like the horse, and the back of her head cracked against the man's face as he held her against him. He grunted but didn't release her. Instead, he spun his steed in a tight circle and headed toward the hill.

Aury shouted, her voice laced with rage and panic. The stream near the Sacred Oak rose like a giant hand, then a mass of cold water snatched Maren's leg. The man shouted something dark and jagged in another tongue, and the magicked water splashed to the ground. As they rode past a slope, he dragged his sword across the grassy knoll. A ferocious rumbling issued from the earth, and Filip shouted as Dorin roared. Aury and Brielle screamed Maren's name, but their voices were already fading. Maren couldn't twist to see what had happened.

"What did you do?" she shouted at the Shadow King.

The steed's hoofbeats thundered as they galloped toward the hill.

The crack in the rock was too small. They were going to smash into it.

And Maren was trapped in the man's brutal hold.

She dug her fingernails into the hand braced across her ribs like a vise. She was strong and had grown up farming and hauling in fish, but her efforts didn't budge his iron grip.

She said a desperate, hurried prayer to the Source just before they smashed into the wall of rock.

The expected pain did not come.

The moss and the hill were gone.

Light-pricked shadows like storm clouds swirled around them. Fear and wonder battled for Maren's attention. She shook from head and toe, but she resumed her frantic fight, cursing the man in every language she knew.

"I didn't realize the Shadow King operated like a

common brigand," she snapped. "And I am Maren the Witch, not Awenydd. You have the wrong person!"

The root-like shadows shifted, and he pulled his mount to a stop. He slid from the horse, lifted her like she weighed no more than a bundle of clothing, and set her—almost gently—on a stone bench. She drew a ragged breath as he moved toward double doors that glowed with runes. All else was darkness.

He whispered over the runes. At the touch of his long fingers, the markings—unlike any runes she'd seen before—glowed a brighter blue. They flashed red, then he started speaking a little more firmly to the doors in a language she didn't know.

He glanced at her. "You're the one who acts as a brigand and who knows nothing of decorum, Awenydd. You don't deserve this boon, and I am loath to set it upon you."

Maren prayed he didn't see the wild trembling of her fingers. She couldn't see him any more clearly than she could this place. What in the name of all the goddesses was she supposed to do now? "Lovely speech from someone who violently abducted an innocent woman."

"There is a way of doing things in the Underworld, and it does not include shouting for me in the Between. Your blatant disregard of propriety during your summoning has set the spirits on a dangerous path."

"Forgive me for not being aware of the precise etiquette for a task no one in the history of our world has done! Now, tell me what you did to my friends back there! Did you...you didn't kill them, did you?" Her eyes stung. The earth had completely walled in the place where Brielle, Dorin, and Filip had been fighting. Could they dig their way out, or were they dying right now?

The Shadow King whirled away from his work on the runes to face her.

Rage chiseled his features into a frightening mask. The points of his ears showed between the thick strands of his hair, and deep within his dark eyes, a wine-red light glowed.

He was utterly terrifying and completely stunning.

His full lips pulled back from a set of straight teeth to show elven-sharp incisors, his mouth now inches from hers. Warm breath dusted her cheeks, sending a tingling sensation down her body. She leaned closer without intending to do so, her lips parting, her heart pulsing in a strange, slow rhythm.

She tried to clear her thoughts, to remember what she had been thinking before he stood this close, but it was impossible. Her mind and body were drowning in his presence, the scent of him, the feel of his power...

"You, Maren the Witch, are the Oracle, the Awenydd, and you," he murmured, his gaze sliding down her temple to her chin, then along her neck, "will learn our ways or die trying, my queen."

A bolt of shock snapped her out of whatever trance she'd fallen into. "Your what?!"

CHAPTER 5

"I'm sorry, did you just say your *queen*? And what is the Oracle or the Awenydd?"

What was he talking about? The chill of fear remained fully present in Maren's heart, but confusion now battled for her focus.

He snarled and pivoted away. "Even your tone is insulting. Typical Upperworld folk. You don't care for anything beyond your realm."

"Must I once again mention how you abducted me? Did you hit your head on something on the way here? Did some of Aury's ice get through those shadows of yours?" Her heart cinched tightly at the thought of them under the dirt, fighting to unbury themselves. "I demand to know what you did to my friends, Arse of Shadows."

The runed doors opened with a gust of storm-scented wind. The elven lord grabbed her and forced her to remount the black steed. He climbed up, settling behind her, and they rode through the magicked passageway, the runes casting an eerie light on the horse's tangled mane.

"Your friends," he said, pronouncing the word as if it were poison, "were simply encumbered. They will live unless they refuse to dig their way out like the low beasts that they are."

A breath left Maren, and she relaxed somewhat. They were alive, then. At least she had that to hold on to. She was too relieved to concoct another lovely insult for this madman.

Under the blush of a twilight sky, rich green meadows extended from the doors and beyond a rippling, sparkling river bordered by tall plants with dark indigo leaves. Tiny dots of blue light glittered along the banks, a sight she'd never seen. Were they glowing mushrooms?

She'd expected a cave, tunnels, mud, and darkness. But this was nothing like that. She'd never seen anything like this. It was as if someone had taken the kingdoms she knew and painted them in colors from a dream world.

Mountains like great ocean waves marked the distant, wispy fog, and a crowd of pale blue flowers surrounded a massive castle with a lengthy curtain wall, a portcullis, and four round, peaked towers. It was like a combination of Loreton Palace's regal architecture and Balaur Castle's rugged edges and stern face. She'd expected only death and decay here, not this sharp beauty.

To the east and west, several towns held clusters of low, stone buildings with roofs of slate and thatch. They were too far away to see clearly.

Shock stole her of speech as surely as he'd stolen her from the living world. "But it's all so...alive..."

"The spirits are only one element of the vibrant Underworld, Awenydd."

His scent encircled her like a spell of its own, a spicy sweetness that made her think of dark corners and fevered touches. She shook her head.

What in the name of the Source was she thinking?

Maybe this feeling of desire, this urge to lean into him, to breathe him in, was part of his magic. It had to be. She wasn't the smartest woman in the kingdoms, but she was wise enough not to swoon over the King of Death. Goddess above, she'd nearly asked him to call her Maren despite the very real fact that he was her abductor! Hearing him say her name would be as frightening as—well—the Underworld. A hysterical laugh almost escaped her lips. She had to flee. Now.

He stared, those burning eyes narrowed. "We are shadow—"

"Elves. Yes, I know," she said. The point of one ear showed between his smooth, dark locks of hair.

"Do you?" he asked sardonically.

He spoke in the Lore tongue—the common tongue —not Maren's native Wylfen, and the way he spoke the language was very different from the way Aury, a Lore native, did. His accent dipped in unexpected places, and something about the sound of it, the way his tongue seemed to curl around the vowels... She'd die before admitting it, but his voice sparked a heat in her.

"We aren't all fools aboveground," she snapped.

The lift of his severely slanted black eyebrows said he disagreed heartily. "You don't even use your true title. Deadspeaker is a disgraceful term. You are the Awenydd."

She wanted to say she didn't like the change, but she did. Awenydd or Oracle did sound rather more pleasant. "How do you even know what they call me?"

"I heard the foul name shouted once. A long time ago..."

His tone had turned mournful, and if he hadn't been a complete nightmare, she'd have worried he'd lost a dear friend because of the very word Deadspeaker.

But as it stood now, she didn't give a rat's right toe. All she could think about was whether or not her friends were all right. Alive was one thing, but who was injured? Had they suffered from the shadow magic?

The king continued. "We shadow elves are fully alive." His quick words made him sound like a tutor tolerating his most hateful student. "And we are mostly immortal, as are the animals of this realm."

"Splendid." She ground her teeth. Never mind how she had ended up beside the Shadow King, perhaps they could solve the riddle of Aury's vision. "Princess Aurora saw a vision in her scrying bowl. I'm sure you know about it. What is happening to the Sacred Oak, and how you are involved? I also wouldn't mind a quick run-through on why you are kidnapping me. I'm here and prepared to help fix whatever is going on with the Source's Conduit of Power."

He nudged the horse with his heels and looked toward the castle near the pale blue poppies. "You are prepared to dedicate your life, then."

Her heart jumped and hit the back of her throat. Umm, what? Her life? "Oh, definitely."

She leapt from the horse and ran in the direction of the rune doors.

Had he lost his mind? Perhaps he was lonely and her non-shadow-elven self was the only one around that might fall for his lusty magic? Running faster than she'd ever moved in her life, she prayed she could work with the doors' runes despite her lack of a wand.

Black shadows spiraled around her torso, the tendrils' touch as soft as a whisper, then she was frozen in place, held tight by the Shadow King's dark embrace.

He walked around to face her, looking much like a man who had paid for a sweet cake and received a scorchpepper.

"I'm the one who summoned you," she said, barely able to move her jaw. "It's not like I don't want to help stop whatever horrors are coming. Aury saw you and the Sacred Oak during her water scrying. Talk to me. Stop being a monster."

What did he mean when he said *to dedicate your life*? She imagined a bloody knife and chanting...

The shadows carried her toward the horse. Her boots brushed the tops of the plants, and though a good portion of her body hummed with desire because of this mad king's foul magic, she forced herself to think only of murder. His, in particular.

She glared at the beautiful Underworld as he seated her on the horse in front of him and they rode onward with the wind in their faces. At least the heat of anger had eased the cold of fear. She would escape this fiend, and if her guess was right, Brielle, Aury, and the rest were already fighting to find a way to help.

"Sleep," the Shadow King commanded.

"Not likely," Maren said, but then the world faded, and she lost the fight against his strange magic.

HAZY MINDED, MAREN WOKE FROM A LOVELY DREAM of gentle hands to find herself in a four-poster bed hung with gold-threaded linen curtains. High ceilings and dark wooden beams lorded over smooth stone walls and brightly colored tapestries showing waterfalls, misty forests, and fields of wildflowers. It actually resembled Balaur castle's interior—her new home at court within the mountains with Brielle and Dorin. She'd expected all darkness in the Underworld and cold, not the beauty of a finely decorated room.

Large beeswax candles flickered in every corner, and a small fire snapped in a hearth decorated with petals carved into the rock. Who knew the Underworld king's castle would be warm? A large coat of arms hung above the fireplace—black tree roots encircling a castle gate on a field of pale blue with black diamonds spread about.

Sitting up, she ran a hand through her hair,

expecting the usual morning tangles. Her hair was thick and quickly became a rat's nest each night. But her locks were smooth and newly brushed.

She swallowed, the peaceful feeling slipping beneath a crashing wave of panic.

She was trapped. In the Underworld.

With a king who insisted she had to *dedicate her life*? What did that mean? Was he going to kill her and offer her to some demon of shadows she'd never known existed? The way he'd taken her and attacked them at the Oak spoke to his penchant for violence.

She touched her face only to feel her skin freshly washed and free of the debris from the madness of her capture. Had the king ordered his servants to brush her hair and wash the dirt from her face while she slept under his spell?

Flinging herself out of the bed, she looked down to see she was dressed in a fine sleeping shift. He had changed her clothes. Or had a servant do it. Either way, she was angry.

And what had they done with her dirty clothes? Brielle had given Maren the split dress she'd been wearing. It had been a birthday gift.

No matter how lovely this room was, nothing about this situation was tolerable. Heat built behind her eyes, and she searched for something to throw or an item that might be good for stabbing. A candle holder. That would work for now. She pinched out the flame, dumped the candle on an ornately carved desk, then upended the heavy metal holder, gaze on the double doors.

"Come visit your guest, dark lord," she whispered, shaking in spite of herself. She tried to pretend she was silver-haired Aury or redheaded Brielle with their courage burning through her veins. "This guest has a gift for your face."

CHAPTER 6

A quiet knock sounded. "Awenydd? May I enter? I have something to break your fast."

It was a soft, female voice. Maren lowered the candle holder. She didn't want to murder an innocent shadow elf. Maybe she could shove her way past the woman and escape. But she had no idea where she was or how to get out of the Underworld. Sighing, she tucked the holder under her coverlet. She needed information before acting. A tiny voice in her head mentioned the end-of-the-worlds problem.

"My lady?" The voice sounded stressed and thready.

"Enter," Maren said, doing her best to sound like Brielle did when she spoke to her ladies-in-waiting— confident but not monstrous.

One of the double doors opened, and a maid stood there with a shy smile. The maid had pointed ears and the same gray eyes most elves had. Her gaze didn't have that odd occasional glow like the Shadow King's eyes did. Her cheekbones were quite sharp and she didn't blink very often—both things Maren had noticed in the Shadow King as well.

Maren stood on tiptoe to see beyond a maid. In a room at the end of a twisting corridor, someone walked past, someone dressed in black. Her breath caught.

It was him.

He shifted his stance, and the side of his face and one shoulder showed. He took a deep, slow breath, his gaze distant and downcast. What was he doing out there? He appeared horribly sad. Was it because of the Sacred Oak and the death coming to them all?

Maren snorted at herself. Yes, of course it was.

"Why won't he just discuss this problem with me?" she hissed at the maid.

The maid—dressed in a well-tailored dress and a clean white apron—ignored her question and bobbed a curtsey, then she set a round tray of steaming greens, roasted potatoes, and a large crockery pitcher of what smelled like white wine on the table by the hearth.

"Welcome to Calon Dywyll," the maid said, "castle home to our king and master. I hope this serves you, my lady." Pulling a goblet from her apron pocket, she blinked at Maren, her eyes wide. She curtseyed again. "I'm sorry for my staring, but I've never seen a human." She paled. "Oh, I shouldn't have said that."

Maren didn't mind. It was such a pleasant change of pace to have servants being kind to her rather than resentful of her non-royal self being set up nicely in places where one normally had to possess a title. "I'm not insulted. I've never seen shadow elves except for my abductor."

The maid smiled shyly and tucked a strand of strawberry blond hair behind her pointed ear. "If it pleases you, you can call me Eefa."

"I'm Maren."

"I can only call you Lady Maren, my lady, Awenydd, or queen. By order of the king."

Maren fell into a chair and picked up an eating knife. "Fine. Surprised you let me have this." She wiggled the blade in the air. "I could kill you and escape, couldn't I?"

The maid giggled like she thought Maren was teasing.

"No, seriously. What's keeping me from that plan?" She made stabbing motions and showed her teeth.

Laughing fully now, Eefa pushed the goblet of wine closer to Maren's elbow. "You don't have an evil presence, my lady. I trust you already."

"You really shouldn't. What did you do with my dirty clothing? My dress was a gift, and I..." She stopped because Eefa's face had fallen.

"We burned your dirty clothing, my lady. I am so sorry if that displeases you."

"Burned it all? Why would you do that?"

"It was quite filthy, and the king doesn't want you wearing anything less than the best."

Maren fisted her hands. Her dress from Brielle was gone.

"I'm so sorry," Eefa said.

"It's not your fault." It was Eefa's king's doing. Maren stuck a potato, then ate it quickly. The herbs were different from anything she'd ever tasted, almost bittersweet but good. "What herb is in this?" she asked, reluctantly curious. "It's like rosemary, but not quite the same flavor."

"Gwraidd brith. Um, that would be...speckled root in your tongue."

The taste was almost familiar. It had a pleasant kick to it. "It's addictive."

"A little is good. Too much will sour the stomach. I would think you could eat it all, but I don't know enough about humans."

Maren carefully returned the fourth herbed potato back to the tray, then took up a bit of the greens. They were good too, but nothing to write home about. She had definitely sped right past sanity and into madness. Why was she eating and thinking about herbs when she was trapped in the Underworld?

She rubbed her temples and took a few deep breaths. There was a solution to this. Already in her young adult life, she'd survived her parents' deaths, a legendary dungeon, and a major battle. Surely, she could find a way through this situation too.

After making the bed, Eefa opened the armoire beside the bed and pulled out a long black gown. The maid brought it over and set the bodice across the arm of Maren's chair. Tiny rectangular rubies glittered across the neckline and down toward the waist in patterns of curling smoke and billowing clouds.

"That's beautiful." It pained her to say it because she was trying to hate everything here, but it was true. She liked Eefa and she liked the dress, no matter how she wished she didn't just to spite the king.

"It is. The king ordered it made for you when he learned about you."

"Hold on. I thought he didn't know about me until I summoned him."

"You shouldn't have done that, if you don't mind me saying. That was badly done. The spirits are in a fuss about it, and there'll be work all night to once again put them at ease."

"Well, let me fix it. I'm the Awenydd, after all." She didn't relish the idea of attempting to appease angry spirits. She'd rather flee to the nearest pub. But for years, she'd communed with the spirits. She didn't want to upset them. The king could kiss her back end, but she wouldn't mind making it up to the spirits and mending the damage she'd done. Plus, maybe she'd learn more about this world and what she needed to do to save the realms and get out of here.

"That's not up to me, my lady," Eefa said.

"I understand."

Perhaps once Maren dressed, the king would call for her and explain everything. One caught more bees with honey, as the saying went.

"Fine," she said to Eefa. "I'll swathe myself in the gorgeous gown from the kidnapping king." Maybe with good behavior—that phrase made her ill—she'd lull him into thinking she was malleable then wring his pretty neck until he told her everything she needed to know.

She allowed Eefa to clothe her and braid her hair so that it sat high on her head.

"I feel taller," Maren said.

"You could never be called tall."

"Honesty. Good. That's my favorite thing about a person. Even when it cuts a bit."

Eefa's cheeks flushed. "Apologies."

"Don't apologize. I meant it. Thank you, Eefa. You've been kind. What's the king's name?"

"What?"

"I don't even know the name of the man who stole me from my world."

Eefa looked to the doors like she worried he'd walk in and slice her head off. "Kynan Meilyr Islwyn. In the Upperworld language, it means Chief Man of Iron Under the Grove."

"Rolls right off the tongue."

The maid's eyes went hazy, and she grinned. "You're so lucky. I can't imagine bedding a man like him. Oh!" She covered her mouth with both hands. "I definitely shouldn't have said that. Please..."

Maren swallowed against a sudden lump in her throat as Eefa curtseyed. The maid stayed there, low to the ground, until Maren took her hand and lifted her.

"You can say what you want to me, Eefa. I'm not a queen. No matter what the king says. I'm a fisherman's daughter and a human witch." Eefa's face was red as a berry, but she nodded. Poor thing looked ready to cry. "Truly. Speak freely to me," Maren added.

Eefa nodded, but her voice shook as she said, "Is there anything else I can get you?"

"A way out?"

"If you leave, we die, Awenydd."

A chill swept over Maren's skin, and she heard the truth in Eefa's words. "Why? I don't understand what is happening. Will you tell me? Why did he take me instead of simply talking with me? Why is he holding back information?"

"I'm not permitted to speak like that with you. Please don't ask me too many questions. Now, I've been instructed to lead you in a few exercises in decorum so you know how to behave as befits a queen of the Underworld."

"I'm sorry, what?"

Eefa smiled nervously. "Take this." She pulled a small book from her apron pocket and set it on Maren's head. "Walk the room ten times with the book in place, by order of the king."

Maren bowed her head and caught the book as it fell. "I don't think so."

"The king demands you practice good posture and the walk of a lady."

Heat built behind Maren's eyes. "The king can—"

Eefa grabbed her hand, then released it quickly as if she shouldn't have touched Maren like that. "Be careful." She looked to the doors, eyes wide. "He will hear you. You do not want to make High King Kynan angry."

"I have no desire to start a fight with a god..." Maren didn't think of him as a god, but many humans certainly did. "But let me tell you right now that I will not be walking about with a book on my head like a daft ninny to please anyone."

"Please, my lady. Do it for me. My king is a good man, and I must do my duty to keep my position here."

Maren gritted her teeth. Good man. Right.

"Please?" Eefa reached for the book, her gray eyes large and sparkling like elven eyes always did. The tips of her slightly pointed ears gave away the tremble running through her.

Maren set the book on her head and fought a snarl. "Fine." She walked the room and did perfectly well. Riding horses and sailing had given her all the balance and agility she needed to pretend to be a fine queen. Now, what would an actual royal, trained from childhood to command, plot, and be generally aware that they were head of the pack, do in this situation? Gather information. It was worth another try...

"Eefa," she said on her final turn around the room, "you can tell me why I must be here and why you call me queen. The king will never know you said a word because I won't tell him." And since they had called her *queen*... "If I have such a title, don't I have any power here? Can I order you to tell me what in the name of the goddess is afoot here in the Underworld?"

That's what Dorin would have done while Filip used his hatchet on the doors. She wished they were here; she wished they were all here, every last one of them.

"I truly cannot speak of it." Eefa smiled sadly. "You're to read the tomes there on the table and prepare to discuss them with my lord king at dinner sometime in the near future, mimicking his use of the proper utensils and tone of voice." She gathered the tray and left quickly, locking the doors behind her.

"Perfect. Sounds delightful."

Smart woman to leave. Maren was ready to tear someone's head from their shoulders. "I have lived at court for almost seven months," she muttered. "And who cares which fork one uses for thine precious prawns?"

She paced the chamber, fear and anger welling in her chest until she was about to burst. She drank more wine, put another log on the fire, then sat at the desk to write down everything she could remember about Aury's vision in the water.

She tapped the end of the quill on her lip. *The Sacred Oak collapsing into the earth.* Collapsing? Was that the word she'd used? What else had she said? Did she mention any damage or seeing any particular magic in the vision?

Cracking her knuckles—a nervous habit she'd had since childhood—she tried to think. It was as though her mind had been strung out on a line like laundry. Every thought was pinned too far from the next, and each time she almost recalled something new, the memory stuck together in all the wrong ways. It was the shock of being taken here. She knew the feel of shock, had felt it for a long time after the murder of her parents at the hands of those who hated magic. The loss of her wand wasn't helping either. It was like a limb had been rent from her body.

She took up pacing once more, treading the stone floor so many times that eventually she'd memorized every bump and mark from the bed to the hearth to the window. The twilight sky had faded to the deep violet dusk of early night. How long had she been there? The sky hadn't changed overmuch. How did light work here? The same sapphire glow of the mushrooms at the river's edge now dotted the meadows beyond the castle's grounds. It was odd that the castle had no walls and—

The glowing plant life threw light onto a shifting barrier of darkness. The castle did have walls, barriers formed entirely of shadow magic. She swallowed. How powerful was this king that he could hold a spell like that as he slept? Did he sleep? She imagined his deep voice and the way his shadows had lifted her like she didn't weigh more than a handful of oats. An odd sensation fluttered through her chest. She couldn't name what she was feeling, only that it was impossibly both uncomfortable and pleasurable.

Suddenly, the grounds surrounding the keep went pale gray.

The earth had turned to ice.

She stumbled back a step as the icy gray flickered and turned back to blacks and greens and blues. Like it had never been there at all. Had she had a vision? Or was the gray ice already attempting to spread? What was holding it back?

"Are you all right?" Eefa said from outside the double doors.

"Yes. Why?" Had they seen it too?

"Because...there are some disturbances around the castle." Muffled voices echoed beyond the doors. "All is well, my lady queen," Eefa said.

Maren went to the doors and tried to open each in turn. They were locked, of course. "Eefa? What's going on?"

But there were no sounds in the corridor anymore.

Finally, Maren gave up asking the doors questions,

and she sat at the desk again. She scratched the quill across the parchment, recording the only other bit of Aury's vision that she could remember: *World turning to ice.* Her penmanship was atrocious, but she was still proud of learning to write under the tutelage of her mother, who had grown up in a merchant's house. She reread what she'd written. That wasn't exactly what Aury had said about the vision. Aury had worded it differently. And there was definitely more, but the memory refused to solidify.

Maren threw down the quill and began cracking her knuckles again. She wasn't built to be a mysterious heroine of the world. Brielle would have recalled every single syllable of Aury's words, and that woman adored saving the day. Maren could imagine her shouting strongly worded suggestions to Dorin. Maren chuckled sadly, her throat tightening.

Maren would escape this room and force the king to talk to her.

Grabbing up the heavy candle holder she'd stashed in her coverlet, she decided to break off one of the door handles and see what would happen when she really angered the Shadow King.

CHAPTER 7

Maren rammed the candle holder into the iron latch, and the mechanism snapped, most of it clattering to the floor. She winced at the sound, suddenly wondering what she was thinking. If he found her out of her room, he'd just call up those shadows again, and she'd be right back where she was. Maybe stealth was in order here. She'd gather some information by snooping about. With no more pin to hold the handle from moving, she swung the right side door open easily and crept into the corridor.

The castle was quiet. Too quiet. Maren strongly preferred happy chaos to silence any day.

No guards stood watch, and only the hiss and snap of a few oil lamps lit the room where Kynan had been when she'd glimpsed him earlier. She slipped down the cool stone floor in her bare feet, gown bunched in her hands. Slowly, she peered around the corner and into the room.

It was a study of sorts with a large round table,

shelves of scrolls and thick tomes, and a dark wooden chair facing a hearth. The table held a scattered array of parchment pinned down at the corners with smooth river stones. A book with green binding lay open beside a leather pouch. She hurried over and began sifting through the items in the bag. She found a gold coin marked with lines that might have been some sort of rune she wasn't familiar with, a tiny wooden box filled with dried blue poppies, and two rings made of a deep red material she couldn't name. The parchment nearest her was written in the Lore tongue—what Eefa had called the Upperworld's language.

After checking over her shoulder to make certain Kynan wasn't skulking about, she set to reading.

The roots of the Sacred Oak bond the worlds above and below and beyond. When the tree suffers, the people, creatures, and spirits suffer.

Nothing new there. She moved that parchment aside and began studying the next. But it was written in some language she didn't know, a language with harsh lines and curves, dots over numerous symbols, and sentences that never ended. She tried to sound out the first word, guessing at pronunciation.

"Gwehyddu'r gwaed..."

"Back away from the Binding page," a deep voice rumbled out behind her.

Her pulse leapt in her throat. It was him.

No magic unspooled from him, no shadows or thrall-type of power. But even when he wasn't using his shadow magic to soothe or tempt, his presence continually affected her; it made her want to get closer and to submit. Obedience was definitely not her nature, no matter how fine he looked. Perhaps he had high royal elven blood. The god Arcturus held that power. So the draw she felt to him at times could be born of three sources: shadow magic thrall, which he could control; the allure of his royal blood, which he could not control; and the one source that stemmed from her alone— simple attraction.

Kynan's dark hair was tousled and mussed, his eyes burning onyx and ruby again, and he wore only a pair of tight-fitting breeches that left little to the imagination.

She cleared her throat. "Listen, Shadow Arse." Her voice cracked, and she looked over his shoulder so she didn't have to stare at that body of his. "I've worn the dress. I've walked the room with the stupid book on my head. I'm done with being your pretty queen. I want to know what in the name of the goddess Nix is going on and how we plan to fix it."

His chest, set with hard muscle, moved in slow, measured breaths like he was trying very hard not to cross the room to destroy her. Source save her, she was staring again. His stomach was flat and etched in rows of yet more muscle that led to a smooth plane of flesh that disappeared below his waistline.

"Umm..." Words fled her mind. She shook her head and lifted the candle holder she'd forgotten she was holding. "You...you can't lock me away. I won't just sit in that room until you decide what you want from me. Explain yourself immediately or—"

"Or you'll strike me with my guest room decor?" His raven-black eyebrows bunched as he frowned.

"Exactly."

His nostrils flared and his jaw worked. "Return to your chamber. At dinner, I'll tell you what you must know and no more, Upperworlder." He practically spat that last word. He certainly didn't harbor any love for those outside his realm.

He splayed his fingers. Shadows sped from the corners of the room to cocoon Maren. She sucked a shocked breath as his cool, gentle magic curled around every finger and toe, her neck and legs, and then sped her back to her chamber.

The doors slammed shut, closing her in.

As the shadows dumped her unceremoniously onto the bed, bumping and dragging sounds made her guess that something heavy was being set in front of her only path to freedom.

Freed from his magic, she jumped off the bed and ran to the doors.

"You can't keep me here forever." She flexed her right hand. If only she had her wand. "Magelord Aurora will come for me, and Prince Filip, too. He'll hack you up into tiny shadowy bits with that hatchet of his, and you'll regret stowing me in this closet of a room like last year's root vegetables!" She swore loudly, using every foul word she'd learned on the docks as a child. It was childish. But it felt amazing.

The doors swung open to show Kynan's fierce eyes and bared teeth. His shadows flared up behind him like wicked wings. "You will cease this degrading behavior at once."

"You picked up a dockside girl, not a queen, and if

you don't tell me what is going on, I'll move on to the curses I learned in the Wylfenden dungeon not so long ago."

He just stared, completely unmoved.

"At any moment," she whispered, "this place will be absolutely crawling with powerful mages, warriors, and witches. They might even bring the gryphons. I hope they peck your eyes from your handsome head."

She was rewarded with a spark of surprise in his eyes before his shadows swarmed her lips and neck, then stole her voice.

Falling back, she put her hands to her throat. There was no pain, just that cool slip of his particular type of magic, but not being able to speak had her heart hammering wildly in panic.

He stepped forward, some of the rage in his angular features dissolving into what she might have called concern if he had been anyone else. Raising a hand, he called the dark, swirling mist to his fingers. "I will release your voice if you agree to stop shouting obscenities, woman."

She kicked at his groin, but he dodged her, then drew her close.

He lifted her chin with his shadow-swathed hand. It looked as though he had dark roots growing from every finger. "Do you agree, or would you like to remain silent for the rest of your stay here?"

She couldn't stand having her words snatched from her throat. And so she nodded.

The shadows immediately left her, and she opened her mouth to spew venom.

He held up a finger. "You agreed," he said, his deep voice a whisper. "Do you not even have the dignity of holding true to your word?"

"I would tell you to go to the Underworld, but..."

The corner of his lips quirked like he almost wanted to grin, but then his frown returned in full force. His gaze strayed from her face down her neck, his head tilting as he examined her. He stood so close, and his magic shifted over her like soft, skilled hands. She took a shuddering breath, hating her desire to submit to him, a longing that laced through her senses. Was that his magic? Or something about his presence?

Confidence beamed from his stance to the look in his dark eyes. He appeared to have no qualms about holding her, and he didn't seem to doubt his actions for even a moment. He was the most commanding, kingly man she'd ever seen.

But he was truly an arse.

"I will summon you," he said, a look of satisfaction passing over his eyes, "when you are needed."

With that, he left the chamber and shut the doors behind him, shadows billowing around the broken handle and the hinges, ensuring she was once again thoroughly snared.

She threw the candle holder at the wall, where it did basically nothing. Shouting in frustration, she picked up the water basin and prepared to toss it and appease her anger. But then she saw the ripples of the water and remembered what Aury could do.

Setting the wide basin back down, she stared at her reflection. "Aury? Any chance you can hear me?" If Aury was searching for Maren as they'd done once in the past with another friend in trouble, this might work. "Aury!" she whispered, pushing her witch's will into the words like stoking a reluctant fire and praying her power might somehow work despite her lack of a wand.

But the water remained silent with no silver-haired friend looking back. It was only Maren's dark blonde hair, too large eyes, and lopsided mouth.

She looked at the decorated ceiling, to the dark shapes that flew in the painted twilight sky above the forest that was crafted in shades of emerald and sapphire. Were those dragons? They didn't have front legs but were instead more like bats in that their wings seemed to serve as arms or forelegs. What horrors awaited her in this realm?

After trying to speak into the water to Aury a dozen times, Maren left the basin and searched every drawer in the corner desk and each cranny between the stones in the walls. She didn't know what exactly she wanted to find, but staying busy was better than going fully mad. She recited every spell she could recall, only managing a slight warmth in her fingertips and between her eyebrows. At least her magic still lived in her even if she couldn't use it without a wand. She drew back the heavy curtains and looked into the sparkling night full of glowing plant life and twisting shadows. How long did night last in the Underworld?

She gripped the window ledge, the stone as cold as ice beneath her fingers. She was completely trapped, and there wasn't a thing she could do about it.

CHAPTER 8

The chamber doors thundered with a knock. "It's time for dinner, Awenydd," a male voice that wasn't High King Kynan's said.

Before Maren could answer, a slew of smiling servants poured in, then proceeded to escort her from the room to a great hall where a round table sat before a massive fireplace.

Golden platters held black grapes, slices of venison covered in an orange sauce, and greens of every variety. Goblets and pitchers were filled to the very brim with what smelled like red wine.

Kynan walked in from a set of double side doors, and her heart jumped. His dark eyes held her as firmly as chains, the disdain in their depths unmistakable. He wore a dark green tunic, a wide black belt with a jeweled dagger and his sword, dark trousers, high boots, and several rings on his long fingers. That sword had moved the earth like Goddess Vahly's sword of oak from the ancient tales. And if she remembered correctly, his sword was black and held a sparkle to it, as if it were made from spirit agate, the stone that the fae controlled, the stone that increased one's magical power.

Because Kynan had tied some of his hair away from his face and knotted it at the crown of his head, his cheekbones seemed even sharper than other elves' features. Magic wove around his temples and brow, visible in wispy shadows and small sparks of golden light. Those same types of shadows rose behind him like a ghostly cloak waving in the wind. His power echoed across the great hall, vibrating from the floor, into Maren's toes, and up her body. He wasn't spinning shadows around her at the moment. This feeling had to result from a blend of the presence his powerful royal elven blood gave him and her simple physical attraction to him.

"Sit, Awenydd." His shadows snaked across the floor, jerked her chair away from the table, then forced her to do as he commanded.

The servants stood to the side, eyes wide.

The shadows relented, and Maren went through about two hundred eleven magical curses she would thoroughly enjoy throwing at this beast of a king if she'd had her wand.

"First, we greet one another and ask about one another's family. That is how one begins a dinner."

"Dinner? What is this dinner? I've never heard of such a thing." Grinning, she picked up her eating knife and threw it at his heart.

His shadows plucked the blade from the air and set

it on the table beside him. "And we do not throw cutlery."

"You wield your shadow magic like a weapon, and you've lost me my wand. So I'm going to use whatever I choose in any manner I choose. Plates, for instance." She pitched hers at him, and it wheeled through the air. He deflected it with his forearm, and it rolled to a noisy stop by the hearth's flickering fire.

Kynan's fingers dug into the carved wooden arms of his chair.

"Am I frustrating you?" Maren smiled wickedly. "Would you rather be abducted and dragged to another realm instead?"

He said something very fast and sharp in a language she didn't know. But she could guess its meaning.

"Go ahead and end me in a fashion that fits your legendary reputation, High King Kynan. But I'm thinking you won't because you need me. Why else would you have stolen me away? And why would you be wasting time teaching me table manners when you could be doing all of your favorite things like frightening small children or perhaps playing with your fancy magic?"

A gasp came from one of the servants, but Kynan's glowing gaze never left her face, nor did his intoxicating magic ever truly leave her body.

"Take up your spoon, Lady Maren, and eat peacefully with me." His voice was warm and melting, and she longed to do exactly as he ordered.

"Tell me what I need to know."

"Do you swear on your life to measure your response with the heart of a queen instead of the spoiled Upperworlder I see before me?"

"If I swear and don't answer in a way that pleases you," she sneered, "then what happens? You kill me? Feed me to the dragons you're hiding down here somewhere? I think you've spent too long in your own realm, and you haven't taken the time to realize that we Upperworlders have everyone's best interest at heart. I summoned you only so that I could do what's best about the vision and the Sacred Oak."

He'd gone still, his eyes spearing her. "The only Upperworlders I respect are those who have passed to their spirit form." Pushing away from the table, he kept his gaze on her.

Then he turned toward the side doors and left. Just like that. No shadows. No shouting.

This was getting her nowhere. If the fate of the realms relied on her, everyone was doomed.

She rose and strode to her chamber, slammed the double doors shut, dragged the side table over to block them from the inside just in case the mercurial king decided to lop off her head, then collapsed into a chair.

This was an absolute nightmare. She paced the floor, and time passed as her mind wrapped around the problems at hand.

LATER, A VOICE AT THE DOORS STARTLED HER. "LADY Maren," a man said, a man who was not Kynan. "Please come to dinner. High King Kynan has retired for the night, and we want the chance to serve you."

"No, thank you."

"But we made such a decadent feast. Won't you simply try a few bites?" The man's accent was the same as Kynan's, but his voice was like her father's had been, calm and sweet.

She opened the doors to find the speaker and another elven woman.

"I'm Ninian, and this is my wife, Nia." They bowed and curtseyed.

Ninian was a slender fellow with freckled skin. Maren had only met one other freckled elf—Costel. The couple looked so sincere and kind that she couldn't imagine telling them no. She took a heavy breath and nodded.

"I'll eat whatever wonders you've created. I suppose I can go back to plotting once my belly is full."

"Thank you for allowing us to serve you. We never could have imagined we'd be lucky enough to serve the Awenydd!" Nia's round cheeks blushed under her dark skin.

A tiny elven woman peered over Nia's shoulder. "My name's Saffir." Her eyes glittered like sapphires.

"Nice to meet you," Maren said. "We're about the same height, aren't we? I haven't seen too many as short as us. We'll have to stick together."

Saffir's smile stretched fully across her face. "Indeed, my lady!"

Ninian and Nia traded a grin, then Maren let them

lead her back to the hall. As they walked, she looked for signs of Kynan but didn't hear his voice or feel his magic. The corridors were softly lit with oil lamps and candles, the walls draped in jewel-toned tapestries of forest and mountain scenes. The scents of incense, pipe smoke, and pine wafted through the air. She tried not to appreciate how nice everything was. She failed.

The moment she sat at the table, a tall, fair-skinned elf with well-muscled arms strode out of another set of side doors and bowed so low his tousled hair almost brushed the floor.

"I'm Deron, your chef." He straightened and nodded —a very serious fellow who was easy on the eyes. "Thank you for agreeing to eat my food this day, Lady Maren. It's my life's greatest joy to cook."

"I can't say I ever loved cooking the regular fare I grew up eating," she said, "but I do enjoy baking for my friends. Princess Brielle gave me some black cinnamon imported from the island of Khem, and it makes for the best croissants."

As Deron nodded knowingly, her chest tightened. She wanted to go home, to see that everyone had truly escaped from Kynan's mound of earth.

The servants set out dishes of pumpkin and bean soup and ladled three different sauces over her venison, asking her to pick a favorite.

"The green." It was delicious and possibly made with that same stuff as the herbed potatoes.

"Ah! I knew it." Deron raised a fist like he'd just won a battle.

Maren almost laughed at how quickly his serious demeanor had fallen away.

"You look cold in your lovely gown, my lady." Nia arranged a dark blanket over Maren's shoulders, tucking the ends around her as she enjoyed a little, round cake packed with currants and topped in powdery sugar.

"This is astounding. You are all goddesses and gods to me now. Just so you know." The cake melted in her mouth. "What is that one spice I can't place? A uniquely Underworld seed perhaps?"

"It's the mace," Deron said, looking like a rooster ready to crow proudly. "Less sweet than nutmeg, its sister spice, and ground fresh by my own hands this morning."

"You can grow nutmeg trees here?"

"Yes, but I have read that they are quite different from the ones in the Upperworld. They are smaller and don't require such warm weather."

"Ah. If I weren't worried for my life," Maren said sharply, "I'd love to learn how to make these cakes."

The servants stilled and looked at her.

"You are valued above all here, my lady." Ninian set down the pitcher of wine he'd been carrying about. "High King Kynan will protect you above all others."

Nia nodded. "Above even himself and the ones he has held most dear his whole life."

"Then why treat me like I'm a fool and prisoner?" It made no sense. "Why am I here?"

Saffir had lifted the venison platter and now gripped the edges, knuckles whitening. "We've been told not to speak of such things to you. The king will explain all in time."

"I don't want to land you in trouble, but this...it's infuriating."

Ninian refilled her goblet. "Have a glass of this vintage, my lady queen. It isn't as strong and will help you sleep tonight."

"Don't mind if I do." Maren downed the drink, then another. She bid the lot good night and walked with Saffir back to her room.

Back in her chamber, Maren asked, "Where is Eefa?"

"Oh, she rests in the later hours while we take over her work," Saffir said, her eyes darting about like she expected someone to pop out of the shadows—which was possible in this realm.

"That's kind," Maren said. She had definitely had too much wine. Her head was spinning, and she felt reckless, ready to do just about anything to escape this castle.

"It's the king's way." Saffir smiled. "He cares for us all. Very good one, he is."

Right. Before or after he abducts people? "I respectfully disagree." Though his staff did seem to respect and care for him. It was at complete odds with what she'd experienced of him.

"You'll see."

Indeed. Maren shook her head slowly. "Well, thank you for the feast. It was wonderful."

Saffir shut the doors, and Maren was left alone in her chamber, wondering if she should have tried harder to escape while Kynan wasn't around. She fisted her hands. If only they'd given her even one piece of information for this puzzle of a situation.

Finding the pitcher of wine on her table, she poured the last of it into the goblet and drank every drop.

Sudden chills swept down her body.

A presence materialized behind her, a sense of someone in the room.

CHAPTER 9

Blood rushing like floodwaters through her veins, Maren set down the goblet and eyed the room for a weapon. She spotted her eating knife on the floor where she or maybe Eefa must have dropped it. She snatched it up. Dizzy as a storm-tossed fish, she held the little blade like it was her wand and turned around. But no one was there.

"Such poor treatment of the Awenydd," a voice whispered on the air.

A face appeared, light eyebrows over gray eyes, dimples in handsome cheeks... Then a body with broad shoulders and an easy stance grew visible. The fair-haired man bent his head in greeting but didn't bow. "Nice to make your acquaintance, Awenydd."

"Who are you?" She set the knife against his throat.

His eyes sparkled with pleasure, and instead of attempting to disarm her, he adjusted the black ribbon holding his hair at the nape of his neck. She wasn't sure what to make of him.

"I'm Tiergan, an alternative to the Shadow King, should you wish a union with another dark lord, a different Binding that would resolve the problems building in our worlds."

A shiver dragged across Maren's back. What was he talking about? "Binding?"

Tiergan tsked and shook his head. "Kynan has told you nothing."

"No, not a thing. Would you be willing to speak up? I'd love to know just what in the name of the Source is going on here."

"I'd say I'm shocked Kynan treats the Awenydd this way," he said, "but alas, our king has his ways, and he hasn't changed in eons."

These men were truly that old. Immortal. Maren's petite knife seemed even more silly now, but she kept it in place anyway.

"What is the problem with the Sacred Oak?" she asked, squinting at him. Definitely too much wine. "My friend is a water mage. During her scrying, she saw the tree collapsing, but we don't know why or how to keep that future from occurring."

Tiergan's gray eyes narrowed, and he glanced to the side like he was thinking. "We aren't certain."

Her announcement hadn't caused him even a moment's surprise. Even through the haze of the drink, she could see that. Perhaps all of the shadow elves knew the end of the realms was coming.

"We only know the last time the Sacred Oak showed signs of rapid decay," he said, "the Binding of a dark lord and the Awenydd healed the roots and saved us all, and the spirits too."

He walked casually past her, the knife nicking him slightly with the movement. No blood showed. She shivered. Had she not cut him, or did these dark lords not bleed?

At the hearth, he took hold of a painted tile above the mantle and swung it back like it was a small door. He drew out a bottle of wine. "Old Underworld tradition," he said. He lifted her wine goblet. "May I?"

She blinked, impressed by that particular tradition. "Go right ahead if it'll help loosen your tongue."

Who was this elven man? Should she scream for help? Would Eefa or other members of the castle staff help? She didn't want him to stop talking though, so she held her tongue.

He spun the goblet, and it became two goblets. Magic.

Did Kynan have manifesting abilities as well? He must have. He was their king, after all. So perhaps shadow lords shared some talents with witches like herself in addition to their shadow magic. It was then she noticed Tiergan's presence didn't affect her like Kynan's did. Maybe the crown bestowed that power.

After pouring out the wine, Tiergan drank deeply then held out her goblet. "Please join me."

"Oh, why not..." She hoped he hadn't poisoned it, but honestly, he seemed far kinder than Kynan.

They sat and drank, listening to the fire crackle. Maren tried to untangle her thoughts.

"Three days ago," Tiergan said, "a shepherd who lives near the Spirit's Well reported a whitened root."

"I saw the ground outside this keep turn to gray ice, then flicker back to its original state. I don't know anything about the well, but I assume the root the shepherd saw belongs to the Sacred Oak."

"Yes. The well is where the spirits rest, peacefully fed by the power of the Sacred Oak's roots. They are content and quiet there, invisible to our eyes. Perhaps not always to your eyes, Awenydd."

"So when the spirits aren't visiting the world of the living to bestow blessings on their descendants or visiting the Between, they rest in the Spirit Well?"

"That's right. Have you helped many of them during your short life?"

"I have." She wanted to gain information, not pass it out. "But let's move on to this Binding subject." The wine in her goblet went down easily. She had a strong feeling she wouldn't enjoy his answer.

"Only one thing can halt the end of our worlds." His voice was gently hypnotic, the sound of it relaxing Maren's coiled muscles and bunched fists. "The Awenydd and a dark lord of the Underworld must complete the Binding, a ceremony much like a wedding."

The memory of Aury's words stung Maren's mind. *The Shadow King's ringless hand...* She swallowed, stomach roiling.

Kynan needed a bride, and he planned to take Maren as his wife.

That was what Aury's vision had shown.

Tiergan's face blurred, and a sweat broke over Maren.

She couldn't marry the Shadow King. He was a nightmare come to life. He'd buried her friends alive and left them for dead.

"How does a marriage fix anything?" Her words cracked as she spoke too quickly, the wine sour in her throat and on the back of her tongue. She couldn't trust him. Perhaps he was lying. *Please let him be the biggest, most disgusting liar in all the realms.*

"No one knows for certain. I am quite sorry to be the bearer of bad news." Tiergan lifted his goblet as if to salute her, then drank deeply.

She stared at the fire, stunned, mind shattering into a million pieces. "I have to escape." But should she? If this was true and only a Binding would save the living and the spirits...

Tiergan ran a finger around the rim of his goblet. "I do have a plan if you wish to hear it."

She spun and gripped his forearm, nearly making him drop his drink. He lifted his eyebrows, seemingly shocked at her casual way. "Tell me, dark lord. I'm all ears."

"Bind yourself to me, spend one night with me, then I will take you from the Underworld myself and place you wherever you choose."

She jerked back and fisted her hand.

The elven man was gloriously fine-looking with his square jaw, wavy light hair, and those dreamy eyes, but Maren had absolutely no desire to bed him, let alone marry him. The very idea felt wrong. But if it saved everyone from the end of life itself, from the spread of that unnatural ice...

"How does the Binding help the Oak and the spirits?" she demanded. He had to know more than he was letting on. Surely! He'd been around for eons, he'd said.

"The magic is shrouded in secrecy and in the long, long years of the past. No one knows. The ancients did, perhaps, but if they were aware of why the Binding of the Awenydd and a dark lord mended damage to the Sacred Oak and the Source's root of magic, they never recorded it in scroll or song, and no Awenydd in history has been able to discover the reason or workings of the old magic."

Maybe she could summon the goddess Vahly and ask. The goddess had spoken with her in the Between once before in order to help Dorin. Perhaps Goddess Vahly wouldn't be against Maren calling for her? Or perhaps the goddess would be offended by something Maren didn't understand and simply unmake her in a dramatic fashion.

Maren had no plans to be unmade. Life—magic, dancing, horses, friends, wine, and food—it was all lovely.

Well, when she wasn't trapped in the Underworld.

"I'll give you some time to think it over." Tiergan stood and straightened his dark green cloak and black tunic. If he hadn't been a dark lord of the Underworld, she would have sworn he was showing off his trim waist with his careful movements.

Suddenly, Tiergan lifted his head and looked toward the doors.

She stood. "What is it?"

"Your rude jailer is leaving his castle. Shall we follow him at a discreet distance and see what he is up to?"

He wanted to follow Kynan and spy on him? She was all for it. "You can magic us out of this chamber?" Maren asked. She went to the armoire in the corner and dug out a black cloak with white fur trim. The cloak was heavy and warm on her shoulders, made for royalty, and this fisherman's daughter was plenty grateful to have it.

He held out his arm and smiled. He truly was a fine-looking lord. "I most certainly can."

She took his offered forearm, and shadows swarmed her arms and legs.

These shadows didn't feel like Kynan's. They weren't cool and soft, but instead were insubstantial mostly. The ones linked about her arms felt like a dry wind. Their color was black like Kynan's shadows, but that was where the similarity ended.

The world dropped away.

CHAPTER 10

Maren stumbled as the shadows cleared, and a strong hand caught her as the world reappeared.

With shadow magic, Tiergan had brought them out of Kynan's castle and landed them on a hilltop overlooking what had to be the Sacred Oak's taproots.

The night here was not as dark as it was in the Upperworld. A hazy violet light filtered through the wispy clouds. It was like dusk refused to fully give up its hold to night.

The urge to run, to flee to the runed doors somewhere out there and try to return to the Upperworld, whipped through Maren. But dashing off would be stupid. Not only had she had four goblets of wine like a gigantic fool, but she was half the size and breadth of Tiergan, and he had shadow magic. It was pointless. Plus, if what Tiergan said was true and she had to wed one of these dark lords to save the realms, well, she couldn't leave. She didn't believe that yet though. She'd seen enough of cons on the docks to know when to wait and gain more information. And this was far more important than a couple of copper coins.

Between two hills, tangled lengths of dark wood gripped the mossy earth and stretched thick tendrils into a swirling pool of silver water. One of the largest roots had turned white, and glassy ice shone along the top and down one side. The sweet-scented breeze lifted specks of the strange ice... Was it snow? The white was almost a gray though, not a lovely white like true snow. The ground around the injured root sparkled with ice as well and appeared gray beneath the freeze's crust.

"This is the Spirit Well," Tiergan said.

Curiosity overwhelmed her fear as she stared down at the place where spirits rested. The scent of flowers and deep well water touched Maren's nose. A quiet rush of whispers rode the night air, but just like at the castle, the spirits were nowhere to be seen. It was a strange thing to Maren, who had grown up seeing them walking to and fro, occasionally stopping to speak to her and ask for assistance. In addition, the Underworld felt rather sparsely populated in comparison to the Upperworld, to use Kynan's term.

As if thinking his name had summoned him again, the Shadow King walked out of the misty pine forest beyond the Spirit Well. He'd dressed up for this chore, it seemed, walking in a stately fashion toward the pool wearing a crown that appeared to be made of shadows that flashed occasionally with golden light. The spikes on the crown stood high above his proud brow. A blood-red cloak dragged the ground behind him, and he wore black leathers and tall boots. His shadows curled around his shoulders and head, and he held something small as he approached the well and knelt. Root-shaped shadows grew from his chest and temples, stretching into the Spirit Well. The water glowed a brighter blue where his root shadows made contact, as if his magic were feeding the spirits and their home with power.

"What's he doing?" she asked Tiergan, hoping Kynan wouldn't discover them here. Would he kill them if he did? The king seemed perfectly capable of such reckless cruelty. Of course, this new dark lord could be just as deadly. He did seem as if he wanted to negotiate though. If murder had been on Tiergan's mind, he could have tried it the moment he'd gained entry to her room at the castle, and he would have most likely succeeded, seeing as he was nearly as tall and broad as Kynan. Even without shadow magic, he most likely could have overpowered Maren and her tiny knife.

Before Tiergan could answer, Kynan set whatever was in his hands into the water. Pearly smoke danced from the surface and spun around him. The scent of something akin to incense poured through the night, musky and spicy. His shadow magic streamed farther into the pool, and his shoulders bent as if the effort weighed heavily on him. A score of the spirits materialized from the pearly smoke and stood behind Kynan. He spoke to the water, not responding at all to those standing near.

"Doesn't he see them?"

"See what?" Tiergan studied Maren's face.

"The spirits. You don't see them either, do you? They're standing behind him."

Tiergan grinned. "Such a powerful Awenydd. Look at your hands."

Her fingers were cloaked in sparks that faded quickly. She turned toward the spirits again, and the flickering light appeared on her fingers once more. It was related to her magic somehow. She strained to hear Kynan's words and only caught the whispers of the spirits.

"She frightened us," a spirit woman said as they tried to communicate with Kynan.

Maren wondered if perhaps he had dreams now and then sparked by the spirits' words. Surely, they communicated with him even if he never truly understood the way of it.

The round ears and clunkier aspects of the spirit's build said she had been a human. Her hair reached all the way to her ankles as she repeated her words.

"The Awenydd is troubled," a spirit boy said, his voice pulling at Maren just as the woman's did. "We must speak with her."

Maren's heart cinched, and before she'd thought it over, she was striding away from Tiergan, down the hill toward the gathered spirits, her hands sparking wildly. "I'm here. It will be all right."

Kynan stood swiftly, eyes wide. "How did you escape your room?" His gaze lashed across her hands. "Address the spirits properly." He looked like he was ready to attack her with his shadows again. They lifted into what almost looked like wings fashioned of tree branches at his back, pointed shapes that made her shiver.

Maren turned to see if Tiergan was coming down, but he had disappeared. "Don't attack me," she said to Kynan, her words not as crisp as they should have been because of the wine. "I see the spirits. They're right behind you. You have me, the Awenydd, in your castle, and you don't even bother taking me to help them? You're a fool."

"How did you even travel this far?" He glared into the twilight.

"Apologies for summoning the king without warning you," she said to the spirits. "I didn't realize that would upset you, and it was done with good cause. Do you know what's wrong with the Sacred Oak?"

Kynan gripped her arm. "Must I restrain you again?"

She pulled away. "Kiss my arse, you horrible thing. The spirits are speaking to me, and if you'd shut your mouth, I'd hear what they have to say!"

The spirits regarded them quietly. Both old men and young stood among children and women of all ages. They wore patient smiles downturned at the edges and eyes pinched with worry.

"We accept your apology, Awenydd. We don't know what's causing the decay," the woman said, her voice like wind in a chimney. "We feel its cold though." She held a needle and thread as if she'd been called away from mending her husband's trousers by the fire.

The boy floated forward, his woolen cap sitting too far back on his head, not even covering the tips of his pointed ears. Maren longed to straighten it, but she couldn't touch the spirits. She'd tried once before and only felt cold where solid form should've been. "Ask the alchemist god," the boy said in a sweet voice accented with the tones of Balaur. "We grow hungry."

A shiver rattled Maren's bones. "Who is the alchemist god?" Maren asked Kynan.

He frowned and looked toward the well. "This is highly unusual..." From anyone else, the words would have been quiet, prudish, and far from menacing, but from Kynan, they sounded like the worst of threats to her very life. Glancing at her again, he set his jaw. "The alchemist god would have to be Arcturus, the god of air."

"I've met him," she said. As Kynan stammered, she faced the spirits. "Will you see if he's about?" she asked the boy. "I'd love to ask him for help. Is that all right? I don't want to upset you again."

The woman and two old men nodded and smiled as the rest murmured niceties about her and sent the boy on his way.

"Thank you," Maren said, replying to a wizened old fellow with a water mage staff after he complimented her hair. "A woman named Eefa braided it."

The spirits shimmered away until she was alone with Kynan, and the fire on her hands faded. Tiergan still wasn't on the hill.

"I can't believe you addressed them that way." Kynan left her to pick a handful of blue poppies. He also pulled several gold coins from his cloak's pocket. He set them into the water, one by one. The flowers floated in a slow circle, and the coins dropped into the deep.

"Tiergan told me about the Binding."

Kynan was up and standing not an inch away from her before she could even finish the statement. "Did he touch you?" Fury rolled off him in the form of actual heat that warmed her cheeks and chest as his shadows spun high into the air. His fingers flexed at his sides, and his chest rose and fell quickly as his dark eyes glowed ruby bright. "Maren of the Wylfen Sea, did he touch you?"

Her face flushed because of the wine, but also due to an emotion she couldn't name. "What if he did?" How did he know she'd grown up on the coastline of Wylfenden?

Shadows whirled around them both, their branching darkness blocking out the scant light of the glowing mushrooms and the hazy deep violet of the sky. Wind blew through the shadows, not touching them, but chilling Maren's skin and setting her teeth to chattering.

And when a portion of the shadows cleared, Tiergan was there, grinning. "Greetings, my king," he said sharply.

Kynan hissed something in his language and drew his black sword.

Tiergan bowed deeply, hand extended gracefully. "I simply brought your Awenydd to the Spirit Well because she wished to see it."

Had Maren asked to see the well? She rubbed her forehead.

"She longs for information about the Binding," Tiergan continued, "and I do think you two should discuss the details."

Kynan lifted his sword. His face was a mask of pain. What was their history? "What I should or should not discuss with the Awenydd is none of your business," he growled out.

"Actually, it's everyone's business, Your Highness," Tiergan said, then he winked at Maren.

The corner of Kynan's lip curled like a scar wolf's. Maren had seen a scar wolf one time when the Wylfenden military had paraded through her village. Kynan was more frightening than even that attack-trained beast.

Kynan drove the sword directly toward Tiergan's chest.

CHAPTER 11

"She had no part in our feud!" Kynan shouted.

Confused, Maren leapt backward and raised her hand before remembering she had no wand.

Tiergan disappeared in flurry of shadows as the sword passed through the place where his heart should have been. Tiergan was gone, traveling by the same means he'd used to take Maren here.

Kynan snarled and sheathed his sword.

"I assume this *she* is me?" Maren asked.

Raking his hands through his long black hair, he walked quickly away from the well and toward his steed. The horse munched the tall grasses, appearing unperturbed at his master nearly committing murder. At this point, that wasn't surprising.

"I was not speaking of you, Lady Maren," he spat.

"Will you at least tell me where you think you're going?" she asked. He looked like he was about to mount up and gallop away. "The god Arcturus is most likely on his way here to the Spirit Well unless the boy wasn't able to summon him. Don't you worry about insulting a god? Or are you as powerful as him and considering yourself an equal?"

He stopped and spun to face her, his broad chest rising and falling. "Do you always ramble incessantly?"

"No, what I truly enjoy is being darkly silent and infuriatingly domineering."

He slid her a glare as he rummaged in his saddlebag. Well, he didn't exactly rummage. He was more of the I-know-precisely-where-everything-is type, so he simply put his hand into the large leather bag and removed the item in question.

"What is that?"

"A gift for the god," he said.

"Ah. Good thinking."

Giving her a quick glance and narrowing his eyes, he removed the linen wrapping from a small glass jar stoppered with cork and wax.

"What's in there?" she asked as they walked back to the well.

"Why were you with King Tiergan? Are you drunk? When did he approach you? Did he breach my castle walls and move you with his shadow magic?"

"You're suddenly very interested in conversation. I'll start answering your questions when you start answering mine, High King Kynan."

Halting abruptly, he stuck the vial under her nose. It smelled like lavender, orange, and something salty. "It's ceremonial oil, often used to cleanse a supplicant who makes a wish at the Spirit Well."

Now she had even more questions.

His jaw muscles shifted as he ground his teeth, then he sighed. "At the well, one can ask a favor of the goddesses and gods. It's a rare but not unheard-of custom here. And before you ask, I want to know how King Tiergan traveled with you because using shadow magic to travel long distances creates a mark on the Underworld. That type of high magic asks for far more energy than using shadows as one's hands or some such simpler magic. The earth beneath us can easily handle a few marks of such high shadow power, but if we take it too far, the regions in which the magic is performed regularly will be scarred and unable to produce life. It is deeply irresponsible to throw such magic about like it has no effect on anyone else as King Tiergan did just now and I presume did with you earlier as well."

Before Maren could clear her foggy mind to demand more information, the spirit boy from earlier shimmered into view. Her hands flickered with magic. The small flames tickled a bit but definitely didn't hurt at all. She could barely feel anything from them.

Kynan blinked at the fire on her hands and looked about. "I suppose a spirit is speaking to you."

The spirit boy smiled at Maren, and the genuine appreciation for her that she saw in his eyes warmed her. "The alchemist god has journeyed to a distant island to aid one who inherited the ancient race of elves' dryad magic."

"I didn't realize that power still existed."

"His sword can do such things," the spirit boy said, glancing at Kynan.

"I've seen its work on the earth and rock. But he can use trees as well with his black sword?"

"Yes. The alchemist god will return tomorrow. He asked that I tell you he looks forward to meeting with you."

"Good. Thank you very much... What is your name?"

The boy shimmered, fading a little as he pursed his lips and scratched his head. "I can't recall."

"That's all right. You've helped me tremendously. Have a lovely day."

He grinned, and Maren remembered Kynan's gift.

"Oh!" She snatched it from Kynan, removed the stopper, and poured the scented oil at the spirit boy's feet.

The lad's entire form brightened, his pale blue color going nearly white. "That smells wonderful! Thank you very much for the honor." He bowed his head and faded away.

Kynan looked Maren up and down. "Though you've quite obviously enjoyed far too much wine this evening, I assume you know what you're about." His gaze snapped to the oil glistening on the damp ground.

"I do. The boy says the god Arcturus will meet us here tomorrow."

"Very good. Come." Kynan turned on his heel and headed back toward the horse. A sinuous length of shadow magic hooked around her middle and slid up her torso, making her breath catch.

"I'm not your churl to order about," she said breathlessly.

He spun and froze, eyes wide as he looked at the shadows wrapped around her waist. The shadows immediately faded and fell away. Shaking his head, nostrils flaring, he grabbed her by the upper arm, verily dragging her to where the steed waited.

She jerked away and glared at him. "King Tiergan never handled me like that."

"He befriends monsters, so that surprises me not. Now, mount, Awenydd." Holding the reins, he stretched out a hand.

Maren mounted without his help and ran her fingers through the steed's mane. Had Kynan's shadow magic just slipped out of his control to tempt her? She glanced at him and found he was looking at her. Her heart bumped her chest hard.

He shifted his gaze quickly. "We will ride to the village of Hiraeth," he said as he pet the horse's neck. The animal snuffled affectionately into his master's shoulder. Setting his forehead against the horse's, Kynan whispered something soft in his language.

Interesting. The horse appeared to genuinely like him. Kynan had probably plied the horse into a feigned affection with apples and sugar cubes, because the steed's fondness certainly couldn't result from Kynan's kind soul. He probably didn't even have a soul.

"Do you have a soul?" she asked.

"I do," he said gruffly as he set his foot in the stirrup and swung a leg behind her. "Do you?"

She glanced over her shoulder at him. "Are you teasing me?"

He didn't respond, only staring straight ahead and calling out to the horse.

The steed galloped down from the rise, then through a field of poppies and herbs. The purple blush of this realm's night sky cast a soft light over a pathway leading through lovely hills and beautiful meadows dotted with black-faced sheep. They rode without speaking, the sound of the horse's hooves on the grit of the road and the chirp of birds filling in the space left by their silence.

The jostling of the ride had her pressed against Kynan, his heat soaking through their clothing to warm her. The pressure of his thighs was frustratingly distracting. She cleared her throat and tried not to pay attention to the way his body fit so nicely with hers, the way his breath left him in a quiet rush with each of the horse's footfalls. If he were anyone else...

She shook off that thought and forced her mind to think of the vision and Tiergan's information.

CHAPTER 12

Her head started to pound, and she longed for water. "You must hate this horse."

She heard his lips part in shock behind her head. "I most certainly do not," he said, sounding insulted.

"He can't enjoy carrying two adults."

"Osian is large enough to handle our weight and more," Kynan snapped. "I know my animals. Do not question my affection toward my creatures."

She tried to make space between them, but it was impossible. "You bruised my arm when you dragged me to the horse. King Tiergan didn't mishandle me." She wanted to punish him, to twist the knife, to make him suffer for burying her friends alive.

"It's a waste of the Underworld's magic to keep ensnaring you when you make foolish attempts to escape."

"You're truly an arse, you know that?"

"Keep your foul tongue silent."

Maren began reciting the foulest shanty she'd ever heard, relishing the tension in Kynan. When she finished, her temples throbbing from the wine, she decided he needed a little lecture. "You started this entire situation off by abducting me and committing violence against my loved ones. You haven't earned the gentler side of me. I had no choice to come here, and you've done nothing to make me think you are more than the darkest of criminals."

He exhaled slowly, his chest moving against her back. "I don't owe an Upperworlder any sort of explanation or gentle manners. You and your kind are the fiends, make no mistake."

Near a particularly noisy flock of black-faced sheep, a quiet village appeared around the bend. The inhabitants were most likely asleep.

"This is Hiraeth," Kynan said, his voice gravelly and dark like he wished he were with anyone but her.

The rough stone buildings of Hiraeth were tidy, and most had thatched roofs. Only a few boasted layered slate roofs. Each had double wooden doors for entry and a bevy of windows shut tight for the evening.

"Why do you hate Tiergan?" she asked, hoping to catch him off guard.

A fountain in the shape of a spinning wheel gurgled at the center of a square, and vines with fair flowers bloomed beside a statue of a small dragon much like the ones painted on the ceiling of the chamber at Kynan's castle.

"Why do you care?" he asked quietly, his breath stirring the hair at the top of her head.

She swallowed, then set her hands on the horse's neck, trying to at least enjoy the warm presence of a pleasant animal. "Tiergan has been miles upon miles more polite to me than you have been."

"A poisonous flower can be beautiful."

"Don't speak metaphorically. What do you have against him?"

"Stay away from King Tiergan."

"I realize we've only just *met*, and I use the term 'met' incredibly loosely considering it was an abduction, not a meeting, but you must have discovered by now that I don't tend to follow orders."

"You're on my horse, are you not?" Said horse steered around a bed of the same type of glowing mushrooms she'd seen at the riverbank. They were clustered around a rosebush beside a villager's shuttered window.

"Only because you'll fetch me back with your shadows if I try to run or fight."

"King Tiergan is not as he seems."

"Why won't you explain? What is your history with him? He told me the truth of the situation, while you intended to keep me in the dark." She snorted. "My turn to speak metaphorically, I guess. But then again, dark is your key component, so perhaps that's not as symbolic as I hoped."

"Gods, you never do stop blathering."

"It's not truly blathering if I'm discussing something rather important."

"And that is?"

"That you plan to take me as your wife!"

"You knowing changes nothing."

"I definitely prefer Tiergan," she said, feeling spiteful and her head still swimming from the drinks. "At least he gives me information and treats me like an equal. He claims the Sacred Oak would be mended just the same if I wedded him instead."

Kynan made a noise in the back of his throat.

"Use your words, Shadow King."

"I fear you've exhausted this realm's supply."

"You're hilarious. Tell me why I shouldn't take the far more pleasant Tiergan up on his offer while you're not looking."

"I will always be looking."

"All right. Stop the horse."

"Cease mishandling Osian's reins, woman!"

Maren leaned close to the horse's neck and whispered toward its twitching ear. "Whoa there, Osian. I need to verbally eviscerate your foul master." As soon as the stallion slowed, Maren jumped off to the ground, her slippered feet hitting the smooth cobblestones of the village road. She stood and crossed her arms.

A flash of movement caught her eye, but she turned and saw nothing but another closed window.

Kynan's nostrils flared, and his fingers flexed over the reins and pommel. "Fine. Say what you must to me. Upbraid me. Get it over with quickly so we can attend to issues that far outweigh your precious pride and selfish nature."

"It's not prideful or selfish to want details on what dangers lie in wait for me and my future. Since you called me queen already, I demand that you refrain from *watching* me until our Binding day."

"I thought you planned to Bind yourself to King Tiergan." He matched Maren's biting tone.

"Let us say for now that I'll wed you. That way, I am queen."

Glancing away, he nodded. "Clever." Then he faced her, his long black hair falling over one shoulder. "But I am no simpleton."

"How do you know I haven't changed my mind and have truly decided to Bind to you?" she said, pinning him with her gaze.

The muscles around his jaw worked, and he flexed his fingers.

"Readying to punch me or to propose? I'd bet none of your past lovers could ever guess which side of you they'd get from moment to moment."

The anger from his face slid away and left behind a distant stare. "Do not speak of my past loves, please."

"Please? How about return me to the Upperworld and explain everything to me in a nice tone, please? May I have the same courtesy you expect from me?"

He dismounted, threw the reins over Osian's head, and watched the sleek creature graze a clump of tall green grass encircling a water trough beside a silent pub. He was quiet long enough that Maren wondered if she truly had used up all the words in the Underworld.

She snorted at herself. "Listen—"

"You're correct. I'm in the wrong. I apologize."

CHAPTER 13

Her mouth fell open. "You're apologizing? To an Upperworlder who cares for nothing beyond her realm?" She threw as much spice into her words as possible. "This cannot be!" She pretended to faint.

Whirling, he grabbed her arm and pulled her against him. The scent of him threaded through the air. The Spirit Well hadn't smelled of incense; that had been his spicy, sweet scent floating on the night breeze.

His magic slid up her body and heated her skin like she was fevered. She struggled to take an even breath as he stared down at her with his black eyes. The deepest part of the center glowed red like banked coals.

"Do not test me," he whispered. "You have no idea the work I must do to keep this place alive. It is all on me. Not King Tiergan."

"He isn't a dark lord as he said?" she asked.

"He is, but his power is nothing to mine."

Maren tapped his chest and tried not to enjoy the

feel of the hard muscle under his leather vest. "Confident sort, aren't you?"

"It is a fact," he said. "That is all. Ask me your questions, and I will answer."

"Why will a Binding mend the Oak?"

"We don't know," Kynan said.

Maren crossed her arms and took a step back. "Tiergan told me the truth."

"He blends truth with fiction, so beware." He pronounced each word sharply as if he were presenting weapons before a duel.

"And if I wed him instead of you, will the Sacred Oak be mended?" She had her own blade to bear.

"Perhaps," Kynan said tightly. He was flexing those large hands again as if this all taxed him greatly. "But it would be more of a...a gamble. His power would take longer to heal the damage."

"So that's more truth from Tiergan."

Kynan closed his eyes briefly. "He doesn't wield Cynnwrf," he said, touching the hilt of his sword, "so King Tiergan's power is far below my own, but a Binding between you and him could heal the Sacred Oak so long as you don't allow the poison to spread much farther."

"What is your history with him?" she asked, prodding further.

"I can't tell you that."

"You said you would answer my questions."

"I will not tell someone else's tale," he said.

He did have some honor stuffed in the corners of his dark self. Maybe. "Whose tale is it to tell?"

"The last Awenydd's. My former queen."

Oh. *Oh.* "Where is she now? Why isn't your Bond to her mending the Oak and the mysterious decay there?"

"She is long dead." That distant look appeared in his eyes again, and he dropped his hold on Maren.

No one was this good at acting. His grief was real. She bit her lip, wondering if she should say something. "I'm sorry for your loss."

Surprise flickered across his eyes. "Thank you. I am sorry for treating you in the manner I did."

"Thank you."

Now, they were getting somewhere.

She still didn't trust the elven king of the Underworld any farther than she could toss him, but this was progress.

A hollow feeling crept across Maren's chest. Would said progress ever lead to her freedom?

If these lords were telling the truth, and she was fated to remain here with one of them to save everyone, then so be it.

Her stomach roiled, and she bit her lip, feeling like she was going to be sick.

"Are you unwell?" Kynan's hand moved toward her elbow, but she pulled back, and his mouth flattened into a line.

"Of course I'm unwell. Think about my last several hours, Shadow King."

When her parents had been murdered, she'd thought she'd die along with them for the pain of it. She'd been untethered from life, feeling lost and as if she were falling through an empty sky as surely as someone who'd leapt from a mountaintop. But when she'd met the wild bunch of royals during the battle with those who had killed her parents, she'd found her roots. She could not lose Brielle, Aury, and the rest now. She refused to go back to being utterly alone.

Unless that truly was the only way to save them.

Sadness pulled at her chest and her limbs, and she felt as though every ounce of magic had been sucked out her, that if she were to lie on the ground, she would simply cease to exist. It was such a profound grief, laced with poisonous shame and shot through with fear.

"High King Kynan?"

The voice startled her from the dark place her mind had ventured into, and she realized Kynan had been speaking to her. She had no idea what he had said.

A slender elven man walked tentatively from a house bordered in blue poppies and bowed low, leaving the doors to what she guessed was his home open behind him. "I'm sorry, but, Your Majesty?"

"Hello, Jeston," Kynan said to the man, though his gaze remained on Maren for a moment longer, what she guessed might have been concern showing in his eyes. "Your middle boy is doing quite well. Has a fine hand with the horses." Kynan's white teeth showed just a bit in a small smile.

Kynan's entire persona altered with Jeston's appearance. His shoulders relaxed, his face brightened, and he lost that coiled rage that seemed to wrap his every movement.

"Thank you so much for welcoming him into your service, my lord king." Jeston gestured to the doors.

"We would be honored to host you and your guest if you need lodging. My wife made a fine stew tonight, and there's cheese as well."

A black and white sheepdog slipped from the cracked doors and stood beside Jeston, wagging her tail. Kynan scratched the dog's ear, and the light glittered off the sigil ring on his smallest finger.

He wasn't a monster to the dog or to Jeston. He was a kindly king without arrogance. He didn't use fear to control this subject.

Why did he treat Maren so differently? Because she was an Upperworlder, if his earlier words proved anything.

But why did he hate Upperworlders so much?

"We have already eaten, but thank you very much," Kynan said. "We have a duty to perform tomorrow at the Spirit Well. We would be honored to rest our heads on your pillows, if my queen agrees?" He turned to Maren, eyebrows lifted and eyes narrowed.

Did he want her to agree or politely decline? She didn't want to offend the fellow. "I...yes, if it's not too much trouble. I'd be happy to sleep on the floor by the fire." She wouldn't, but she wasn't about to be picky. She'd grown up in a humble home. It would be familiar if not comfortable. Besides, a villager's floor was far better than a king's prison of a chamber.

"We have an extra room," Jeston said. "It's no trouble at all."

Kynan bowed his head before glancing at Maren. "Jeston and Beca handle the inn's overflow crowd during harvest and festival days."

"Ah. Lovely." She smiled at Jeston, then took a turn petting the dog, who wagged her tail harder and pressed against Maren's leg. "Thank you very much."

It was odd to act like all was well when Maren was here against her will, but she couldn't figure out what to say that might help her. Jeston would certainly take sides with his king, or worse, she'd force the fellow's hand and have him go against a powerful ruler who held his middle son's wellbeing in his grip, not to mention everyone else's.

And if what Kynan and Tiergan said of the Binding was true, she had to stay and learn to live with that.

She wouldn't get help here finding out if marriage was truly the only way to do this. She needed an outsider, an ally, someone who either wanted to defy Kynan or one who could be talked into telling the truth even if it went against their king.

She refused to simply accept what Tiergan and Kynan said of the mending of the Sacred Oak and the Binding. She wanted Filip to tell her more of what Costel had taught him and to have the ear of her new family with this mad decision of what to do and how to move forward.

If marrying a dark lord was the only way to save the realms, then of course she'd do it.

She pressed her eyes shut and fought a terrible shiver. She wasn't about to sacrifice her life in the Upperworld without hearing it was truly necessary from a wholly reliable source.

"I prepared the room you'll share with your queen, my king." Jeston welcomed them inside quickly, keeping his voice down. A chorus of light snoring came from a closed set of doors where she presumed the rest of his family was sleeping in one large bed as her family had when she was a child.

"What did you say?" she asked, feeling disjointed and blurry at the edges. "I'm sorry. I'm dead tired, and it sounded like you said *share*."

CHAPTER 14

"As in share a single room?" Maren asked, earning her a scowl from Kynan and a nod from Jeston.

"Is that not acceptable?" Jeston asked.

"No," she blurted at the same moment Kynan said, "Of course."

Kynan's nostrils flared as he glanced her way. "Of course we will share a room. It is more than enough for us, and we thank you."

There was no chance in any realm in any world that she was going to share a bed with Kynan. She'd sleep on the floor with a giant smile on her face before she did that.

"I'm so grateful for your generosity," she said to Jeston. He and his wife would have to launder the bedding, clean the room, and feed them in the morning. This gesture would set their other work back by a half day, and that was tough on a villager's life. She had been a humble villager and knew it well.

Jeston led them by candlelight up a narrow set of wooden stairs to a balcony that overlooked the main room. He swung open yet another set of double doors and placed the candle on a round nightstand by the single bed that, no, she was definitely not sharing with Kynan.

"Why are there so many double doors in this kingdom?" She fought a jaw-cracking yawn as the black and white sheepdog appeared again. "Every room in this realm has double doors." The dog made herself comfortable by the fire.

Jeston looked to Kynan as if he were asking permission to speak. Kynan gave him a smile.

"It's the way of shadow elves," Jeston said. "We remember one best enters and leaves a room with a friend. A reminder that we are not alone. We live so near the spirits that it can feel as if death breathes down our necks, but we don't have to be alone in that, or in anything. We shadow elves support one another from one place to the next."

"O un lle i'r llall," Kynan said. "From one place to the next."

The men bowed their heads to one another like they were equals, and Maren's heart gave a squeeze.

Everyone in the Upperworld was wrong about the Underworld. It wasn't all horror and terrible creatures. Here was camaraderie, community, a sense of true loyalty—and even a dog. Seeing the shadow elves acting this way should've perhaps made her feel pleased at the potential her future might hold, but it only made her miss her new family that much more. Tears sprang to her eyes. No matter what, she would return. She'd never stop trying unless what the shadow elves said was true and the very act would mean their deaths.

Bidding them good rest, Jeston took his leave with the dog at his side. Kynan hung his cloak on the stand in the corner as Maren sighed. Here came the whole "I'm king here and it would be untoward for me to demean myself by resting anywhere but the bed" talk...

"You take the bed," Kynan said. "I'll sleep by the doors. My subjects are mostly loyal, but they're not perfect."

The mighty Shadow King was taking the floor for her and guarding the way in to keep her safe? She blinked, her heart ticking faster at the protective fire in his eyes.

"Thank you," she said, feeling awkward as she sat on the bed. "Humans aren't either. There are always those who have so much anger that they strike out at their leaders or the innocent."

"Which role do you see yourself in this night? Leader or innocent?" Using a blue crockery pitcher, Kynan filled two wooden cups. He handed one to her.

She just stared at the cup. "I'm not the elves' leader and you know it."

He bumped her hand with the offered cup, and she took it. "In a way, you most certainly are, Awenydd."

"I shouldn't be."

"Why not?"

The water was cool and sweet; she finished the cup, smirking. "I've never been the leader type. I'm more of the 'borrow the neighbor's horse and ride into the night for thrills' type. Or the one who enjoys too many ales and can't get out of bed until thumped soundly by my fellow fishermen."

His eyes narrowed sharply, and his chest heaved in a shocked breath. "Thumped?"

"Get your mind out of the gutter, High King Kynan of the Iron and the Hill Whatever and So Forth. Thumped means to be hit lightly on the head."

He looked like he'd swallowed a mouthful of fish oil. "Ah."

"Really? That's it? I was waiting on something like 'Of course your behavior includes a distasteful proclivity for thievery and hedonism, for you are an Upperworlder.'"

His lips pursed, and his eyebrow shifted up a fraction. "Would I have been wrong?"

That horrid, desirous magic flowed from him in waves that she had to press back with her witch's will. "No. Fully accurate. But not all Upperworlders are as fun as me. Most of them are pretty uptight. A bit like someone else I recently met."

His jaw muscles tensed, and he turned away. "Would you like assistance with your gown? I should have provided more suitable clothing," he said, his tone sharp but directed at himself.

The gown had lacings in the back, and she fumbled to undo the knot Eefa had crafted. "Maybe."

He faced her and nodded, lips in a tight line as he moved behind her. His fingers brushed her lower back, and she swallowed. The gown loosened, and he stepped away.

"Will that do?" His voice was deep and rough.

She cleared her throat, the places his fingers had touched feeling more alive than the rest of her. "Yes. Thank you."

He looked to the doors, giving her privacy. "Get some sleep. We have much to do tomorrow."

She slid the gown off and pulled on a linen shift Jeston or his wife had left for her on the bed.

Kynan removed his leather vest and sword belt, leaving his shirt on with his leather trousers. He retrieved a folded blanket from a set of shelves by the hearth, shook it out, and settled onto the cleanly swept floor. Propping his head with his arm, he angled so that he could see both the doors and Maren, although his eyes were currently closed. He looked younger relaxed like that with his dusky black lashes resting on his sharp elven cheekbones.

Maren peeled off her damp shoes, then climbed under the bedcovers to lie on her stomach, leaving one bare foot hanging out of the blanket as was her habit. She pressed her face into the pillow and wished for a bucket of croissants and her wand. If she got her wish, she'd eat every last one of those buttery buggers, then magic herself into the Upperworld faster than one could say *"Handsome Underworld kings aren't all they're cracked up to be."*

CHAPTER 15

Maren woke to a warm set of muscled arms. Still foggy with leftover dreams of feasts and dancing, she snuggled into said arms and grinned. Ah. Lovely. The man behind her smelled like spice and maybe leather... She must have met him at Brielle and Dorin's ball last night. Maybe he was a deliciously fine-looking lord like Dorin.

Her mind cleared as she woke further, and her blood went cold.

She shot up and twisted.

Kynan lay on his bent arm, one eye cracked open. "Calm yourself." His voice held no emotion. It was impossible to tell if he'd been enjoying being beside her in the bed or if she was a nuisance to him. "I did nothing untoward. You were shivering, your teeth clattering loud enough to wake the household."

Nuisance, then. She glared and climbed out of bed as he propped himself up on an elbow. Ignoring his alluringly sleep-rumpled mass of black hair and very nibble-worthy lower lip, she crossed her arms. "I doubt that I was shivering that hard. It's not even chilly in here."

He looked at the ceiling. "If you tell me you didn't enjoy the warmth of my careful embrace," he said, his tone revealing exactly nothing of his feelings, "I'll know you for a liar."

She had savored his warmth, but goats would pen poetry before she'd admit it. "L-let's be on our way," she stammered, cheeks hot.

A knock sounded at the doors. "Forgive the intrusion," a female voice said.

Kynan stood. "Are you all right with Beca entering?" He offered the blanket he'd used last night and eyed Maren's thin shift.

Maren took the blanket and draped it over her shoulders. "Please come in," she said toward the doors.

Beca walked in and handed Maren a satchel, a dark blue woolen dress with a split skirt for riding, some neatly worked stockings, a gray cloak, a pair of sturdy shoes, and a split skirt shift to go under the dress.

"Thank you so much for this. That gown is lovely, but not the best for riding."

"My pleasure, Awenydd." Beca gave them each a curtsey.

"I will see you paid for your trouble and the clothing, Mistress Beca," Kynan said.

Beca nodded nervously like she longed to impress and wasn't sure she would, then hurried out of the room.

Maren's slippers sat by the glowing embers of the fire in the hearth. Someone had set them close to the heat to dry. She glanced at Kynan, but he'd turned his back to give her privacy.

She tucked the slippers, her shift, and the folded gown into the satchel, then proceeded to slide on the split shift, dress, and cloak. So much easier than a gown. Her hair was a disaster. She tugged at it, trying to free the worst of the knots.

Kynan rose, removed his shirt, and walked to the table sitting under the window. He poured water from a slender pale green pitcher into a basin, then washed his face roughly. Maren tried to shut her open mouth as she gazed at his amazing male form. Goddess, he was lovely. She put a finger on her chin and forced her lips shut.

"You agree to willingly wed me, then?" Kynan said.

He didn't turn from the washing basin to look at her. The muscles in his back coiled and twisted under his smooth skin. Was he nervous? No, the Shadow King was never anxious about women, surely.

"No," she said sharply. "I want to speak with people I trust to make certain you're telling the truth and that they also agree it is the only way."

"Impossible."

He splashed his face again, and she tried to stop staring at his long legs, very trim waist, and bare torso. He was built like a warrior, scarred here and there, and lean from a lifetime of hard training. She'd seen enough of warriors to know the look by now. It was a look she solidly approved of.

"Have you even tried?" she asked. "Tomorrow's

sunset marks Samhain, no? The veil will thin. I'm sure Aury can speak to me through her water scrying then." She wasn't sure, but she had to hold on to hope.

Drying his face with a linen cloth, he pursed his lips. "Perhaps. I hadn't thought of the effect Samhain might have on our predicament. It's a clever idea, Awenydd. We can ask Lady Hafwen."

"Who is Lady Hafwen?"

"A shadow elf who facilitates the Binding," Kynan said. "She knows more than me about pushing the boundaries of our realm and yours. She is the only one of her kind here, very powerful and a friend to me unlike any other. She was there for me through a painful time in my life."

"What? Were you abducted too?" She narrowed her eyes.

He threw the cloth onto the table, then grabbed his undershirt. "You vex me, woman."

"And I'll never stop doing so. If you were in my shoes, would you?"

Looking out the small window, he crossed his arms. "Perhaps not."

"I didn't think so. You don't strike me as the forgiving sort."

The corner of his mouth moved like he might have been fighting a smile.

"Where does Lady Hafwen live?"

"It's not a far ride. Just beyond Calon Dywyll, nearer to the entrance to this realm. To the north."

She was surprised he supported her desire to

communicate with the Upperworld. She didn't say as much for fear of startling him out of this unusual bout of good sense and open-mindedness.

A knock sounded at the doors. "My lord king?" It was Jeston.

"Enter as you please." Kynan finished pulling his leather vest into place.

Jeston and Beca entered the room with trays of simple bread rounds, bowls of something hot, and shallow dishes filled with dark purple berries.

Beca tucked a lock of chestnut hair behind her pointed ear and curtseyed low. "It's been just lovely having you both here, my king, my queen."

"A pleasure to see you, Mistress Beca." Kynan gave her knuckles a quick press of his lips, and she blushed red as an apple.

Maren didn't blame her. Kynan's commanding presence combined with the fact that he was the most powerful lord in this realm and the Upperworld was incredibly attractive.

Maren accepted a cup of hot tea from Beca, then sat when the woman bid her to take one of the chairs by the fire.

"Eat the oats before they're cold, my queen. Don't mind us."

Maren nodded and tucked in. The food was simple and filling. She didn't realize she'd missed humble meals. Life at her friends' various courts had her consuming every type of spice and oddity the royal chefs could work up, and it was all very good. But this kind of meal was comforting in a way that fine court dishes never were.

Leaving the door ajar, Jeston and Beca went to ready Osian and another horse they said their neighbor would be more than pleased to loan.

Maren finished her berries and hot oats only to find Kynan's gaze on her.

"You enjoy village fare?" he asked.

"I do, actually. Why, is it too humble for your fancy mouth?"

He scraped his bowl clean, then held it up for her to see. "What do you think?"

"It's comforting, isn't it?"

He frowned as if he didn't understand.

"I grew up with this kind of food," she said. "I've lived with royals for a while now, and their courtly treats are wonderful, but this reminds me of home."

His gaze softened, and an easy smile spread over his lips. He looked so different when he smiled. How could he be both Underworld king and kind lord? Which side of him was a lie?

"I enjoy every bite of any food that crosses my path." He wiped his lips, then took his weapons belt from the hook and secured it around his waist. "I often forget to eat, as busy as I am, and once I sit to feast, I find myself famished."

Maren ate the last berry and watched him make the bed as if he were the maid.

"You really do care about your people, don't you?" she asked.

As he turned, his eyebrows lifted. "What makes you say that?"

"The way you treat Jeston and Beca. How you are grateful for simple fare. The way you, a king, just tidied a bed."

His eyes closed briefly. Then he went to her chair and went down on one knee.

CHAPTER 16

She gripped the chair's armrests, shock freezing her.

"Once again, I apologize for my behavior. You are not like the other Upperworlders. I never should have stolen you in the manner I did. I never should have taken you at all." His throat moved in a swallow, and he looked down as if he were struggling with what to say next. When he met her gaze again, she couldn't deny the truth in their dark depths. "Please accept my apology and know that if I could go back and ask you to come with me in a less beastly way, I would."

Kynan was changing right before her eyes. Chatting, sharing information, apologizing in earnest. Or was he playing a role?

"I...I accept your apology," she said quietly. She wanted to believe him. Stones, with those pleading, dark eyes and that deep, soft voice, the idiotic side of her wanted to wrap him in a hug. "But your actions will speak for your true feelings."

He nodded and reached for her hand as he had with Beca. She tentatively held out her fingers. He brushed his lips across her knuckles, and a shaky breath left her. Her other hand fisted tightly. His gaze locked onto hers, and that fascinating ruby light glowed in their depths.

"I will show you my genuine remorse and my true heart, my lady, if you will allow it."

She snatched her hand back. "That's lovely, but..." She couldn't deny that a part of her wanted to drape herself over this chair and let him kiss her hand all day. "I'm still the uncouth Awenydd. I'll do my best to keep from offending you and your people, but I'm bluntly honest by nature. I can't hide my true thoughts from my face. I am no hero."

He almost grinned as he pulled her up with him, keeping a distance between them. "I don't mind honesty. I only hope that you will work to learn our ways."

Maren shook her head. "Are you always this mercurial?" She gazed at him, taking in the earnest look in his eye, the shift of his shoulders, and the way he held himself. But she couldn't find the lie in his body language.

"Like the weather here, he is." Beca bobbed her head as if in apology for interrupting and waved her hand at two young girls, who set to gathering the trays.

Kynan pulled his shirt over his head, then set a hand on the back of Beca's head briefly as if he were blessing her. "It's nice to have a second home."

Beca's eyes shone. "Where is Ivar? And the rest of the lads? Are they off on a big hunt?"

Lads? Was he close with his personal guards like Filip?

"They're with Lady Hafwen," Kynan said to Beca. "We'll see them shortly, as we are headed that way to discuss elements of the Binding and the timing of the event after we visit the Spirit Well."

"Trouble for the lads again?" Beca clicked her tongue.

"Indeed." Kynan's mouth tipped down at the edges as he donned his vest, belt, and cloak. He held one of the double doors open for Maren.

"Who is Ivar?" she asked.

"Oh!" Beca shooed the girls down the stairs, then trailed Kynan and Maren away from the room and toward the front doors. "It's his familiar. A wyvern."

Maren's stomach flipped, and she recalled the ceiling in her room at his castle. "You have a pet dragon too?" She'd thought only Filip claimed that astounding feat.

"Not a dragon," Kynan said. "A wyvern. And who do you know who has a dragon familiar?"

"Prince Filip of Balaur and Lore, Princess Aury's husband."

Kynan turned on the last of the stairs, lifting his eyebrows. "Impressive."

"They call him the elven mage because he can communicate with her silently."

"The dragon truly is his familiar, then..." Kynan nodded. "Interesting. I didn't realize that type of relationship still occurred in the Upperworld."

"It's the only instance of such a relationship that I

know of." Maren followed Beca and Kynan toward the post where Osian and a new mount were tied.

They bid farewell to Jeston and Beca and met Maren's horse, Afal, which she learned meant apple. They rode out of the village then rode off.

As they trotted along the winding road between two deep green, sheep-dotted hills, Maren wondered what this Hafwen would be like. Would she be willing to help Maren even though it meant delaying the Binding and posed a risk to the possible solution? What if Hafwen demanded that her dear friend Kynan Bind with Maren on the spot?

Maren swallowed and tried to hope for the best as they headed for their meeting with the god of air.

A SHIMMERING, PALE FORM AWAITED THEM, POWER emanating from the white-blue glow of the male silhouette. Maren's fingers sparked with magical fire, the sign her particular type of magic was active here in the Underworld. The urge to bow her head to the ground nearly had her leaping from Afal's back.

"It's the god Arcturus," she whispered, sliding from the horse.

Kynan let Osian and Afal graze. He joined Maren where she grinned at Arcturus. He was a very handsome god with chiseled features and a patient and curious look in his large eyes. If she ignored the differences in their demeanor and facial expressions, Kynan and Arcturus could have been brothers. Too bad she'd ended up taken by the evil twin.

"Greetings, Awenydd." Arcturus's voice was rich, and it echoed as gods' and goddesses' voices always did. "I thought perhaps I'd see you again. You've witnessed the decay from the poison, I suppose."

"We have," Maren answered.

Kynan looked left and right, most likely trying to see what Maren did.

"Do you know its cause?" she asked.

Being surrounded by two gods—because really, Kynan was a lesser god—with all their shimmering looks and the power practically shining from their impressive bodies was rather disconcerting. Maren really and truly missed her wand. It wasn't delightful to be so weak in the face of these two. She felt like an ant meeting with eagles.

Arcturus shook his head, his shoulder-length hair brushing his shoulders. "It's a poison. Magical in make. The damage is spreading quickly."

With a grave look, he turned and pointed to the whitened root and the ice. The frozen area had indeed expanded to reach another large root of the Sacred Oak, and a strange swirling of spirits surrounded that edge of the well.

Her stomach rolled over. "They're suffering."

"Who?" Kynan asked.

"The spirits," Maren said.

Arcturus nodded. "Ask the Shadow King to feed them again if he is able. They grow restless, and I fear for the safety of the nearby villagers."

So when Kynan had been kneeling at the well,

sending his shadows into the water, he must have been feeding the spirits his energy. "What will they do?" she asked Arcturus.

"They will find energy where they must. The spirits don't have the self-control that some of the living do."

"You mean they'll kill the villagers if we don't stop the decay?"

"Of course they will," Kynan said, taking hold of the conversation. Then he seemed to remember the invisible god Maren was speaking to and bowed low. "Apologies, god of air."

"Please tell him there's no need for apologizing. His actions speak to his heart."

"You think him a good sort, do you? Because I don't. Forgive my bluntness."

"You'll have to decide that yourself. I'm not often in this realm. I prefer to reside in the well or traveling through the air in the living's realm. But I know little of the living's realm of late..." His form faded and began to disappear.

Panic jolted Maren forward, and she nearly reached out a hand. Kynan's grip stopped her from doing what her gut knew was wrong—trying to touch the ancient god. "Should I wed High King Kynan to heal the Sacred Oak?"

She could feel how tense Kynan was beside her. To think she might someday know his mannerisms and his body as well as her own...

Only Arcturus's silhouette was visible. The roots, Spirit Well, and the mossy ground showed through him.

"I cannot influence you one way or the other. You must choose. But I can tell you that the decay resulted from a foul, magical substance cast at the Oak by a dark witch not so long ago. She is no longer among the living or the spirits and has passed completely from existence."

The ancient god disappeared.

CHAPTER 17

"The old witch," Maren whispered, bowing her head toward the spot where Arcturus had been.

She ignored Kynan to think. In the battle she'd fought alongside Brielle and the others, they'd risen up against a legendary witch who'd possibly had access to a concoction the enemy had brought with them to the field.

"It's Magebane," she said to Kynan. She shivered hard, wrapping her arms tightly around her middle. In the Wylfen dungeon, the evil apothecary had subjected her to Magebane. The concoction had sucked the very magical essence from her being and left her wishing she were dead. Terrible, vicious stuff, it was. "That's what's killing the Oak. I have to talk to Costel. He knows much about poisons and foul magic substances."

"Who is Costel?"

"He is a knight of the Balaur court, Prince Filip's

man, and he is a friend. He's a scribe as well and knows everything there is to know about, well, everything."

Kynan cocked an eyebrow.

"Truly. The elven knight is mostly brain with a dash of brawn."

"There is no time. You witness the spread yourself. You spoke to the god. I see that he is gone now." Kynan eyed her hands, which were now free from magical sparks.

"He is, but—"

"But nothing. He surely told you the situation is dire. We cannot wait to untangle the truth about this Magebane. We must commit to the Binding now before it grows worse." Dark circles she hadn't noticed hung below his eyes. "I've experienced the horror of what happens when the spirits grow hungry."

"The spirit boy did mention being hungry."

Kynan's cheeks paled as a wind rose and tugged at Maren's cloak. "I will not allow my people to go through that pain again. Hungry spirits suck the energy from the living. All the energy. They pull every shred of life from you and leave you as a husk. It's a horrific way to die. The cold. The agony... And when the spirits grow hungry, they don't know themselves. They are animalistic, functioning on instinct alone and nigh on impossible to defeat. I have destroyed them before, but I almost lost my life. I don't know that I could do it again. It's a tragedy for all involved." He knelt at the well's edge.

"If I Bind with you or with Tiergan," she said,

watching Kynan's shoulders tighten, "can I visit the Upperworld occasionally?"

Kynan's shadows branched from his back, hands, and head, darkness coiling before rolling into the Spirit Well. It didn't seem to affect the decay at all, but at least the gray ice wasn't visibly spreading at the moment. "No. Once we are Bound," he said, stressing the word *we*, "neither of us can leave while the other lives."

Either Kynan or Tiergan was lying. "Then you have to allow me to return first. Before we Bond."

"I do not. And I will not. They would keep you, selfish beasts that they are."

"They?"

"Your humans."

"Most of them are elves."

"Your Upperworld folk. The elves there are no better than humans, I'm sure."

"How are you so sure? They wouldn't hold me back if our Binding was the only way to keep the realms from crumbling into nothingness. They've all had to sacrifice in various ways, and they would understand that my life is no different."

Kynan stood quickly.

Maren gasped, stepping back and keeping tabs on those shadows of his.

His eyes pinched like her flinch hurt him, but that couldn't be right. "You're willing to sacrifice your life, then? You're prepared aside from your intent to visit them?"

"I don't know if I'll ever be truly ready." It was the

truth. This had all happened so quickly. It wasn't as if she believed her life and her freedom were more important than every soul in the realms above and below. "But if I don't agree to the Binding, the world will end anyway, and where does that leave my precious freedom? Not much to do when the world turns to icy despair. Sounds far too chilly for my liking."

Kynan made a noise of what might have been reluctant amusement.

"You look ready to fall over from fatigue." Not that she cared.

She blew out a breath and climbed atop Afal's broad back, and they began their journey to meet Lady Hafwen.

CHAPTER 18

On their way to Lady Hafwen's manor, they rode through hills covered in trees Maren had no name for, their leaves in shades of purple, dark red, and deep gold. It was autumn here too, although flowers—blue poppies, snow-white wood anemones, pink campion, and some sunny yellow ones —bloomed as if they didn't care about the season.

"What are those yellow flowers called? I haven't seen those in the Upperworld."

"Hawkleaf. It's bitter as a tea but cures a persistent cough."

"And that purple flower there?" She pointed to a bank of delicate blooms clustered like children whispering secrets.

"Mistpetal. Looks like mist in the distance."

Maren looked up and did indeed see rows of the light purple growth along ridges that appeared very much like fog.

"The mistpetal can help one sleep," Kynan said.

"Do you have healers in the Underworld?"

"We do," he said, "but they can't work magic as the fae in Illumahrah do." Two lines appeared between his thick brows.

"You don't like the fae, do you? How much have you interacted with them, seeing as they are basically your neighbors?"

Kynan glanced at her, looking dangerously annoyed again. "Not at all if I can help it."

"You sound like Prince Dorin of the mountain elves. He loathes the fae. Except for his friend, Prince Werian. Werian is difficult to resist for long."

Kynan's gaze pressed against Maren's cheek, then slid roughly down her body. "You failed to resist this fae prince?"

She barked a laugh. "Are you jealous? I'm not yours yet, you know. And I may never be, so just wipe that look off your handsome face, High King Kynan."

Her heart cinched. Saying *yours yet* out loud just made it all seem so real.

She'd had a close relationship with one boy in her youth before she'd been imprisoned for being a witch. He'd been sweet and he'd made her laugh. It had been simple. Innocent. She still remembered him in her prayers to the Source. Since she'd left Wylfenden with Brielle and spent time in Balaur and Lore, she'd found one man who'd caught her eye. They'd danced at the summer ball and traded kisses in the dark, but the connection hadn't been deep. It hadn't satiated her need for someone who was hers and hers alone, someone who understood her and saw her as she truly was.

Could Kynan be that someone?

Or was she destined to be without a love?

Stomach twisting, she shut her eyes and let Afal trot as she saw fit.

"Awenydd?" Kynan's warm hand touched her shoulder, and when she opened her eyes, his face was soft with worry. "I can take you on my horse and tie Afal alongside if you need rest."

"No. I'm...I'm fine." Horrors—she was about to cry. She straightened her back and cleared her throat. "I'm all right. Thank you."

"What were you thinking about?" Kynan said, his voice uncharacteristically tentative. "Maybe I could help?"

"I was...I thought I'd find love in one of the new kingdoms I've been visiting. I saw myself settling down with a lower noble perhaps, someone with land, even just a humble parcel. I imagined myself maybe not as a mother, but with a house full of jokes, games, music, and cats."

"Cats?"

She shrugged.

"I'm not mocking you. I just...cats," he said.

"You don't like them?"

"One adopted me at Lady Hafwen's manor. A barn cat that was missing one ear and smelled like week-old milk." He was almost smiling. "Lady Hafwen claimed that I needed Ceridwen to learn patience."

"That's a fine name for a barn cat."

"She was a force of nature," Kynan said, "make no mistake."

Maren grinned, imagining Kynan with an ancient cat on his lap, pawing his stomach and yowling for milk.

They rode onward through paths that wound up the foothills of the mountains. Mists like spirits shrouded the peaks, and a waterfall danced down the black rocks to the west.

It was the most beautiful scenery. Only in dreams had she seen such atmospheric vistas.

"I wasn't being fair," Kynan said suddenly.

"About what?"

"You told me what you thought your life would be. I told you about Ceridwen."

"You don't have to tell me."

"I think I do; I should. As a youth, I didn't imagine my future mate. I was too set on learning how to sword fight and use my power. But later, yes, later I saw myself with a powerful woman who could be my partner at court and in life. Someone who loved the outdoors as I did and who appreciated simple joys when they weren't busy with the more pressing moments of life."

They came to a steep slope, and Osian decided that hurrying up the hill was not negotiable. Afal followed, galloping up the rise.

She popped her knuckles and chewed her lip. Did she want Kynan to see her the way he had envisioned his mate? Could he truly envision her that way if this worked out?

The road opened into a level acre of land where low trees heavy with fire-colored fruits led Maren and Kynan to a large manor house with a roof of layered slate that rose in three peaks. It was small compared to Kynan's, but no less majestic. Time had worn down the dark stones that made up the walls, and parts of the roof showed signs of ruin. Somehow, that only made the place more approachable. Maren smiled at the arched windows that sat in a group of three above double doors. A collection of wooden outbuildings crowded the western side of the property.

A dark shape the size of a large falcon flew from the peaked roof and swooped toward them.

Envisioning sharp claws and sharper teeth, Maren ducked her head, hugging Afal as the horse danced nervously.

"Ivar!" Kynan stretched out his arm, and a black-scaled wyvern landed lightly, its leathery wings shuffling.

"He's beautiful."

The wyvern's two feet boasted large talons as inky as the rest of him. His scales and eyes glittered like they were made of glass, and the creature whipped its tail to show crystalline spikes in a smoky hue. Kynan scratched Ivar's chin, and a nickering sound echoed from the wyvern's throat.

"Sut wyt ti, fy ffrind gwyllt? Would you like to meet the Awenydd, your new queen?" Kynan crooned, running a ringed finger down the wyvern's scaled sides.

Ivar's gaze flicked to Maren's face, and she lifted her hand in reflex, forgetting she didn't have her wand. The wyvern was gorgeous, but he was assuredly deadly-looking—much like his master.

Kynan glanced at her hand as she dropped it, concern tightening his eyes. "You lost your wand when I took you. Is that correct?"

"Yes." She didn't try to lessen the fire in her response.

"Next time we're at the Spirit Well, we'll ask the Sacred Oak's roots for another."

She gave him a smile to thank him for his kindness, and he bowed his head as if he accepted her gratitude.

"How much time do we have before the spirits grow too hungry and begin to seek energy beyond the Oak?" she asked, smoothing her trousers.

"There's no way to know for certain. When I last fed them with my magic, they seemed sated, so I'd guess we have five days or so."

Maren's head ached from tensing her jaw. She tried to breathe and focus on today.

Ivar extended his jet-hued wings and flew into the air, displaying a spot of white that marred his right flank.

"Is that what Beca meant when she mentioned trouble?" Maren asked, pointing.

The wyvern gracefully perched on a branch of a dark-leaved tree towering above the crumbled corner of Hafwen's abode. Shaking his wings, he dislodged seedpods that flurried down to land on Maren's and Kynan's shoulders and laps. Maren lifted one. The pod had the shape of a heart and was pale blue like the poppies here.

"The damage on the Sacred Oak's roots and subsequent lack of magical energy affects the creatures here in different ways. The last time a decay like this one spread, we lost all but five wyverns."

"When was that?"

Gaze distant, Kynan adjusted his hands on the pommel, the reins laced between his large fingers twitching. "Long, long ago."

"How long?"

"Four hundred ten of your years."

A stillness stole across Maren's chest, holding her as surely as his shadows had. "And...and you stopped that decay by marrying the Awenydd of that time."

"I did."

"How did she die?"

"You are the Awenydd. You must ask her. It is not my place to tell."

Maren sighed. She'd thought maybe he'd open up about his history.

"Greetings, my king." Flanked by two female servants, a well-dressed woman Maren guessed was Hafwen strode from the double doors. She was tall with unbound hair that reached to her waist. As she stood from her deep curtsey, she looked at Maren. The woman—a shadow elf, as her pointed ears and incredibly sharp cheekbones displayed—had one light gray eye and one made entirely of...gold. Maren would've bet her collection of spices that there was a good story behind that eye.

The woman stopped suddenly and stared at Maren, sending a chill of fear down Maren's spine. She could almost taste the magic on this woman, who looked ready to commit murder.

An odd but incredibly comforting thought swept through her mind.

Kynan would protect her.

A secret warmth nestled around her heart.

CHAPTER 19

"You're here..." the woman whispered.
Would Kynan be quick to draw his sword as he'd been when Tiergan had appeared at the well?

But the woman's glare melted, and a broad smile stretched her cheeks. Exhaling with relief, Maren smiled back.

With a nod to Maren, the woman looked at Kynan. "My day has been filled with wyverns and copious amounts of very black tea. How is your day progressing?"

Kynan dismounted and took the woman's hand and kissed it. "Lady Hafwen, it's lovely to see you. Our day has been filled with travel and much discussion on my shortcomings as well as plant remedies. Thank you for tending to Ivar and the lads. Ivar looks much improved. Here, meet my new queen, Maren the Awenydd."

Hafwen smiled mysteriously. "I heard about you, Lady Maren."

Maren slid from Afal's back and tied the horse beside Kynan's mount. "I'm glad to know that abductions aren't so commonplace here that they go unnoticed." Maren raised an eyebrow in challenge.

Nodding, Hafwen lightly hit Kynan's stomach. "I like her very much. You need someone to set you down a notch, my lord king."

Kynan's dark eyes glowed faintly, but he bowed. "As you say, Lady Hafwen."

Hafwen curtseyed low to Maren, who returned the gesture, suddenly glad for the time she'd spent at the royal courts of her friends. It was a strange feeling to be one of the royals here... Or was that a good feeling? She wasn't sure yet.

"Tell me why I've been blessed to receive you as guests today," Hafwen said. She turned to her servants and whispered something in the shadow elf tongue. They hurried inside.

Kynan held out a hand indicating that Maren should walk ahead of him. He glanced backward as if to check that they weren't being watched or followed before he trailed her inside.

The manor house smelled like crushed leaves and rain. A rectangular table rested under the windows, and a cooking fire sat in the center of the large room. Smoke unspooled from the stacked logs and exited the building through an opening in the peaked roof. Countertops filled with small cauldrons, glass vials, and bowls stood beneath rows upon rows of hanging dried herbs.

"You're a witch like me." Maren grinned despite being a bit shocked at finding an elven witch. In the

Upperworld, only humans were born witches. She felt like she'd stumbled upon a friend's home.

One servant collected their cloaks, then disappeared through the doors and down a corridor.

"I am." Hafwen lifted a slender, pale oak wand. "Where is yours?"

"Would you like to answer that, High King Kynan?" Maren poured pepper-infused honey over her words.

"This is going to be very interesting." Hafwen traded a sly look with Maren.

Yes, yes it was.

"I've made apologies," Kynan said gruffly.

"Missing one's wand is akin to missing one's leg." Hafwen's tone said she was more than willing to relieve him of a limb so he properly understood the severity of the situation.

The servants brought in a tray of tea that smelled minty. One poured out the tea and handed it over to each of them.

Maren took a sip, and the heat was absolutely divine. "Can you help me reach the Upperworld during Samhain to obtain a new wand? My friend, Magelord Princess Aurora of Lore, is a master water scryer. I think she could manage to see and talk to me to plan a meeting if we could handle this end of the magic. I would like to speak to her and my other friends about this Binding before I commit to anything."

"Once again, I apologize," Kynan said, his eyes open and sincere. He looked at Hafwen. "I had no idea that her wand would be necessary." He sipped from his mug. his throat moving as he swallowed. Her fingers wanted to run along the tan skin near the silver embroidery on his shirt. "The last Awenydd had no wand."

"She wasn't a witch," Hafwen said. "If she'd been missing her shadow elf heart, then she'd have been dead to the magic. It is the same for a witch and her wand."

Kynan nodded, looking appropriately chastened.

What were they talking about? "Shadow elf heart?"

"We shadow elves have two hearts."

Maren's mouthed moved, but she couldn't find anything to say. Two? Perhaps that was how they could also be born as witches.

The corner of Kynan's lips twitched. "Yes. One elven and the other shadow."

"All shadow elves control shadows?" Maren asked. "Because of the heart situation?"

Hafwen nodded, sheathed her wand at her belt, and finished her tea. She set the mug down and crossed her arms. "If that shadow heart ceases to function, a shadow elf loses their magic."

"And we, witches, lose our magic when we lose our wand. Well, mostly. Can you do any magic without your wand?" Maren asked Hafwen. "I find it nearly impossible."

"Other than the power you have to speak to spirits," Kynan said, raising both eyebrows. "That is magic you perform at the highest level without any sort of wand."

"True." Maren couldn't deny she enjoyed the respect in his eyes. It was pleasant to be around someone who appreciated her power and didn't fear it. She was glad he'd seemed to realize that her way of casually speaking to the spirits didn't offend them. He hadn't chastised her after meeting with the god Arcturus.

"To clarify, all shadow elves can work shadow magic to some degree," Kynan said. "It's like any talent. Some can sing every note presented to them and others only a few. There may be one who can tally faster than anyone else in their guild. That sort of thing. Magic is a talent."

Hafwen looked to Maren. "And High King Kynan is the most talented of us all."

A thrill went through Maren, and she schooled her features to hide it. There was something exciting about knowing the most powerful shadow elf was set on courting her.

Kynan inclined his head as if to acknowledge Hafwen's compliment. He made no move to deny it.

Hafwen tapped her fingers on her elbow. "Lady Maren, you must visit the Upperworld to gain a new wand or retrieve your old one if it is undamaged. You can't function as the Awenydd without it. If you did go through with the Binding as a wandless witch, the power to heal the Sacred Oak would be greatly diminished. My witch intuition confirms that." She set a hand over her womb and one between her eyes. Maren knew that feeling well.

"I hadn't thought of that," Kynan said.

"Tiergan didn't either," Maren said, watching Hafwen and Kynan trade a heavy look at the mention of the other shadow lord. "There's no way to gain a new wand here?"

"No. We must find a way for you to go above. Hmm. It might actually be easier for me to transport you both into the Upperworld for a short time during the veil's thinning because then you'll have the power of his blood beside you, Lady Maren."

"His blood might help me cross?" Maren asked.

"It definitely should. From one place to the next, and all of that." Hafwen smiled at Kynan, repeating the phrase Maren had heard him say to Jeston, the meaning behind the double doors. "But High King Kynan, you'd have to leave your sword here in the Underworld, of course," Hafwen said.

"That wouldn't be a problem as long as you're certain you could bring us back," he said.

"If you have your sword, can you return from the Upperworld as you wish?" Maren asked.

"Yes," Kynan said.

Maren frowned. "But you can't leave at will?"

"No one can," Hafwen said before Kynan could answer.

"Unless it's Samhain," Kynan said.

"And then, only when very rare and difficult magic is successful," Hafwen added. "I'm not certain I can do it."

"How did you leave the Underworld when you set out to take me?" Maren asked Kynan.

"When the Awenydd is needed and is born to the worlds, the realm releases the Shadow King to claim her as his mate."

Maren swallowed. Mate. It was such a descriptive word, and it painted bright images in her mind... Her face flushed hotly, and she drank down the remainder of her tea just to have something to do with her hands.

Kynan's gaze danced across her cheeks and neck and

she wondered what he was thinking. "From what I have read," he said, "the issue of leaving this realm has only arisen a time or two. Normally, the Awenydd is a shadow elf. The sword gives me unmeasurable power for that endeavor, but the Source created the sword with limits. I cannot simply drag it into the Upperworld and bring chaos. And I must claim the Awenydd on the first attempt. I cannot claim you as my mate twice."

"WHAT DO YOU NEED TO MAKE THE ATTEMPT?" Kynan asked Hafwen.

"Peace and quiet to think for tonight and tomorrow. You two are welcome to remain here, and perhaps you can take Ivar out hunting, High King Kynan. He has missed you. At sundown tomorrow, I will work my magic and see if we can push you both through to the shade of the Sacred Oak. Will you return to wed High King Kynan, Lady Maren?"

She said it so boldly. There was still Tiergan's plan to consider. He'd promised a way out for her if she wed him instead. He seemed a slimy git, but if that git returned her to her found family, she would strongly consider him.

But could she give up on Kynan and choose Tiergan? Truly?

Kynan wasn't the man she'd thought he was. He wasn't a monster. Not perfect, certainly, but he'd apologized and brought her here as a display of his respect for her wishes. Her stomach fluttered, and she put a hand on her side and tried to be logical about this.

"May I speak with Lady Hafwen alone?" she asked.

"Of course." Kynan set his tea on the tray, then left the room with a quick, polite bow.

Hafwen gestured to a pair of three-legged stools with seats of linen and wool. "What is this about? I'm dying of curiosity."

The stools were surprisingly comfortable. "I met with King Tiergan."

Hafwen's back went rod-straight. The light caught her golden eye. "He is a foul one. I'm sure he seemed kind and affable, but don't be fooled."

He hadn't seemed kind, but he had been forthcoming. She had always appreciated honesty, and so far, what Tiergan had told her had been the truth—truth that Kynan had been very, very slow to reveal. Tiergan didn't seem to hold the prejudice that Kynan had against Upperworlders.

"What did he do to the king?" Maren asked. "I can tell they have a history."

"I shouldn't tell the story. It's the spirit of the last Awenydd's tale."

"But how can I trust you and the king if I don't know all the facts?" It would take more than just a story about long-ago events to earn her trust, but Hafwen didn't need to know that. Maren would most certainly summon the last Awenydd as soon as possible regardless.

"King Tiergan lured the last Awenydd away from High King Kynan."

Maren blinked, at a loss for words. "I... How? And

why didn't it break the world and ruin the healing of the Binding?"

"The damage from whatever dark magic had hurt the Underworld at that time healed soon after their union was set. Then King Tiergan used shadow magic to tempt the Awenydd," Hafwen said.

"I've felt that same sort of power from the king." Maren didn't try to disguise how angry that had made her, how much her body had wanted him and her mind had warred with itself. "He has since apologized for his behavior, but I haven't fully forgiven him yet."

"Understood. That Awenydd and the king only wedded one another to heal the Underworld. She didn't love him, so she was more easily swayed to King Tiergan's side."

A strange flutter danced through Maren's stomach, but she wasn't sure why. "But the king did love her?"

"I believe so," Hafwen said. "When she left with King Tiergan, the king released her. She was dead by the next moon."

"Did King Tiergan kill her?"

"No, but on Samhain, he worked the magic I will attempt, and he shoved her into the Upperworld with no hope of returning to High King Kynan if she changed her mind. I'm surprised she survived the crossing. Besides all of that, the loss of one Bound to another is painful. The king suffered greatly in both of his hearts, as well as in his mind and body. His very soul threatened to leave him early. Then we learned of the Awenydd's death at the hands of the humans."

Bunching her dress in sweating fists, Maren listened

closely.

"The humans," Hafwen continued, "thought that Awenydd was a demon working for the king to steal souls from the Upperworld. Fools. I have no idea where they get their wild ideas."

"Demons aren't real?"

"No. There are only shadow elves, our shadow elf lords who hold magical power, an occasional shadow elf witch," Hafwen said, giving her a wink, "and the spirits and animals, of course."

Maren's smile faded, and she cracked her knuckles nervously. "The humans murdered the king's lost love, and it was King Tiergan's fault."

"You may watch the events in my crystal plate if you wish. I warn you. The story is full of horror. Kynan lost himself for years..." Hafwen's gaze grew distant, as if she'd forgotten Maren was there.

"May I see this crystal plate?"

"Of course, Lady Maren."

"Please call me Maren."

"High King Kynan would lecture me until my final day if I disrespected you."

Because Maren was fated to mate with him and to save the realms. Not because he liked her.

"All right, then," Maren said. "Thank you, Lady Hafwen."

Hafwen grinned and handed over a flat plate formed from one piece of hazy white crystal.

"Is this similar to scrying?" Maren asked. "I've seen Aury, I mean, Princess Aurora, perform that type of water magic."

"Yes," Hafwen answered, "but it only shows the past here in the Underworld. Nothing beyond this realm. It is an old artifact, handed down to me by the one who came before me."

Maren raised her eyebrows. "Another witch?"

"The one who gave me this as well." She pointed to her eye made of gold.

The eye was fascinating, but Maren tried not to stare. "I've survived tragedy, and I don't always want to talk about it."

"I broached the topic," Hafwen said. "I'm at ease with sharing."

"I'm listening."

"The other witch hated me at first. Just for being born. We shadow elves rarely have younglings, and it was even rarer still to have two witches alive in the Underworld at the same time. She thought my arrival spelled her end."

"But it didn't?"

"No. She lived long years after viciously attacking me. I even forgave her. I think I look rather dangerously elegant with a golden eye."

"You most certainly do."

She preened and pointed to the plate. "Look into the plate and think on the story I told you. It should become faintly visible soon enough. You will feel lightheaded, especially since you have no wand to support your energy flow."

Maren nodded and focused on the crystal. Sure enough, the story Hafwen had told came to life inside the smooth surface.

CHAPTER 20

Maren stared into Hafwen's crystal plate, and suddenly there was Kynan.

Under a luminous cloud bank painted in sunset hues, the Shadow King watched as his former Awenydd walked away. Her dark braids swayed, and her slim silhouette cast a faint shadow across Kynan's boots. Tiergan grinned like a fiend in the distance. As the former Awenydd embraced her new mate, Kynan leaned against the castle wall, his face pale.

"Why didn't he fight for her?" Maren asked quietly.

"He knew."

Ah. He had known she didn't love him.

"But he didn't realize the extent to which King Tiergan would go to exact revenge on his rival, High King Kynan," Hafwen said. "If the king had known the lord's plan, he surely would have fought for her. The histories laid out in our scrolls say that when the last king died, both King Tiergan and High King Kynan had a claim to the Shadow Throne."

"Both of them?"

"They're descendants of twins born to a long-ago queen, the only Shadow Queen. King Tiergan sent assassins to kill High King Kynan on the eve of the selection, a ceremony involving a competition that determines who is strongest in shadow magic. But before the competition, High King Kynan revealed the fact that he had pulled Cynnwrf from the Moon Bog."

"Moon Bog? That certainly has a ring to it."

"It's a deeply magical place, bursting with legends."

"What happened when High King Kynan drew the sword?"

Hafwen leaned her hip against the table and crossed her arms. "King Tiergan knew he had lost the competition before it had begun. No one could defeat Cynnwrf. He was not an honorable loser either. He claimed he hadn't had the chance to attempt drawing Cynnwrf."

"Is that true?" Maren asked.

"No, he lied. A renowned scribe left a detailed account of King Tiergan's travails and failures in the Moon Bog. King Tiergan has been railing to the Source and the Oak about his supposed poor treatment ever since."

Maren was speechless for a moment. How did he rail at the Source or the Oak? "Can...can these shadow lords communicate with the Source and the Oak directly?" She'd spoken with gods and goddesses, but talking to the Source and the Oak? That was an entirely higher level of communication.

"So they say. But supposedly it is a rare occurrence

and not completely within their control," Hafwen explained.

Maren couldn't fathom railing at the Source about something so self-centered. "King Tiergan is a true pile of dung, then."

"Indeed." Hafwen opened her mouth, then closed it. Then she sighed. "You don't trust High King Kynan yet, do you?"

"I'm trying." Maren gave Hafwen a hard look. "Remember, I was taken by force, and he used the sword to bury my friends. He took me, and I didn't know for certain if they were alive or dead."

"That wouldn't have killed them."

"So he told me, and I understand that it wouldn't. But it was an attack on my loved ones all the same," Maren said. "Claiming me like that, it wasn't an auspicious start."

Hafwen shrugged. "It is the way of the Shadow King and his Awenydd."

"If the king leaves here without his sword, will he be able to defend himself in the Upperworld? My incredibly loyal and wildly violent friends will certainly attempt to relieve him of his head and most likely all of his limbs. It won't simply be revenge for themselves but also to protect me."

Hafwen's smile made her eyes crinkle at the corners. "You are well loved."

Heart swelling, Maren forced her voice not to tremble. "I lost my parents to the worst sort of king and his men. I had thought myself as good as dead when they imprisoned me and began to stack the wood for my burning."

Hafwen tilted her head and took the crystal plate from Maren.

"But Princess Brielle rescued me, and the entire lot of those mad royals welcomed me like kin."

"You are doubly blessed then. Born with the gift of Spirit Sight and given a new family."

Maren took a breath and eyed the doors, wondering if Kynan would return soon.

"The king," Hafwen said, "will be capable of defending himself. Shadow elves are far stronger than humans, mountain elves, or fae. Even without his full power, he is near to unstoppable."

She lies. A voice rang through Maren's head, and she froze. *Hafwen lies, and he lies, and they lie on and on. You are becoming a goddess.*

The breath went out of her.

They haven't told you that, have they? the voice said. *They want to harvest your power. This was the same path they took with the last Awenydd. They pushed her too far, and she ran to me. Think on what you saw in the crystal. Did you see shadows curling around the former Awenydd? Any sign at all of my magical wooing, of what they accuse?*

No, she hadn't. *King Tiergan?* she said through her thoughts. *I'd prefer it if you stayed far, far away from my mind, thank you very much. I've befriended Lady Hafwen, and I think she could do something nasty to you if I asked nicely.*

A dark laugh echoed through her head like Tiergan thought she was an adorable kitten that had tried to scratch his cheek.

Well, this development was just lovely. Not only did

Maren have to decide whether or not this Binding was a necessity for life to continue in both realms, now she had to deal with a silver-tongued shadow lord in her head.

CHAPTER 21

Maren smoothed her face. Should she tell Kynan that Tiergan was speaking to her? Did he have such magic too?

"High King Kynan," Hafwen exclaimed happily, standing. "We missed you. Are you prepared to take Maren and Ivar hunting?"

Maren's traitorous heart skipped a beat then decided to catch up by hammering itself against her chest.

"I am," Kynan said as he walked in, his cloak rippling behind him and his gaze on Maren. "If my lady is willing."

She cleared her throat, attempting to hide her reaction to those half-lidded, very dark eyes of his. "That would be fine."

His smile was created for a bedchamber, not for company, and the sight of it definitely didn't help Maren's pulse settle down. He turned away, though his gaze lingered as if he didn't want to stop looking at her.

"Lady Hafwen, I'm impressed with the lodgings you've given Ivar and the lads. They'll not wish to return to Calon Dywyll after such fine treatment."

Hafwen's gaze snapped from Maren to Kynan, then she grinned mischievously, curtseyed, and bid them goodbye.

Outside, Kynan untied Afal from a post at the end of a stone wall and offered Maren a hand up to the saddle. He passed the reins to Maren, his fingers brushing hers and sending a wave of heat through her hand and up her arm. She tried not to breathe deep of his scent, that incense and spice aroma he had, but her body won over her mind. She inhaled, eyes shutting briefly at the feel of his magic like the touch of sunlight on her skin. She shook her head fiercely.

"This is growing fully ridiculous."

"What is?" Kynan threw a leg over Osian's back and straightened.

"Nothing. Nothing at all." Her cheeks burned, and she began cracking her knuckles.

He frowned at her hands. "Queens do not fidget."

"This one does."

Kynan eyed the sky. "Stay close to me."

"Why?" Maren urged Afal toward Osian.

"Ivar approaches with his kin. He insists I must show your rank to them."

"What does that mean?"

Kynan's lips pressed tightly together, and he looked nervous, which was interesting and wholly unexpected.

"Spill it, King."

He coughed and raised his head as a cluster of six

black wyverns winged through a bank of tattered clouds. Scales in varying shades of black and gray, they had the same general head shape as Jewel, Filip's dragon familiar, but the wyverns were much smaller—the size of hawks—and their front legs and wings were joined.

"We will need to perform the claiming ritual," Kynan said.

"Now?" They couldn't marry now—or Bind, whatever they wished to call it. She wasn't ready. She'd never be ready, but she truly wasn't prepared now. Her hands began to sweat again, and Afal danced under her, Maren's stress most likely pouring into the poor thing. "Sorry, Afal." She petted the horse's smooth neck and did her level best not to shriek or run or explode.

"No, this won't be the Binding." Kynan's words and tone were measured and even, as if he were trying to calm her. "This is only between us, because he is my familiar."

What did this entail? "Can't it wait?"

"I'm afraid not. He feels threatened by the power in your blood, and he worries for my safety."

"Ha! He fears I'm going to hurt you?"

Kynan's gaze cut to her face, and she immediately recalled what Hafwen had told her about the former Awenydd and how her leaving had pained him. "Yes. If we don't perform the ritual to his liking, he may very well make an effort to kill you."

Fantastic. Adjusting her hands on the reins, she steadied herself. "All right. Tell me what to do."

Kynan dismounted, very quickly tied his horse and hers to the post, then took her from Afal's back like she was a child, his hands sure and firm around her. "Stand very still."

Heart leaping in panic, Maren froze as the wyverns dropped from the sky and landed on the low stone wall beside the horses. Afal and Osian shifted and stomped nervously.

Ivar flapped his wings and shrieked, a deep and grating sound that burned Maren's ears. The other wyverns mimicked Ivar as they soared in a circle overhead. Ivar must have been their chieftain or king or whatever wyverns would deem such a role. They were gorgeous, but incredibly, painfully frightening. Those sharp white teeth. Those wild talons.

She shuddered. Kynan pulled her back against his chest.

"It's all right," he whispered in her ear, his warm words sending pleasant shivers down her body. His chest pressed against her, and she leaned into him, not caring much if that was the wise move or not, because the wyverns had her wondering what death by hawk-sized dragons would feel like. "I'll only hold you for a moment. Be very still."

"What are you doing?"

"Hush, my lady queen." With a gentle movement, he brushed her hair away from one side of her neck, allowing it to fall over her right shoulder. He tipped her head sideways, then set his sharp elven teeth over the pulse pounding under her jaw.

A strange sensation, like the most poignant sort of longing, spread through her chest and down her stomach. Her legs quivered, and goddess above, he smelled divine. The tip of his tongue touched her skin, and she pulled in a quick breath as he suddenly moved away. A chill swept into the place where his heat had been. She silently derided herself for wishing he'd remained.

Ivar let out another screech and extended his wings.

"You have nothing to fear from Ivar," Kynan said quietly. He took Maren's hand and reached his other toward the wyvern. Ivar flew over and landed on Kynan's arm. "Shh, my friend. Hi yw fy nghymar a rhaid i ti ei pharchu. Fe laddaf er ei mwyn pe bai raid ac fe wnei dithau hefyd."

"Wh-what does that mean?" Maren asked.

"I told him that you are my mate and that he must honor you. That I will kill for you if I must, and he must do so as well."

The way he said that word, mate. It made breathing challenging.

Maren wiped sweat from her upper lip and tried in vain to keep her shaking to a minimum. "I wasn't designed for this kind of life. I'm meant to be on a boat, lying in the sun with a very large bottle of wine."

Kynan's gaze went skyward, but she didn't think he was looking at the other wyverns.

"Did you roll your eyes at me?" She almost laughed, teetering on the edge of madness.

He locked his gaze on her, and a black lock of hair fell over one of his eyes. "You drive me to behave in the basest of manners."

Ivar lunged forward, and Maren jerked backward, stopped from falling by Kynan's firm grip on her arm.

"Now, Lady Maren! Place your teeth on his throat!"

On a wyvern who was thrashing his head around like he was about to lose his mind and kill everything in sight? "What? I can't—"

Kynan's hand moved from her arm to the back of her neck with a speed that made him blur before her eyes. He pushed her forward, giving her little choice. Pulse pounding in her temples, she parted her lips and followed orders. This was no time for rebellion.

She felt cold, reptilian scales brush her mouth, and she eased her teeth around the wyvern's narrow throat.

Ivar stilled.

Then the creature maneuvered his wings around Maren's shoulders and head and cooed. Her heart shivered, then melted, and she actually wanted to hug the creature.

"That will do." Kynan's voice was laced with a command, and the sound of it plucked a string threaded through Maren's heart.

What was that feeling? She moved away from Ivar, who now appeared content and was calmly looking at Kynan. The other wyverns landed on the stone wall and began chirruping at one another.

Kynan returned Ivar's gaze and cocked his head, smiling and nodding. "Aye, she is to be my queen."

Maren couldn't believe what she was seeing. "Are you two having a conversation?"

"We are. He doesn't think like elves, fae, or humans, but he is no less intelligent. He might be more so."

"Does he want to hunt? I wouldn't mind seeing that if you're certain he won't decide I'm delicious."

Kynan's gaze landed on her body and slid slowly to her face. His mouth shifted, but he made no comment. He flexed the hand that had been on her neck, and his chest moved in a deep breath.

Desire swelled in Maren's blood. Earlier, she'd thought she had adjusted to the feel of his high royal elven blood and his intoxicating presence, but now... Her feelings for him were shifting. The attraction she'd felt when she'd first truly looked at him grew into a longing that made her entire body ache with need.

"He will obey you in everything," Kynan said quietly, his voice dark and low, "to the best of his ability. You have nothing to fear from him."

"What about you? Lady Hafwen told me your hatred of humans goes very far back indeed." She didn't want to reveal that Hafwen had told her about the former Awenydd, so she didn't elaborate.

Kynan lifted his arm, and Ivar took flight. Turning gracefully despite his large size, Kynan took her hand. He reminded her of a fae dancer, incredibly dangerous and altogether thrilling to watch. He pressed a kiss into her palm, and heat shot up her arm and directly to her middle. She stepped closer.

He looked up at her, his cheekbones sharp and his jawline casting a shadow on his broad chest. "I am yours if you will have me. You need never fear me again. I will not force our Binding on you. I will court you and endeavor to enchant you."

"With that magic of yours? Your lure?"

"I cannot control the way my presence may affect you, but I do my very best to court you without any shadow power influence. I swear it. I will not use the shadows on purpose to lure you."

So he could indeed use his shadows in that manner. She'd guessed as much.

That plucking sensation snapped at her chest again. So odd. "I don't want to ask this, but I'm feeling something strange." She tapped her chest. "Right here."

"Do you need food? Are you unwell?"

"Why do you always go to that? I'm not a sickly person. Most witches aren't."

"Humans are weak unless they are armed and in large groups."

"We'll untangle that one later, but to go back... I'm feeling a strange tug of sorts when you say certain things. Are you ensorcelling me right now despite this promise of courting?" Her cheeks went hot, and she gritted her teeth. She hated flushing; it told everyone too much about the intensity of her feelings.

"Ah." Kynan's smile was sly as he stood. He kept her hand a moment too long, then slowly released her fingers. "It's the bond you have now with Ivar. Since he is my familiar and he swears fealty to me and you just put yourself as a step between us, the bond of the familiar will sing to you at times."

Ivar squawked overhead, landed on the post, then began running his long snout along his side like a hawk tending its feathers.

"I'm not sure about this."

"It's true."

"I believe you, I suppose; I only mean that I don't like it."

"Because you haven't yet decided to wed me or not." His eyebrow twitched, and his dark gaze dragged over her cheek like a rough fingertip.

"Exactly." Her voice was a little louder than she'd meant it to be.

"There's naught to be done about it now. Shall we hunt?"

After untying the horses, he held out a hand to help Maren mount, but she waved him off and climbed up on her own. With one glance her way, Kynan readied himself, then rode into the nearby pines, the wyverns above him flying through the faint shadows of his magic. She nudged Afal with her heels, and they caught up quickly as the sky disappeared behind a thick canopy of sweet-scented conifers and the jewel-bright leaves of red maples.

"How does the Underworld have a sky?" she asked. "The roots of the Sacred Oak extend into the Spirit Well, so we must be underground."

"The Underworld doesn't follow Upperworld science. This is another realm entirely. We are both under the Upperworld and in a different layer of creation that exists outside Upperworlders' reach."

"That's why entering and exiting the Underworld is nigh on impossible."

He nodded and pointed to a light spot in the dark forest. "You will love this, my queen."

"What is it?" she asked.

He tsked. "It's a surprise. Ivar!" The wyvern wheeled from the canopy and circled down to hover over Kynan. "Go, friend. Find a meal we can all share."

Ivar shrieked and veered away, his fellow wyverns following his lead. A long patch of white marked one of the smaller wyverns toward the back.

"That last one is having trouble keeping up. Is it the poison?"

"It is. I must remember to tell Ivar to keep a keen eye on him."

Maren felt a smile tug at her lips. Kynan sounded like a concerned father fretting over his youngest child.

Suddenly, Maren found herself rather excited about what Kynan's surprise might be.

CHAPTER 22

The trail crossed a river that came to the horses' hocks, but the creatures were obviously well trained and used to water because they went along, emerging on the other side with no missteps. The pink-purple light of the Underworld sky peered through the branches and touched Maren's face. She lifted her chin and breathed deeply of the forest scents.

"You like it here." Kynan's voice was quiet and measured, as if he were asking a question.

"I want to say I hate it because, well, you know, but truly, it's gorgeous. I've missed riding in the woods."

"You don't have the opportunity in the Upperworld?"

"Not lately. I've been spending time on the edges of the Balaur, Lore, and Agate courts, waiting for the others to finish meetings or participating in martial and magical training. I love the decadence of a fine bedchamber, but my heart aches to ride free in the wilds like I did as a child from a humble home by the sea. I also miss the water and sailing."

"If you choose me," he said, his eyes flashing, "I will build you a rich lodging in this forest, and you will have a stable of your own horses for riding. Whatever you need, whatever you desire, it will be given freely. My realm is your realm to enjoy and tend. There is a sea here in the Underworld too, but we'll have to visit that place to be sure you would enjoy a home there in addition to your lodgings and at our castle, Calon Dywyll."

Our castle. Maren was a fisherman's daughter. A witch who'd nearly died in a dungeon, nearly burnt at the stake. And this king was offering his whole world to her. It was unbelievable.

Unable to fashion a reply to Kynan's mad plans and wild generosity, Maren instead decided to mine for information. "First, what does Calon Dywyll mean?"

"Dark Heart."

Fitting. "How does the afterlife work for the spirits? What do they do in the Spirit Well?"

"When they aren't using the well to pass into the Upperworld to bless their loved ones and descendants, they dream."

"That's what I thought. I wasn't certain it was true." The spirits blessed their descendants with luck, helped them imagine solutions to problems, and gently guided them with that magical ability they had to sway their loved ones to do this or that.

"You've spoken to them. Haven't they told you as much? I only know from old writings."

"They don't speak of their dreams. I asked a spirit once, but he disappeared before I even finished the question. His leaving chilled me..." It wasn't a delightful memory to say the least. She'd thought he had killed her for asking, because her flesh had grown so cold so quickly. "So I don't think asking is a good plan. Ever."

"Understood. The spirits must have our respect for their wishes. Without their presence, the Underworld would crumble and then the rest of the realms along with it."

"Everything truly is a circle."

"Indeed."

Her next question was snatched from her mind as a tree appeared at a fork in the path. A wide trunk with rough bark supported an absolute storm of dazzling golden leaves that rippled in the crisp, autumn breeze.

"This is the Awenydd's tree," Kynan said.

"I can't possibly be linked to this magnificent creation. I'm just...me." She slid from Afal's back and walked under the bountiful boughs of sun-colored leaves. They were as soft as down, and as her finger made contact with a slender branch, power surged up her arm. "Oh! Well, that's very nice." She wrapped both hands around the branch and let the power flood her. Releasing the tree, she whispered, "Thank you." A quiet hum touched her ears, and the sound lifted her heart. She whirled around, and Kynan smiled. Her already thrilled heart jumped at the sight of his eyes like sparkling black stones made of jet.

"It blessed you with power, I see." His gaze traveled the length of her. "Power suits you, my queen." He lifted her hand, and she followed his focus to see that her skin glowed gently in soft yellow tones like the tree. Easing her closer to him, he ran his fingers through her loose hair, lighting her blood up as surely as the tree's magic but in an entirely different manner. He held out a lock of her hair, and that too shimmered with light, the edges of every strand of her honey-colored hair a fiery red.

"What did this tree do to me exactly?" Maren decided not to worry about how close he was standing or how his hand was lingering at the side of her face. She just felt so, so good.

"You're the Seer of the Underworld. You tell me."

"I feel stronger, that's for certain. I should visit the Spirit Well and see if I can help there like you do with your shadow magic."

"Do you want to leave? What about Samhain and speaking with your people?"

"I still want to talk to them. I have to let them know what is going on and see what they believe about all of this and if Filip's man Costel has had time to research the scrolls more thoroughly. But, High King Kynan... Just a warning..."

Curiosity filled his eyes. "Yes?"

"They will definitely attack you," she said.

The hint of a dimple appeared in his left cheek. "You don't want them to do so?"

Her cheeks warmed. "I...no, not now. I can't..." She waved her hands around, indicating the realm at large. "I can't absorb all of this so quickly. You. Who I thought you were and who you actually seem to be. This place. The poison. My upcoming sacrifice of my own free will to save everyone… It's too much." Closing her eyes, she fell against the tree's large trunk and let the sweet hum fill her ears and the magic pour into her body.

Leaves shuffled as Kynan came closer—his scent told her it was him—but he didn't touch her or try any of his frustratingly alluring magic. "You can remain here," he said, "and sleep under the tree if you wish. I will go to the Upperworld for you and do whatever you command. I swear it. I am fully committed to gaining your trust and forming a bond between us that isn't only due to a required sacrifice or duty."

She opened her eyes to see the light cascading through the golden leaves onto his sharp elven features, his pointed ears, his raven-black hair tied away from his face… His eyelashes were thick and his eyes burning with earnest fervor. She took a shaky breath.

"Thank you. But I long to see them. It hurts my heart to be away from them." Source save her, she sounded like a child. Where had all her street smarts gone? Where was the hard shell she'd developed on the docks? She'd been too long in the company of kind people.

He turned away slightly, his gaze downcast and his shoulders tight. "You'll have to leave them because of your fate and mine. I'm sorry for that as well."

A very large lump in her throat made swallowing difficult. "It's not your doing. It's just the way it works, right?" Unhitching herself from the tree, she touched his arm. "I'm not fooled by King Tiergan." She couldn't deny what her gut said any longer.

Kynan's gaze snapped to hers. "No?"

"He's too smooth with his words and ways. I know a snake when I see one."

The moment she said the truth, she realized she'd known Tiergan was not the right choice for a while. Kynan was a good elven man. No one could lie this well. Not a chance.

"What exactly will happen after we wed? How does the Binding work? I'm guessing it isn't me in a pretty frock and you carrying me over the threshold? Just tell me there isn't a lot of blood involved. I've seen the Balaur elves in their wedding ceremonies and I'm not chomping at the bit to participate in that sort of thing."

Blinking slowly, he frowned. "No bloodletting."

"But there is something disturbing."

Grimacing, he held out his hands. "It is an eternal Binding in the Underworld. What did you expect?"

"Puppies."

A loud and gorgeous laugh shook him, and startled birds flew from the tree. She couldn't fight a grin.

"No darling animals, I'm afraid," he said, running his thumb over his chin. "We will stand with Lady Hafwen at the Sacred Oak's roots and join our hands."

"Doesn't sound so terrible." She glanced at his crossed arms and the one hand visible over his muscled forearm. Four rings adorned his long fingers. One was his sigil ring, simple in design but large. Another boasted runes too tiny for her to read, and the one beside it held a massive ruby. The largest of the bunch looked like an oak leaf tooled in bronze.

He looked up into the tree's branches. "When we join hands, we will use our two strongest magical elements to draw up the other two."

"Your air and my fire?"

"Yes. And the Spirit Well serves as the element of water, while the Sacred Oak's roots work as earth. Drawing up the other elements requires us to enter a realm similar to the Between."

"Do you go to the Between often?" she asked.

"As Shadow King, I visit once a year to offer a sacrifice."

"What do you give?"

"I offer the spirits my blood, which is full of the magic that helps them travel. The magic in my blood is strong due to hereditary power, my crown's influence on me, and my sword," he said. "Cynnwrf will make our Binding incredibly powerful and should heal the Oak and the spirits quickly."

Hafwen had said something similar. "Do you see the spirits when you're in the Between?" Maren asked.

"I don't," he said, "but I sense their presence as I do at the Spirit Well."

"I'm surprised that I never saw you there."

He glanced at her, then away as if suddenly shy—an emotion she would have thought impossible for him to feel. "I glimpsed you once."

Maren stilled. "When? How old was I?"

"Perhaps newly a woman?" he said. "Not a child

certainly, but younger than you are now. I am not proficient in the way humans age."

"What did you think when you saw me?" She felt foolish asking. Why did she care? But the question had fled her mouth before she could think it through.

He still wouldn't meet her eyes. "Your skin glowed in a similar fashion to the tree's effect on you." His deep voice was quiet, almost a whisper. "You were, you are," he said, glancing at her with something akin to awe in his gaze, "a beautiful soul." Looking away again, he took a breath. "I had thought, at the time, that I was merely fooled by the natural but base desire for that which is lovely. That my feeling was only lust. After all, I hated humans. I felt only shame. Now, I know..." At last, he met her eyes. "Your beauty is deep and true."

She felt lighter than a single feather, as if she could float on the breeze.

"Thank you," she said, not knowing what else to say.

He must have sensed her confusion, because he continued on with their earlier thread of conversation. "As for the Binding... The region where we will Bind is a place of deep magic and is rather frightening, as one loses one's corporeal body upon entering and the mind changes. One must hold fast to the growing Bond between the elemental pair. There is pain and desperation. Only through the Binding can one survive it and come out with one's mind intact. The Awenydd must listen for the voice of her shadow lord to find her way back."

Maren pulled her gray cloak tight, cocooning in the soft warmth of the homespun wool. Her mind had nearly cracked when she'd lost her parents and been thrown into the Wylfen Castle dungeon. Would she survive the Binding? She simply had to. There was no other choice. It was that or watch the world turn to ice and crumble, brittle and lifeless, at her feet.

Kynan took her arm and spun her, and suddenly she was in his arms. He pressed her to him and gently eased her head against his chest. "Do you hear that?"

His hearts beat steadily. She nodded, her own heart matching the rhythm of his.

"I am alive," he whispered, his deep voice low and lilting with the Underworld accent. "I have dreams and desires, too. I'm not just a cold king."

He was saying this to comfort her, and she smiled sadly against his vest. He must have wanted her to know that he too was risking all to save the realms, that they were in this together.

"You are my dream now and my desire," he said. "These hearts of mine beat for you and will not allow anything to hurt you. No matter what."

"What if I choose not to go through with the Binding?"

"Then the world can turn to ice, and you can live out the last of our days as you please with me at your back, sword in hand to defend your choice."

"Truly?" She pulled away slightly.

His eyes flashed with defiance. "Yes, for you are my mate even if you deny me and deny your fate. Nothing is more important than your wishes."

She savored his devotion, reveling in the comfort of knowing at least one soul understood her turmoil even if it wasn't the most noble of feelings. But they couldn't think like that.

"What about Eefa, Jeston and Beca? Deron, Nia and Ninian, Saffir? Hafwen?" she asked quietly.

Kynan bowed his head. He didn't speak for a while, but finally he looked up and sighed. "You're right. We can't abandon them. Or your family either. I want to hold you higher, but—"

"But that's not the type of king you are," she said, "and it's not the type of queen I'd choose to be."

He cupped her face and watched her lips as her heart beat faster and faster. His shadows flared up her back and cooled her neck before going hot and smoothing over her shoulders. He gasped and pulled the shadows back into himself. His mouth was so close...

"I have trouble controlling my shadow magic lure around you. I'm sure you've noticed."

It was difficult to talk; her whole body hummed with desire. "I did."

He broke away, letting his hands falls to his sides. She stepped toward him, but stopped, unsure about this, about everything. With a sad smile, he turned and walked beyond the tree's golden boughs.

She couldn't help but feel like she'd missed an opportunity.

Near a stand of pines and maples, he whistled for Ivar. The wyvern glided through the speckled light of the forest toward them, a hare clamped firmly in his mouth. Ivar dipped his snout slightly, and Kynan removed the hare from the wyvern's teeth. Reaching into a small bag tied to his weapons belt, Kynan retrieved a piece of pink meat.

"We reward him for offering us the first feasting on his kill," Kynan explained as Ivar gobbled the meat with quick snaps of his gleaming teeth. Kynan whistled three times, and the rest of the wyverns flew into view. They landed in the branches of a towering red maple. "Shall we camp here for the night?" he asked Maren.

"I'd like that." Feeling both weighted down and jumpy, she led Afal to a stretch of dark green grasses, then unbuckled the girth and slid the saddle free while Kynan set Ivar's kill on a flat rock. He cleared a circle of dirt with his boot, readying for a fire. "I have something I need to do," she said, feeling breathless. What was the best way to broach this sensitive topic? Perhaps it would be best to just say it quickly and be done.

Kynan drew Osian near Afal. He flipped a stirrup over the saddle and loosened the girth.

"I want to summon the last Awenydd," she said quickly, "and learn about what is required of me from her point of view. I also want to know if, in her current state, she has discovered anything more about the workings of the Binding and the Source's magic. There could be wisdom she's found in the afterlife, information that would be helpful to us."

Kynan dropped Osian's saddle to the ground, his eyes widening then turning to slits.

Was this too much for him? Had she pushed him too far?

CHAPTER 23

Moving so fast that he blurred before Maren's eyes, he adjusted the saddle, then cleared his throat as if he were trying to pretend he wasn't thrown by her statement.

"As you wish." He looked at her, his eyes unblinking. "But I will go farther into the forest to find kindling and firewood, if you don't mind. Ivar and the lads will keep watch over you. I cannot... I don't know..."

Maren set a hand on his forearm, her heart cinching at the pain laced through his words. "It's fine. You go. I'll handle this. I'm sorry it disturbs you, but we'd be foolish not to at least attempt to glean information from her spirit, don't you agree?"

"I do." He glanced from the forest to her. "But she may lie."

"I might be able to tell if she is lying. The spirits are not very good at hiding their emotions from me."

He nodded. "Of course, Awenydd. I will remain and keep watch for you."

"No, just have Ivar keep an eye out, all right? I'll be fine," she said.

"You're certain?" he asked.

"You'll be a distraction. Honestly."

With a sigh, he nodded again. Then, after a quick bow, he started into the shadows of the tall trees and left her to it.

She found a log to sit on, staying next to the horses because they made her feel safer somehow with their familiar scent and soft munching noises. Closing her eyes, she focused on that cool and calming thread of magic in her chest.

"Awenydd of the past, could I please speak to you?" It was odd to try to reach spirits here. There was no need for the Between, so she wasn't entirely certain how to progress. "Forgive me if this isn't the way it's done, but I need information to save the realms."

A wind stirred Maren's hair, and she opened her eyes to see the willowy, dark-haired woman from Hafwen's scrying crystal glowing before her. Maren's hands snapped quietly with the fire of her gift.

"Why do you disturb my rest?" The former Awenydd glared and clenched her fists. Her spirit eyes were white orbs lacking any kind of emotion besides pure fury.

She was very tall. Maren hated that it bothered her.

Maren chanted silently in her head, *I am the Awenydd now. She can't hurt me.*

It wasn't working.

Her knees knocked together, and she fought a full-body shiver. "I need to know how the Binding heals the Underworld."

"The ceremony mends the Oak's roots."

"But how?" Maren asked.

"Why does it matter? It brings balance to the core of all magic. Once long ago, the Underworld had a great crystal called the Calon y Dderwen," she said, her voice as sharp as a fillet knife, "and the crystal did the work of balancing the core of the Sacred Oak. I learned that here, after death, but Kynan should have heard of it even if he thinks the crystal is only a legend. The ancient and long-dead King Broderick threw it into the Dark Sea." She grinned and chills rattled down Maren's back. "He was a madman. Just like Tiergan. Like me."

She tore at her glowing hair, and her eyes widened far more than any living being's eyes were capable of doing.

"I can't stay," she muttered. "I won't stay. I hate this place! Do not summon me again. You must Bind yourself to a shadow lord and embrace your fate." The spirit's face and hands grew hazy, and the leaf-covered ground showed through her wispy form.

A crystal? Maren took a shuddering breath. "What did the Calon y Dderwen crystal look like? Could it be retrieved?"

"You're bothering my rest in an attempt to preserve your freedom, and it's pathetic," the former Awenydd said. "Why the Source blessed you, I'll never know. It's a blight on the history of the Awenydd."

Maren glared back. "I want to keep the family I've

found," she said through gritted teeth. "There's nothing pathetic about love."

The spirit's eyes flashed, and Maren knew she'd said something very wrong.

"You are an ignorant fool! Love is the reason for all of my pain! Tiergan tricked me, and I nearly died breaking the Bond with Kynan to be with him. Tiergan threw me to the humans." She spat on the ground as if the word were the worst sort of curse. "You humans are the stain on the realms. Your kind should be destroyed. In fact, I hope your Binding fails, Awenydd, and the worlds fall into cold nothingness!"

The previous Awenydd zipped out of view, gone in a blink. Maren couldn't say she was sad to see her go.

"Everything all right?" Kynan's voice made Maren startle, and she nearly fell off the log.

"She wasn't pleasant," Maren said, "but she told me one important piece of information."

"What's that?" His boots crunched across twigs and fallen leaves.

"A crystal that can permanently balance the elemental magic at the core of the Sacred Oak exists."

"Where can we find it?" He looked half hopeful and half afraid.

"At the bottom of the Dark Sea."

He grimaced. "You speak of the Calon y Dderwen. I had thought that was only a story, told around bonfires to children."

"She said the crystal is real. I assume we don't have the time to seek it, since the god Arcturus said the damage is spreading quickly," Maren said. "And I'm guessing the sea isn't a small one?"

"It reaches leagues and leagues from my kingdom to King Tiergan's," he answered.

Her mind whirred as she tried to imagine the whole of this realm. "How big is the Underworld?"

"I don't know what terms to use to explain that to an Upperworlder."

She had to smile. "Ah, you said the word *Upperworlders* and it didn't sound like a curse for once."

"Are there other Upperworlders like you?" His voice was quiet, soft.

He wasn't being mean-spirited or sarcastic like she often was. She could tell he was honestly curious.

"What do you mean exactly?" she asked.

"Like you," he said. "Are there other Upperworlders who think of the spirits with the respect one shows a friend? Those who listen and decide carefully? Folk who would sacrifice everything and Bind themselves forever to a horrible monster to save all living things?"

Smiling and feeling bashful, she met him at the cleared circle of dirt and helped him arrange the kindling and logs he'd gathered. "My friends are better than me. Proven heroes, the lot of them. And you are not a monster. You just occasionally behave like one."

He tilted his head as if he were considering that, then he used a flint and striker to coax the kindling to flame. "I forgot to mention your humility. Are there truly Upperworlders who hold the same level of humble attitude you do?"

Her heart warmed at his praise. The fire grew, light

licking over the trees' rough trunks and the underside of the leaves that hadn't yet fallen.

"No," Maren said, laughing. "My friends are heroes, but they aren't exactly humble. You know, you're quite good at courting when you want to be, High King Kynan."

The edge of his mouth lifted, and his eyes glowed a very dark red that made heat rise to her chest and cheeks. She found herself breathing too quickly.

"Let's have our meal and rest, all right?" she said. In truth, the meeting with the former Awenydd had bled her energy stores dry.

While Maren took a seat on a stump by the fire and held out her hands to warm them, Kynan dressed the hare with expert movements. Soon they were eating Ivar's contribution to the wilderness feast as well as a small round of yellow cheese and a half loaf of black bread Kynan must have picked up in Hafwen's kitchen. It was obvious Kynan had spent plenty of time on his own in the woods without servants such as Eefa or his chef, Deron, to aid him.

"This is delicious. Did you spice it, or is it just the perfect spice of hunger?" Maren chuckled at herself and gobbled down the last of her portion.

"It's only your hunger. You've been through a great ordeal, and I imagine your body needs extra sustenance. I'll gather some berries and nuts while you sleep."

"You don't have to do that. I'm fine." Her stomach growled, and Kynan grinned.

"I'll return shortly." He stood and studied the ground near her feet.

"What is it?"

"I can create a bed of sorts for us—for you, I mean. With my shadows. It will keep the insects away, warm the ground, and serve as a cushion. Not as comfortable as a bed, of course, but much better than lying on the hard ground. Would you like that?"

"Very much. Thank you." She stood and removed her cloak. Shaking it out and preparing to use it as a blanket, she watched as Kynan worked his air magic.

His fingers undulated over a spot by the crackling fire. Obsidian shadows and golden sparks drifted from his palm and fingertips to form a swirling darkness in the rough shape of a sleeping mat.

"Well, don't look at it like that," he said. "The shadows serve you. They won't harm you in any way. Or trap you." He glanced away as if ashamed for using his power in that manner recently. "Once my promise is made, there is no breaking it, Maren."

Facing her again, his eyes burned into hers, and a spark of desire shot through her body, making her gasp. Goosebumps ran down her arms and legs, but they were pleasant.

She stepped back, blinking and trying to gain control of her feelings. Was what she felt for him the beginnings of love? How could she fall for someone who stole her from her entire life? But, another part of her whispered, he did it to save everyone in both realms. She looked at him again, at the dark kindness in his gaze and remembered his apologies and the way he was with his people. She did care for him. It was undeniable.

With a patient smile, Kynan returned to the deeper

forest to search for more food. Ivar perched on the maple above Maren, just beyond the small clearing. The firelight sparkled across Ivar's black scales. His hide resembled spirit agate, the same stuff that made up Kynan's sword and decorated the cloak that Rhianne—Maren's fellow witch friend—wore in battle.

"Do you have any magic, Ivar?" she asked, feeling a bit silly for talking to a wyvern. He squawked at a lower volume than his usual high-pitched noise, then he stretched his wings like he was showing them off. "Yes, you're very handsome."

The wyvern left his perch and flew to her side, landing lightly on the boulder beside the stump Maren had claimed near Kynan's bed of shadows. Ivar squawked again, then nuzzled her arm like a big scaly cat. She laughed and ran a hand over his head and down his side.

Ivar jerked away, and she jumped. He leapt into the air and hovered, flapping his wings wildly and calling to the other wyverns, who quickly joined him.

Her pulse knocked against her throat. "What is it?"

The wyvern stared at her with some meaning she couldn't figure out, then all the wyverns flew—fast as arrows—into the wood in the direction Kynan had gone.

CHAPTER 24

The trees' beauty didn't match the chill spreading through Maren's bones. As she ran, Ivar looped back every once in a while to make sure she was there, but he was obviously in a hurry, huffing like he was frustrated with her. She should've grabbed Afal, but she hadn't realized how far they'd be going.

"High King Kynan!" Her voice sounded reedy and seemed to fall into the forest faster than it would have in the Upperworld, but that was probably just her fear twisting things.

Ivar and the other wyverns wheeled away from the canopy and dove. Maren ran, the lack of a cloak not bothering her since she was sweating from exertion.

She pulled to a stop, heart hanging in her chest.

With his sword plunged into the ground, Kynan stood in front of a spirit that blinked in and out of her view. A gray hue tainted the normal spirit's blue-white glow. Shaking, Kynan gripped the hilt of Cynnwrf as shadows peeled away from his body and flew into the flashing image of the spirit. His crown flashed erratically like lightning in a dangerously unpredictable storm.

What could she do? What was happening?

Ivar roared at her, a sound she hadn't heard from him, a noise that shook her from her inaction. She raced to Kynan's side, braced one hand on his forearm, then looked into the face of the strange spirit.

The spirit's eyes were nothing but empty pits of darkness, and the body had no true shape at all. It could have been elf, human, or fae—there was no way to tell.

"You're hurting your king!" Wind blasted against her cheeks, and her hands blazed brightly.

The spirit howled at her, its blank gaze sending arrows of ice into her chest. She held tight to Kynan, who hadn't reacted at all to her arrival. His skin was corpse-cold.

"Stop this!" she shouted at the spirit. "I can help you if you just tell me what you need!"

Another howl tore from the ghostly maw of the thing, then it rushed toward Kynan. Maren shoved Kynan out of the way then she surged toward the spirit to meet it bodily. Ivar's wings brushed her cheek as he hovered low over Kynan.

"Stop!" Maren held out her hands and pressed her witch's will through the spot between her eyebrows and out her palms as well. Heat built where she focused her power and then left her in a stream of strength.

A shriek dragged its way out of the spirit's insubstantial mouth, and the being shot backward.

Spikes of hoar frost spread over the ground below the spirit's fluctuating light.

Fire-cloaked hands outstretched, Maren drove the spirit out of the air and toward the ground, lower and lower and lower. The sounds of its misery tore at her heart, but it had to be stopped. Light flickering into nothingness, the spirit at last disappeared.

The frost on the ground crackled, then halted, remaining but not reaching further into the live growth as the fire on Maren's fingers dissipated. The silence was broken only by Kynan's labored breathing.

He was on his knees, his shoulders slouched and head bowed. She put a hand on his back. He looked up at her, his eyes shockingly light, as if the spirit had drained the dark power from him.

"Kynan. Can you hear me?"

He bent his head and shook it as if to clear his thoughts, his hair falling over her arm. A shudder rocked him, and he reached for his sword, missing by an inch. Maren drew the sword from the ground, and magic buzzed through her palm. She set the hilt into Kynan's hand, then wrapped his fingers around the cool leather grip as his eyes shuttered closed.

"Just breathe." She put a hand on his head, and his tangled hair, like black silk, looped around her thumb. Her mother had always done that when she was a child, touched her head when she was upset or sick. "The spirit is gone now," she whispered to Kynan. "Take your time."

Leaning against her thigh, he breathed slowly, his chest moving in and out. He was so heavy, such a large man, that she had to dig her heels in to keep upright. At last, he got to his feet and gave her a quick hug. His lips pressed gently to her forehead.

"Thank you, Awenydd. Maren." He spoke her name again, turning the sounds to song. "Thank you from my soul, Great Seer."

She didn't know what to say. The spirit had her mind traveling down dark roads.

Kynan started to walk back to their camp, his steps growing steadier as they went. "This is a sign that the damage is spreading quickly."

"How did that spirit end up here, so far from the well?" she asked.

"She spoke to me before she lost her senses."

"The spirit?"

"Yes."

Maren shuddered, wishing for her cloak. "Was this the first time a spirit has spoken to you?"

"Aye, and to be honest, I hope it's the last." Kynan sheathed Cynnwrf, removed his cloak, and wrapped it around her shoulders before they continued onward. "I only see the spirits when they are hungry, when my duty to dispatch them arises. Sometimes, I wish I could see the spirits as they are meant to be, at peace and whole-souled."

She inhaled the scent of him and sighed at the lovely warmth. They walked slowly with the wyverns flying through the branches above. Every once in a while, a wing would brush a cluster of leaves and a flurry of red, orange, or brown would twist across their path.

"The spirit informed me," Kynan said, "that she'd

been to the Upperworld to bless her thrice-great-grandchild. Upon her return, she grew tired and fell into listless wandering. She claimed the air was dry of energy, that the Underworld itself was going cold."

Kynan's shoulders were straight again, and his stride grew more confident with each step. Maren exhaled, incredibly glad he didn't seem permanently injured.

"Do you think this means the area near the well is full of hungry spirits?" she asked.

"It's hard to say." His gaze flicked to Ivar, his eyebrows knitting. "This specific spirit needed immediate succor because of her travels."

Back at the fire, Kynan's shadow bed was gone—most likely lost because of his struggle with the spirit—and the flames had died, leaving only glowing embers and the occasional spark that drifted into the deepening night. Kynan stoked the fire with a stick while Maren gathered more kindling from the base of the maples. Soon enough, they had the fire crackling again. Kynan spread his hand in Maren's direction, and his shadows formed a bed once more.

"Please, sleep. I can tell you are exhausted," he said.

"You must be tired too." She returned his cloak and took up her own from the stump. "I can keep watch if you want to sleep first." A yawn escaped her mouth even as she finished saying the last word.

His eyebrow lifted. "I'll rest, and Ivar will keep watch. I'll be fine. I promise." A sweet smile spread over his mouth.

She nodded and lay on her side in the bed of shadows. The magic was warm like Kynan's cloak and smelled of him too. Pulling her own cloak over her like a blanket, she snuggled into the strange softness of the shadows. They cushioned her body and kept her away from the cold ground and damp leaves. Before she could ask more about Kynan's experience, sleep stole her away.

When she woke on the morning before Samhain's sundown, with Kynan readying the horses and the fire already tamped down, she knew it was time to return to Hafwen's manor.

Would they visit the Upperworld tonight?

She ran fingers through her painfully tangled hair and gulped down a pile of bright red berries Kynan had left for her on a stone beside the smoking remains of the fire. She joined him in saddling the horses but was hesitant to speak first.

Sleeping all night inside his magic felt oddly personal, very intimate, almost as if she'd spent the hours in his arms. It reminded her of the night at Jeston and Beca's house. The memory of Kynan's sleepy eyes and the feel of his body against hers robbed her of words.

"Morning, my queen." Kynan glanced at her with wary eyes as he plucked a clump of mud from Osian's hoof.

What uns he worried about? The visit to the Upperworld? Most likely. Or he could tell she was feeling awkward... Goddess, she hoped that wasn't it.

"Good morning." Her voice was too bright. She sounded like a fool. "Do you feel all right today?"

"Aye." He tied half of his hair at the crown of his

head, looping the length of it with a thin strip of leather. "It will take more than one tragedy to drain me of all of my power." His eyes were black, but the hint of ruby red simmered in their depths.

"I'm sorry I had to end that spirit's existence." Beside Maren's foot, Afal stomped the ground. Maren plucked some clover and encouraged the horse to lip the treat from her palm.

"Don't apologize." He smoothed Osian's mane, then checked the animal's hock. "You saved me. Besides, the spirit was lost the moment it grew too hungry to think clearly. There is no returning to a peaceful afterlife when they cross that line."

The ride back to Hafwen's manor was quiet, but Maren's mind was not.

They stopped once, and she showed Kynan how, as a child, she had learned to catch creek brewers by wiggling a thumb in the dark nooks of the bank.

"We have the same fish as you do in your kingdom of Wylfen," he said.

"Wylfen is no longer my home, but yes." She held up the large, fat fish. Its brown scales didn't look like much, but it would be delicious cooked. "Ours have a blue fin though, and this one is much darker."

"Shadow fish."

She whirled. "Was that a joke?"

"Maybe."

A laugh that felt as though it belonged to someone else filtered through her lips. She couldn't wipe the image of the starved spirit from her mind long enough to enjoy what little pleasures cropped up on their trip back.

As they rode onto Hafwen's grounds and two stable lads approached, a sharp wind cut under Maren's cloak and chilled her to the bone. She and Kynan traded a look. That wind wasn't born of autumn but of a deep cold come too early.

They were running out of time.

CHAPTER 25

While Kynan and Hafwen continued a long discussion on what to do in the Underworld if things went awry and Kynan became trapped in the Upperworld, Maren went on a walk through the mostly dormant orchards just past Hafwen's northeastern courtyard.

The air had gone from pleasantly crisp to a deepening chill, and though the gray ice wasn't here yet, the cold wind announced loud and clear that the decay had grown worse in the last hours.

A row of nearly bare-branched apple trees bled into a lane crowded by a bush she didn't recognize. The leaves remained despite the season, dark green and glossy. She touched one and tried to calm herself. They had a plan. No need to panic. She was the Awenydd, after all. She was fated for this challenge.

A frustrated shout came from the slender dirt road that passed around the back of Hafwen's manor. Maren glanced back toward the manor house, wondering if

Kynan or Hafwen had heard the disturbance, but no one appeared. She hurried out of the orchard and toward the sound.

A shadow elf with close-cut brown hair and homespun clothing braced his back against the side of a small cart filled with root vegetables and pushed, trying to move the front right wheel from a mud puddle. "Yah!" he shouted at his mule, who tugged hard once, dislodging an orange potato-looking thing that rolled onto the road.

The elf looked up at her approach, eyes hopeful, as his mule stomped its hooves impatiently.

"Greetings," she said in the common tongue, wondering if he'd understand. So far, everyone here had the ability to speak it. Kynan had said it was because many of their historical documents held the common language, so children were taught from a young age.

She tossed the potato back into the cart.

"Good day, my lady," the man said, eyeing her clothing and probably trying to figure out who she was. His gaze caught on her ears, but he looked away quickly as if he didn't wish to be caught staring.

"Do you need a hand? You almost have it out. I bet the two of us can manage it."

A smile sped over his mouth, and Maren's witch intuition gave a tug, her womb warming and the spot between her eyebrows tingling. Was that a warning? Or was she meant to meet him for some future reason?

"I'd appreciate the help, my lady, and thank you. I'll lift and you push once I say the word?"

Nodding and keeping an arm's distance from him in

case her intuition had given her a warning, she walked around the rear of the cart. She turned and put her back against the rough-hewn wood slats.

The elven man grunted, and the cart groaned as he lifted it a fraction. "Now!" he shouted to her. "Yah!" he called to the mule.

With a lurch, they shifted the cart from the mud, and the wheel rolled up onto the road.

"Success!" If Maren had had her wand, she could have helped him without pulling every muscle in her back. She shook her head, smiling and actually rather glad to do something simple for the moment.

"Thank you, my lady." The man bobbed his head in gratitude, then let his gaze travel the length of her body. "And if I may be so bold, but you are the one everyone has been whispering about, aren't you?"

"Probably, yes." Unease filtered through her positive mood, and her stomach twisted. She turned to leave, ready to be away from this fellow.

"You should Bind with King Tiergan—"

"Thank you for your opinion, but there is much you might not know."

"I lived in his humble sub-kingdom when I was young. He was a good lesser king across the Dark Sea."

"In what way was he good?"

"He looked out for us lowly subjects, farmers, fishermen..."

Fishermen? What were the chances he knew she'd grown up as the daughter of a fisherman? Not likely a coincidence. She turned and began to walk away quickly, sweat beading on her upper lip. "Thank you," she said over her shoulder. "Good luck to you."

Were those shadows in the grasses by the road? She whirled and squinted at the darkness lining the man's arms. Was she being ridiculous, or was that shadow magic?

CHAPTER 26

A shrieking call sounded above. Black wings stretched wide, Ivar peeled away from the steely sky and dove at the man.

Maren's heart thudded painfully as she called for Kynan and grabbed up a stick.

She ran at the man to help Ivar, but the shadows unfurled thickly, and Ivar landed on the ground, rolling, as the man, the mule, and the cart disappeared.

Kynan burst from the orchard, face alight with rage and his sword drawn. "Maren!"

"It's all right," she said, helping Ivar untangle himself from a briar patch near the mud puddle. "He's fine. I'm fine."

Kynan ran to them, then bent and set a hand on the back of Maren's head. "You're certain? What happened?" The concern in his eyes made her want to curl into his arms.

"There was a man with a vegetable cart. His wheel was stuck, and I was helping him free it from the mud.

But then I noticed shadows gathering around him and there too." She pointed at the ditch and the autumn grasses by the roadside. "Ivar must have decided, and rightly so, that this man wasn't what he seemed. He came to my rescue."

Ivar nudged her hand with his cool, scaly snout. She rubbed a spot behind his short black horns, and he purred loudly like a big cat.

Kynan touched Ivar's back and examined one wing, tsking. "You are a brave one, Ivar. Thank you for protecting our Lady Maren."

Ivar cooed up at Kynan, whose smile was as bright and happy as dawn. But the smile faded fast as Kynan stood and glared down the road.

"That was no simple farmer. I'm sure you know that with your street smarts."

Maren got to her feet and nodded. "My intuition warned me. It doesn't always rise to help me out, but sometimes, it can be incredibly useful. I was a fool for questioning its warning. I had thought maybe I was meant to meet the man, but shortly, I realized he wasn't a good sort."

Turning toward her, Kynan looked into her eyes. "That was King Tiergan."

"What?" Maren gripped Kynan's wrist without thinking.

Kynan took her hand and rubbed the back of her knuckles softly. "No elves besides him and me can do such powerful shadow magic."

"You can disguise your looks?" she asked.

"I can, but I never would."

"Why not? It might come in handy."

"It's a twisted form of our magic," Kynan said. "It bends the soul. The cost is not worth the reward."

Maren exhaled, feeling shaky. "I can't believe that was Tiergan. I can, but...he's so reckless, showing up here and trying to win me to his side with tales of his competent ruling in his kingdom."

"That's what he told you?"

"Yes," she answered. "He pretended to be a former subject and spoke of his kindness toward lesser subjects." She shook her head. "I suppose when I wasn't buying that lie, he decided to attack me with shadows."

"He might have tried to lure you." Kynan's voice had dropped an octave, and his fingers tightened on Maren's hand.

A shudder went through her, and Kynan stepped closer. She breathed in his scent and savored his warmth. "But you're certain it was him?" she asked.

"There is a slim chance it could have been a shadow lord who has remained removed from society for ages, but I doubt it. None of the others come here and trouble me. They've all sworn their fealty except King Tiergan."

"What would have happened if Ivar hadn't defended me?"

Kynan tilted his head and bared his teeth for a moment, flashing his elven incisors. His arm circled her protectively as he gazed into the distance, eyes glowing. Fingers flexing against her back, he took a breath, then another. Finally, he spoke. "You haven't experienced a full lure. Though I have at times failed to control mine around you, those moments were nothing compared to what King Tiergan and I are capable of using to ensnare a person through desire."

The feel of even the accidental slip of Kynan's lure had been embarrassingly powerful. She couldn't imagine one of them using the magic with full force. "I'd have gone to him? Believed I was in love with him?" she asked.

"Yes, that, or that you desired nothing besides him. But you are remarkable, Awenydd. Perhaps you would have been strong enough to break the lure." He pressed her closer into his arms. "I hope we never have to find out."

She curled her fingers into his shirt, then realized what she was doing and backed away a step. "Thank you. For introducing me to Ivar and for coming so quickly when I called for help."

His gaze went half-lidded, and she fought the urge to sigh like a ninny. "I'm glad you hailed me and me alone."

"Where is Lady Hafwen?" Maren asked.

"She is in the root cellar, gathering materials for the potion."

"Ah. Does she agree that you should do more than simply set your sword on her dining table before we go?"

His eyes glittered with amusement. "She does."

In preparation for their magical passage from the Underworld to the Upperworld, Maren suggested they hide the sword.

"Where I grew up, one didn't leave belongings out

in the open unless one cared to lose them," she said as they gathered in Hafwen's main hall.

Beside Hafwen, Ivar perched on a large chair; the other wyverns had remained outside at Hafwen's request.

"It's a wise idea. I have the perfect spot," Hafwen said. "Remove those two larger stones, High King Kynan, if you will."

Ivar's eyes shifted with every move as Kynan slid the largest of the flat cooking stones to the side to reveal a bronze handle set into the packed dirt between the stones of the floor.

Kynan removed Cynnwrf and its sheath, then knelt beside the fire. He handed the sword to Maren. The weapon hummed with power. Even through the thick sheath, the feel of it sent lightning through her fingers. Her Awenydd power ignited, and her hands began to flicker with her particular brand of magic, mostly fire element and a dash of air.

"Are you certain I should be touching this?"

CHAPTER 27

"This feels very much like a duty for a shadow elf," Maren said, holding the legendary sword, a weapon that only had one superior, which belonged to the greatest goddess of all time, Vahly, Earth Queen.

Kynan glanced at her, his gaze appreciative. "Who better than my future queen to help me ensure the safety of my greatest weapon?"

Maren dipped her head and held tightly to the incredibly heavy length of steel and leather.

"The latch there will be quite rusted shut, I'm afraid," Hafwen said, eyeing the small floor hatch set in the flagstones of her great hall. "I should've oiled it ages ago."

Kynan took the ring, heaved on the thing just once, and then a small door swung upward with a great screech.

"Showing off again, I see." Hafwen raised an eyebrow.

The opening below the floor appeared to be no more than a humble storage space. A large amphora rested against the wall that Maren could see over Kynan's shoulder, and a tapestry, rolled and covered in sackcloth, sat nearby. Kynan twisted and held out a hand, and Maren gave over the sheathed sword. He placed the blade in the hiding place using slow movements. No one took a breath until the stone that hid the spot was back in place.

"Will you still have your shadow magic without it?" Maren asked.

Kynan stood and rubbed a thumb under Ivar's chin. "I will."

Remembering the power of Cynnwrf from the day Kynan had restrained Filip, Dorin, and Brielle before claiming her, Maren wrapped her arms around her middle, incredibly glad that Hafwen would be watching over the sword while they were gone.

As the three of them started off on horseback to ride toward the rune doors that served as entrance and exit to the Underworld, the last hour of the day painted the edges of Hafwen's manor in shades of deep gold and dark amethyst. Maren twisted in her saddle to enjoy the view of the weather-softened manor house and the browning grasses before facing the upcoming challenge.

The road offered mist, twists, and turns, dark greenery and the sound of the river falling over its well-worn stones. The mushrooms began to glow green-blue, and the sheer beauty of this strange realm took Maren's breath.

"My kingdom pleases you?" Kynan asked.

"It's ridiculously lovely. I can't wait to tell everyone how wrong they are about the Underworld."

Hafwen rode up beside them, adjusting the hem of her split skirt so that the hem hung neatly over her boot. "Do you think they'll believe you?"

"Why wouldn't they?" Maren ran a hand along Afal's soft neck.

"They might think the king has some magical sway over you," Hafwen said.

Kynan's brow bunched, but he didn't disagree.

In the glow of the Underworld's lengthy twilight, they rode for a long while in silence as Maren's mind turned over the potential outcomes of the night. It was Samhain, and anything and everything felt possible. There was a crackle to the air, like if she had her wand, she might thrust it high and end up breaking something.

"Almost there now." Kynan rode alongside Maren. The sparks in his shadowy crown matched the golden seed heads drifting across the cobblestone road.

"What are those seeds from?" Maren asked, longing for a distraction. Too soon they would be at the passage place where their potential failure lurked like another hungry spirit.

Hafwen's tall silhouette cut a slash in the view of the misty mountains to the north. She looked over her shoulder at Maren, her golden eye reflecting the light. "From a type of flower called River Ladies."

"Lovely name."

"It is. And like most of us ladies, they're poisonous when they want to be." Hafwen grinned.

Maren shook her head, smiling. Kynan's shoulders shifted with his quiet chuckle. It wasn't even a true chuckle, the thing he did when amused. It was more of a head dip and a quirk of the lips that was gone before one could mention it.

Kynan didn't seem any different without his sword. His shadows flowed around him from time to time just as they always did, and his crown looked the same. Perhaps leaving the weapon wasn't as difficult as he'd thought it would be. Kynan spoke at length with Ivar to be certain the wyverns would defend it.

The road led them to a cave with close walls. They dismounted, left the horses tied to a stand of beech trees, then continued on foot until they reached the runed doors that Maren remembered well from her first day here. The runes glowed blue-white as they had on the other side.

Hafwen untied a small amphora from her belt and uncorked it. A bright scent like freshly cut greenery followed a wave of sage that hit Maren's nose. The potion wasn't unpleasant, but it wasn't subtle either.

"I hope we don't have need to hunt once we are above." Kynan raised his sharp chin, and Hafwen painted his cheekbones and the pulse points on his throat with the concoction.

Hafwen squinted in the rune's light and painted a breaking rune on Kynan's forehead. "I packed more food stuffs for the both of you."

"Won't the breaking rune hurt him?" Maren popped her knuckles and chewed the inside of her lip.

"Not if I add the uruz with his sigil beside it and intertwine them." Hafwen used the tip of a fingernail to draw the auroch rune alongside an array of diamonds and a few slashes that must have represented a wyvern to complete his sigil. "Symbols have as much power as the old magic runes if the wearer believes in them."

"In a way, we all have a witch's will?" Kynan asked.

"Careful," Hafwen and Maren said in unison. They laughed together, and Kynan's eyes sparkled as if he were delighted to be warned by them.

As Hafwen moved toward Maren, Kynan looked at the runed doors, rubbed his hands together, and moved his shoulders up and down, looking like a warrior preparing for battle.

Hafwen's touch on Maren's cheeks, forehead, and throat was soft and quick. "How many times have you painted runes on bodies?" Maren asked.

"I like to try new magics on myself when I have the time." A wicked grin broke across Hafwen's lips. Maren could easily imagine Hafwen in the deep forest, working spells and rune magic never before seen anywhere in any realm.

"What is the most fascinating new spell you've managed?" Maren wished they had longer to talk.

"I accidentally changed my voice so I could speak only to owls," Hafwen said.

"That sounds less than handy."

"Yes, they really didn't care to chat with me. It took seven days to wear off."

Kynan frowned. "Was that around the time I asked you to feast with Mayor Symon and me in Hwyl last year?" He pronounced the word *hoo-eel*.

"It was, sadly," Hafwen said sarcastically. She drew something small on Maren's right cheek, then eyed her work. "I'd suffer the owl language for a moon to avoid dinner with Mayor Symon."

Kynan snorted.

"Who is he?" Maren asked.

"The council leader of the largest town in the Underworld," Hafwen said. "Hwyl is a hub for trade, leather works, brewing, mining... You name it, they produce it."

Kynan's mouth bunched, and he looked into the dark.

"What is it?" Maren asked.

"Nothing. Is she prepared?" Kynan ignored her and looked to Hafwen. What was he avoiding?

Hafwen nodded as she set the cork into her amphora. She retied it to her belt and moved Kynan and Maren so that they stood side by side facing the doors.

Whatever Kynan was keeping from Maren, it wasn't important at the moment. Now, they had to focus on entering the Upperworld. "What did you use for my sigil since I have no noble house?" she asked Hafwen.

"A hand of fire and a fish."

Maren grinned. "For someone who just met me, I think you hit the target there."

Hafwen's smile was sad. "It's time now. Samhain has arrived."

Kynan's eyes shuttered, and he took a slow, deep

breath. The rune doors flashed blood-red, as if he'd performed his shadow magic again even though he hadn't moved. Maren guessed the runes were working.

In the corridor beyond the doors, a small space in the distance showed flickering orange light. "I can see a bonfire!" Maren lunged toward the doors and the corridor beyond, but Kynan grabbed her arm.

"You must join hands and repeat after me." Hafwen raised her wand. Purple and black smoke billowed from the end, and pale blue sparks the same shade as Underworld poppies flashed in the tiny clouds.

They chanted in turn, just as Hafwen had instructed them back in her hall.

"To the sun's domain, I go,

To leave the twilight world below.

With me, I take my essence and hearts,

With me, I hold my sign and mark.

Return in three moons hence, I will,

Or remain forever lost to the hill."

Maren wanted to remark on how the spell rhymed in the Lore tongue and ask why Hafwen had bothered with that instead of using their language, the words of the shadow elves, but the runes were sparkling the deep ruby of Kynan's eyes, and then they were walking under the archway and into the corridor toward the Upperworld. The moment for questions had passed, and now they would either fail or succeed.

If they failed, both realms would fall.

If they succeeded, she would give up her family and live forever with Kynan.

She glanced at his profile, so strong and defined in

the flickering light beyond the hill's magical opening. She didn't balk as strongly against a future with him now. Certainly not. The idea of being his wife, his mate, sent a fiery thrill through her blood.

His nostrils moved, and he looked down at her, an emotion she couldn't name washing across his eyes. He swallowed and tightened his hold on her hand. She squeezed his fingers back and tried not to be afraid that she would fail them all and everyone she had ever known would be turned to gray ice.

CHAPTER 28

Maren and Kynan walked side by side toward the slender crack in the wall of the Underworld. The black walls seemed to lean close, and Maren's breath stuck in her throat.

Would Hafwen's potion work? Or would they be trapped between realms?

She held tightly to Kynan's hand. Surely the Shadow King wouldn't be crushed by his own world's entrance. Maren hoped that was logical thinking. Her mind was racing and far less reasonable at the moment than it usually was.

A deep cold stole over Maren's fingertips and toes, setting her to shiver. The hazy view of the Upperworld showed that same flickering light of a bonfire. Was it only a trick of the eye?

The chill deepened, then they were through.

They had successfully reached the Upperworld. Maren was home.

The Sacred Oak stood tall, golden and brown.

Spirits flitted through the Forest of Illumahrah, smiling and carrying handfuls of blue poppies to bless their loved ones. A living couple talked under the tree's wide branches, the woman laughing and throwing back her head of silver hair.

Recognition shot through Maren, and she stared running. "Aury! Filip!"

With a yelp of joy, Aury wrapped her in a hug, and Maren accidentally bumped the mage staff strapped to the princess's back.

Filip slid his hatchet from his belt and whirled on Kynan. "Prepare for your end, Dark King." Filip stalked forward, knees bent. Pure, murderous intent gleamed from his light eyes.

"No!" Maren pulled away from Aury and grabbed Filip's leather bracer. "He's not the enemy here."

Aury stared into Maren's face. "You're ensorcelled."

Shaking her head, Maren waved Kynan over. "I'm not under a spell. Ask me anything"

"What recipe did I want from you?" Aury slowly drew her staff from its straps, her gaze slipping to Kynan's face.

"Cinnamon rolls," Maren said quickly. "I swear. I'm under no influence. He isn't perfect, but he is doing the right thing now, and if you hurt him, we will all die."

Filip straightened, and the fury tightening his features disappeared, but he didn't put away his hatchet. He eyed Kynan up and down, like he was sizing him up. Both elven lords had dark hair and pointed ears at about the same length, but that was where the resemblances stopped. Kynan was stillness, danger, and shadow. Filip was lightning just about to strike.

Aury's silver hair escaped its braid as she circled Kynan. "You have no sword, King of the Underworld."

Kynan spread his arms wide. "I do not come here to fight." His voice was deep and steady.

"You might not have the choice." Aury cocked her head.

"Please, Princess Aurora," Maren said, feeling like some courtly manners might help things, "may I introduce High King Kynan Meilyr Islwyn?" She couldn't believe she'd actually remembered his ridiculous name. "Prince Filip, he has been looking forward to meeting you." That was a fib, but it was better than bloodshed. She had to smooth over this new beginning between the Underworld and the Upperworld.

Bonfires flickered outside the Sacred Oak's moon shadow, and the stars pierced the black of the sky.

Filip exploded into action, striking out at Kynan with his hatchet, his movements blurry with speed. Kynan slipped his head to the right, dodging the blow. Kynan launched his shoulder into Filip, grabbed his leg, then slammed him to the ground.

Whirling her mage staff, Aury pushed Maren out of the way. Water in the shape of a sickle's head sliced through the air above them. Kynan's shadows spun from his chest and back, grabbed the ice, and dashed it to bits.

Panic lanced Maren's chest. "Please! Stop! We need him to save the Sacred Oak!" Why weren't they listening to her? She got to her feet and tried to get between Kynan and Filip, who was already up and spinning his hatchet again.

There was a shout beyond the light of bonfire. Rhianne—a human witch and princess of the fae court —ran toward them, brown hair flying and wand thrust into the air. Her fae prince husband, Werian, leapt into a smaller oak's branches and began firing arrows from his bow. They too had fought with her and the others against Brielle's father, the Wylfen king, a man who was now dead and the world better for it.

"Stop, you wonderful fools!" Maren's throat burned from shouting. "Princess Rhianne! Prince Werian! I'm fine! The Shadow King is on our side!"

Kynan's shadows deftly plucked every arrow from its path and spun easily around Filip's and Aury's attacks of steel and ice.

"Listen to me!" Goddess, if she only had her wand!

As if he'd read her mind, Werian pulled something from behind one of his ram horns and tossed it down to her. "Catch!"

Maren snagged her wand out of the air, and a rush of warm power ran from her hand to her heart and back again. She wasn't always the best with fighting magic, but maybe this time...

She pointed the wand at Aury and thought simply, *Down*. Aury fell to knees, mouth agape. Maren did the same to Filip, who railed against the magical bonds she'd set on him.

Werian jumped down from the branches and landed beside Rhianne. He put a hand on Rhianne's arm.

"Look," he said, his fae voice carrying like song through the forest.

Rhianne stopped hurling magical curses and stared at Maren.

"Finally." Maren dropped onto a log beside the bonfire. "Thank you, Prince Werian." She'd always liked him. Such a flirt and a heart of gold. "Just sit, everyone. Please. I've had enough of everyone's mad tempers."

"We were only trying to rescue you." Aury took a seat beside Maren and set her mage staff on the ground near her boots.

"I know." Maren looped her arm in Aury's as the others came near.

Kynan bowed at the waist, his cloak rippling in the autumn breeze. "Princess Aurora, Prince Filip, Princess Rhianne, Prince Werian, it's a pleasure to make your acquaintance." He didn't miss a beat, did he? Impressive that he'd caught Werian's and Rhianne's names. The firelight glittered in his eyes as he stood. Neither his gaze nor his tone said he was happy to meet any of them, but at least he was trying to be diplomatic. "I don't blame you for striking out at me," he said. "I apologize for claiming the Awenydd in a way that you found alarming."

"Does anyone not find abduction alarming?" Rhianne looked ready to punch Kynan right in the teeth.

Werian snorted a quiet laugh.

"It is the way it's always been done," Kynan said. "Granted, I have not claimed an Upperworld Awenydd in my life." His gaze slid to Maren, and her heart thumped against her ribs. "I have promised my soul and hearts to your friend. I endeavor to court her properly, but we must inform you that time is indeed rather short."

Rhianne sat on another log near the fire. "Tell us everything."

Werian slung his bow over his back, then took a water skin from his shoulder bag. He handed it to Rhianne, who took a sip and gasped.

"What is that?" she asked.

"Scorchpepper brandy." Werian wiggled his eyebrows. "Filip and I created it last night for this evening's festivities."

Filip grinned and glanced at Aury, who narrowed her eyes. He shrugged and held out his hands.

"Now is not the time for drinking, my darling," Rhianne said to Werian.

Aury reached for the skin, and Werian handed it over. She tipped it up, then wiped her mouth with the back of her hand. "I humbly disagree. This seems a time when drinking is absolutely required. Although next time you tell me you're training, Prince Filip," she said, her voice thorned, "and instead are in the kitchen concocting plans with Prince Werian, know that I will have both eyes on you."

"Since I have to tell you the terrifying news, I need a swig too." Maren waved a hand impatiently. The scorchpepper brandy burned its way down her throat and left behind a lovely heat. Her muscles relaxed, and she squared her shoulders, ready to tell the tale.

She handed the brandy to Kynan, who took a neat sip.

Maren explained everything from the icy, dead roots of the Sacred Oak at the Spirit Well to the Binding and how the joining of her magic and Kynan's would heal the damage. She mentioned Tiergan briefly and Hafwen as well.

"The poison is the Magebane from the last battle?" Rhianne tapped her wand against her palm and paced.

"The god Arcturus told us at the Spirit Well," Maren said. "His description fits the old Matchweaver, the one you told me about." Maren leaned toward Kynan. "Rhianne is the new Matchweaver."

"I know of the Matchweaver." Kynan nodded respectfully at Rhianne, but he looked pained doing it.

Werian's eyebrow lifted, and he angled himself between Rhianne and Kynan.

Maren continued the explanation, giving details about the Spirit Well. "...and so I must Bind myself to High King Kynan before the gray ice spreads and takes us all."

Kynan crossed his arms, his gaze never leaving Maren's face. "Already we've met with one hungry spirit. Maren saved my life. If anyone else had met that spirit, they would be nothing now. Both starved spirits and their victims experience a death with no chance of an afterlife."

Filip stood beside Aury, his brow furrowed and his knuckles white on his weapons belt.

"You can't return here after the Binding?" Aury's eyes shone as she stared at Maren.

The tough Magelord Princess wouldn't cry, but the threat of her tears was more than enough to make Maren weep. She fought the urge, forcing her eyes to hold on.

"I don't think so," Maren said, her voice trembling a little.

Kynan shifted his weight from one foot to the other. "Lady Hafwen and I will search for a way around that magic. I promise you that."

Filip came up behind Maren and squeezed her shoulder. His Balaur braids swung over one cheek. "I thank you for being willing to sacrifice. You are a true star in the sky, Lady Maren."

"Thank you, Prince Filip," Maren said.

Filip kissed her hand.

Kynan, dark-eyed and deadly, took a step closer, his shadows whirling possessively around Maren. A flutter of pleasure danced across her body.

Filip gave Kynan a respectful nod and drew away.

"Where did you find this?" Maren held up her wand, eager to change the subject.

"Rhianne located your wand shortly after your... disappearance, shall we call it?" Werian aimed a foul look at Kynan.

"Your wand called to me," Rhianne said. "I can't imagine how lost you've felt without it." Rhianne had fought alongside Maren in the battle against Brielle's father, the foul king of Wylfenden. Rhianne was a much more powerful witch, a woman who could do so much more in this realm than Maren.

Maren pressed her fingers into the oaken wood's

soft grain and savored the feel of its warmth and the hum of its power. "I'm myself again. And the Binding will work properly now that I have this. Hafwen explained that element of the ritual before we left. I'd assumed I would have to beg for another." She smiled, gratitude flooding her. "But tell me, where is everyone else? Don't the people of Lore celebrate Samhain? I would think the Sacred Oak would make a fine place for the event." Maren had only been a subject of Lore since the early summer. In her home kingdom of Wylfenden, everyone had celebrated Samhain with bonfires and dancing.

Filip looked toward the fire. "We set guards around the area to keep all of our subjects safe."

"We hoped we'd receive a message from you tonight," Rhianne said, glancing at Aury. "We wanted privacy and security." She gave Kynan a careful look.

"Wise," Kynan said. "Please don't hold off your celebrations on my account though."

"Can we send for Sir Costel now?" Maren asked. "I was hoping he might have more information about this situation. Has he done any more research?"

"To see if you truly do have to return with High King Kynan?" Aury asked. She didn't seem to care if she offended Kynan.

"Yes, that," Maren said, "as well as anything about any earlier damage to the Oak."

Aury raised a hand, then stood and began walking away from the bonfire. "I'll send a messenger now and open up our celebrations to the fae, elves, and humans gathered," she called over her shoulder. Aside from the two large contingents of elves who had come with Dorin on this visit and those who accompanied Filip in his court alongside Aury, no elves lived in the Kingdom of Lore or its sub-kingdom, the fae's Agate Court. Witches were rare, so the local inhabitants were mostly humans and fae. "Not too many will brave the area at night with the enchanted fog and all, but about a dozen arrived with drink and food when we first rode up." The fog in the Forest of Illumahrah cloaked scar wolves and could addle the mind, if one believed those superstitions.

Filip joined Aury and they began talking excitedly as they disappeared into the moonlit night.

Maren blinked, feeling light and happy but worrying she may have had a little too much of Werian's brandy. "Prince Werian, I think that brandy was crafted for fae and elves only. This small human witch is already dizzy just from that one dram."

Werian pushed a thick lock of purple-tinged black hair out of his face, arranging it between his horns. "Does that mean you want more?"

Rhianne smacked his stomach with the back of her hand. "Leave off, you naughty thing."

He kissed her head and drew her into the small clearing on the far side of the bonfire as a group of finely dressed nobles and a few common folk wandered over. Laughter and shouts of greeting sounded as the Samhain celebration grew. A group of fae with lyres, flutes, and skin drums began to play a quick tune that made Maren bounce her leg, her body wishing to dance.

Kynan sat beside her, his face unreadable. She

touched his leg briefly, suddenly feeling shy and awkward with him here and Werian and Rhianne dancing provocatively just a few feet away.

"Would you like to join them?" Kynan asked.

"Do you enjoy dancing?" She truly couldn't picture it.

"Not at all."

Her own laugh surprised her. "Then why suggest it?"

"When one is courting," he said, "one must behave in a pleasing way to one's intended."

Maren grinned wickedly.

CHAPTER 29

"Maybe try that invitation again," Maren said to Kynan. She couldn't help chuckling at his obvious discomfort.

Standing in a graceful move that had his cloak sweeping dramatically across the fallen leaves, he held out a hand. "Lady of my hearts, please dance with me."

"Well, when you put it that way." She took his hand and dragged him toward Werian and Rhianne, who were spinning like tops and laughing like the world wasn't about to end.

"I suppose having a lovely time won't inhibit our chance at saving the Sacred Oak," Maren said.

"Certainly not." Kynan pulled her close against him, and she gasped. He looked down at her, his eyes shimmering ruby red and the scent of him making her head swim. "The stronger your feelings are for me, the more powerful our Binding will be."

She slid her arms around his shoulders and toyed with the hair at the back of his neck. His breath caught, and his eyes closed briefly. When they opened again, the ruby light intensified.

Maren grinned. "So this is all for the realms, then? Not for our own pleasure."

Bending his head to hers, his lips nearly touched her temple, then her ear. But he didn't kiss her or make contact with his mouth. "Exactly so," he said.

The nearness of his body, the warmth of his breath, and his presence made her shiver with delight.

"We're incredibly selfless," she said.

A quiet laugh rumbled through his chest. "As kings and queens should always be."

Music soared through the night air, lilting and increasingly fast, and the fire snapped and reached bright fingers toward the canopy of colored leaves, beams of moon glow, and the scattered light of the stars.

Kynan drew her even closer, then tipped up her chin. "May I take you into the shadows for a moment?"

"Is this the brandy talking?"

"Perhaps." He drew her outside the bonfire's circle of flickering light and under the wide trees of the fae forest. Beneath an oak with a broad and mossy trunk, he brushed a thumb along her jaw and pulled her very close. "May I kiss you?"

"And I ask again, is this the brandy talking?" It was such fun to tease this serious king.

"This is my admiration for you," he said quietly. "For the way you are loyal to your friends and for your courage when you weren't born to such reckless acts as giving up your way of life for all the world. For your quick mind and adaptable spirit," he whispered, his words deep and low under the trill of the music. "Your humility and the love you have for those entrusted in your care. The spirits trust you. Ivar and every other creature we've come across immediately longs to be near you. I may be the Shadow King, but I am certainly no better judge of character than the spirits. I would kiss you, my lady, because I find my eyes, body, soul, and mind drawn to you in a way unlike any experience in all my centuries of life. It may not be wise. I do not care. I can't deny the power you have over every inch of my being."

His shadows smoothed down her arms and torso, then along her legs. Their sparkling magic, cool then warm, made her body shudder with pleasure. The heat of desire scorched its way downward, igniting her blood and throwing all her good sense to the wind. She parted her lips, lost on what to say, her body aching with need for his every touch, word, and promise.

He crushed his mouth to hers.

With each stroke of his tongue on hers, with every caress of his hands on her hips and neck, he sent waves of delight and abandon through her.

Here she was with the Shadow King himself on Samhain. Glittering black and gold with power, his crown peaked above his head. Shadows spiraled away from his back like great wings that stretched until they melded with the night. More shadows tickled the backs of her knees and swept up her sides and lower back, spreading a tingling feeling that was truly incredible. The muscles in his arms tensed as he held her close. She felt the beat of his hearts against her chest. The stoic king was losing control, and the knowledge that she was responsible for his wanton behavior thrilled her beyond belief.

The drums thundered, and the people's laughter turned into song. The fae, humans, and elves, wove a bilingual ballad that spoke of darkness, of fire, and of hearts longing to be near those lost and those found once again.

In the pale light of the stars and moon, Kynan urged Maren against the oak, his hips sharp against hers. Thoughts shattered as soon as she tried to form them, waves of pining crashing across her body. He hitched her dress up at the leg, then ran a rough hand up her thigh over her woolen stockings.

"If we don't stop now," he said, his voice like far-off thunder, "it will be very difficult indeed for me to return to the celebrations." His shadows flickered in and out of view around him, as if he were trying to restrain his luring magic but was failing gloriously.

She truly didn't have a chance against him either. What was it about his stoic demeanor that drew her in? Strength, yes. That was admirable. He'd been through a loss and come out with his heart still open. Such strength. And the way he was with his familiar. Ivar loved him, and creatures didn't love so easily. Especially dragons, and wyverns were basically the same animal.

"I would rather claim you properly after our Binding in a room that befits your noble heart, my queen." Kynan sounded as if the admission pained him.

"I would like that." She felt so oddly bashful around him.

But instead of leaving, he looked at her, his eyes wild. He breathed out through his nose, his chest rising and falling so fast, and suddenly he kissed her again. He devoured her lips, his hands splayed over her cheeks and jaw as he seemed to pour every bit of his feelings for her into the slip, dive, and crush of his mouth, teeth, and tongue.

He drew away abruptly, panting and eyes glowing. "Apologies. I had meant to stop, but you're more temptation than I can handle, my queen."

"Don't apologize for that." She felt light as a feather and as sparkling as the starry sky.

He smiled and nodded, and she knew it was time to go even if she didn't want to.

They walked hand in hand to the bonfire, where the song had ended and the younger fae and a few human lads had started jumping the fire.

Rhianne had one arm around Werian, and with her other hand, she was sheathing her wand. She raised her eyebrows at Maren and grinned cheekily. Had she cast a spell?

Maren stopped. "Oh."

Kynan's grip on her hand tightened. "What is it?"

"I think Princess Rhianne might have...urged us on, so to speak." Her cheeks couldn't grow any hotter.

"Ah." He looked at Rhianne and bowed his head.

"You're all right with that?" Maren asked.

"I am if you are," Kynan said.

"Maybe we needed a push in that direction."

"Are you as stubborn as I am?" he asked, humor trickling through his words. "If you're even a tenth as stubborn, then we might never have grown closer." The side of his mouth lifted.

Kynan escorted Maren to where Rhianne and Werian stood eating cooked apples that had been cut crosswise to show the sign of the goddess Vahly. "Why are they leaping over the flames?" Kynan asked.

Rhianne handed them each an apple, her eyes sparkling with the aftereffects of her special type of magic. "The fire burns away the foul deeds they've done and gives them luck in the coming winter. At least, that's why we humans in Lore do it. What are the fae's beliefs about the bonfire?" she asked Werian.

A young fae with pointed ears showing through his light hair and spirit agate rings on every finger leapt over the fire and tripped as he landed. Laughing, he let his fellows lift him to his feet. He must have tried the scorchpepper brandy as well, because she'd never seen a fae trip so easily.

"To ensure fertility." Werian's half-lidded gaze found Rhianne, and his hand snaked around her middle.

Rhianne looked skyward. "Fae."

Kynan gave Maren an *I told you* sort of grimace. He definitely disliked the fae.

Maren stood on tiptoe to whisper into his ear. "I don't think you can point any fingers regarding loose behavior this evening, High King Kynan."

His mouth twitched, and he dipped his head in acknowledgment.

"And the mountain elves of Balaur jump the fire for prowess in battle," a low voice said from behind.

Maren turned to see Dorin and Brielle approaching from the forest. Kynan gasped, his eyes widening at the sight of Dorin, but Maren's heart was too full to worry about explaining that he was a dragon shifter. She ran to Brielle and hugged her tightly. The bonfire's light shone brightly over Brielle's red hair and cast shadows along Dorin's dragon wings.

"I heard the news," Brielle said in Maren's ear. "Do you need me to loose one of my knives and stop that Shadow King's heart? Because I am perfectly prepared for that."

"That won't be necessary," Maren said, "but thank you. I'm actually growing rather fond of him."

Maren bowed to High Prince Dorin. He took her hand and squeezed it gently. "I am very glad to see you again, Lady Maren."

Kynan bowed his head. Maren had to credit him for not staring too hard at the scant amount of scales on Dorin's cheek, and, of course, the wings. "Greetings, Prince Dorin."

Dorin didn't acknowledge Kynan's bow and instead stared him down. "You abducted a subject of my brother and sister-in-law's kingdom. I would like to hear your explanation myself."

"I respect that," Kynan said coolly. "Lady Maren is the Awenydd."

"The Deadspeaker."

"In my kingdom, that term is offensive. She is the Great Seer of the Underworld, and as the Shadow King,

I was called to claim her as my mate in an effort to halt the ruin of both our realms. Only in times of trouble do I claim a mate. The claiming is an ancient rite and one that demands quick action to avoid..."

"Yes?" Dorin stepped closer, wings shuffling in irritation.

Kynan's gaze cut to the sharp points on the ends of those wings. "To avoid interference from Upperworlders."

"Upperworlders."

"Indeed."

Brielle touched her leg, and Maren knew well that the redheaded princess had a thigh-strap there and about a dozen knives.

"Let's calm ourselves," Maren said. "I appreciate everyone's concern. I tried to kill High King Kynan myself when I was first taken."

Brielle nodded approvingly.

"But now," Maren continued. "I understand the ancient rite. The king has apologized and shown a change in his behavior while in my company."

Dorin's wings expanded slightly, as if he were ready to lunge at Kynan. His eyes sparkled with malicious intent. "As long as you're certain, Lady Maren."

"I am. Thank you."

Dorin gave Kynan a curt nod, which Kynan returned. Maren supposed that was as good as it would get between those two for now.

Shoving a cup into Dorin's hand, Werian said, "I can handle one stormy fellow. But two? Come now, drink up and be merry."

Werian attempted to hand another cup to Maren, but Kynan stopped him.

"Lady Maren? Is the fae bothering you?" Kynan said.

Maren took the cup. "No, he's not. He is lovely."

Werian winked. "You speak the truth."

Shaking her head, Rhianne pulled Werian away and into a new round of dancing.

"My lords and ladies!" Sir Costel ran up the path, waving a parchment. A bag slung over his shoulder banged against his leg, and his frizzy hair flopped about his pointed ears.

It was time to see if Maren had been a fool to trust Kynan, or if he and his Underworld associates had indeed been telling the truth about the Binding and the Sacred Oak.

CHAPTER 30

"Once we've spoken to Sir Costel," Kynan said to Maren, "I would love to hear Prince Dorin's tale."

Costel bowed in the Balaur style with one leg extended. "Good Samhain to you." His gaze snagged on Kynan, and his mouth fell open, gaze wandering from Kynan's strange crown to the shadows just barely visible around his shoulders. "I..I…"

"A pleasure to meet you, Sir Costel," Kynan said. "The Awenydd has told me about your sharp mind."

Costel gripped the parchment too tightly, then seemed to realize what he was doing and smoothed it on his stomach. "I, yes. Thank you. Is Awenydd what you call the Deadspeaker? And what are your powers, Lady Maren, while you are in the Underworld? What is it like there? How did you manage to break through to this realm?"

Maren grinned widely. Because Costel was so often training and educating Filip's unit of warriors, she wasn't that close to the elven knight, but he was such an endearing fellow with his obvious thirst for learning.

"Maybe one question at a time would be best," Maren said.

Costel laughed at himself. "Of course. Apologies. Can we sit somewhere and talk? I'd like to show you this writing I found."

Brielle waved them toward a table where servants had started setting out more food. "Please set the trays on the table nearer the second bonfire," she said to the servants, who bobbed quick bows and hurried to their work.

Kynan was quietly explaining all to Costel as they walked.

"I can't believe I get the opportunity to speak with you." Costel spread the parchment on the table and set his bag beside it. "See this here?" He pointed to a scrawled line that Maren couldn't read.

"Is that the elven language?" she asked.

Dorin leaned over to eye the writing. "Ancient elvish, yes."

Kynan's lips pursed as he read silently. He glanced at Maren. "Can you read this?"

"Not at all," she said.

With a nod, Kynan began to translate aloud. "'The Sacred Oak longs for balance, and the Binding of the King of Shadows brings such peace. When the Master of Cynnwrf joins with the fire-blessed Awenydd, all elements are set into the circle of life. There is no stain that can touch the completed circle.' It's not an ideal translation, but that's as close I can manage."

Costel eyed Kynan's belt. "Do you not have Cynnwrf, Lord King? Your sword's magic is similar to the goddess Vahly's oaken sword." He faced Maren, his wild, red hair flopping about his pointed ears. Maren was sure Costel had heard all about what Kynan's sword had done to restrain Filip, Dorin, and Brielle. The only reason they hadn't brought it up was surely to protect their own pride.

Kynan nodded. "I was forced to leave the sword with Lady Hafwen, the shadow elf who performs the Binding. The weapon would have made crossing into the Upperworld impossible."

"Ah." Costel's shoulders dropped, but then his eyes brightened. "Would you be willing to teach me about the Spirit Well?"

"Of course."

Kynan and Costel rambled on about the well and the roots while Maren studied the parchment with Brielle at her side.

"Why are you here, Maren?" Brielle kept her voice very low.

"I wanted to see the truth for myself before I agreed to Bind myself to him. I wanted to hear it from Costel, from our sources."

"'Our' meaning Upperworld?"

"Yes. I find that I do trust Kynan. We've...had some experiences in the Underworld, and I'd be lying if I didn't say I trust him. Maybe that sounds foolish, but you can't say a word considering you decided to woo a dragon-shifting elven prince." Maren elbowed Brielle, who snorted.

"True. It's wise of you to check our history for information on the Binding. But, Maren…" The corners of Brielle's mouth tipped downward, and she swallowed. "I can't just let him take you away forever."

Maren's heart trembled, and she gripped Brielle's hand. This was the true reason Maren had been so determined to return—to see her friends one last time. "You saved my life. I'm glad I can repay the debt by healing the Oak."

"You know there is no debt." The fire of anger lit Brielle's eyes.

"I know, but if I have to give you all up…" Maren's throat tried to close up, and she coughed. "Then I'm glad it's for a good reason."

"You won't be miserable in the Underworld?"

"I'll miss you terribly, but maybe we can find a way to visit one another. We still have hope."

Brielle yanked Maren into a fierce hug that nearly broke every rib in Maren's body. "I love you, friend. And if that Shadow King so much as makes you frown, I will somehow, some way, smash into that realm and use him for target practice."

Maren held on, pressing her face into Brielle's shoulder, wishing things were different. "I know you will. Now, when are you and dragon boy going to start making babies?"

"How did you know?" Brielle pulled away but kept her fingers laced around Maren's upper arms.

"I didn't! Congratulations!" Maren looked to Brielle's belly, but it was as flat as ever.

"It's early. Keep it to yourself for now, all right?"

"That baby is going to be the cutest thing in any realm," Maren said.

Brielle's smile stretched wide. "Definitely." She laughed at herself and hugged Maren again.

Suddenly, Kynan grasped his chest and cried out, his shadows erupting around him like great claws. "My sword..."

Maren ran to him and took his arm. All the color drained from his face, and the sparks in his dark and shadowed crown died down to pale flashes.

"What is it?" She held tight to his leather vest. "What about your sword? What's wrong? Kynan." His gaze lost focus, and his weight dropped. Dorin and Werian each caught an arm and helped him to remain standing. "Kynan! Answer me!"

He met her gaze and found the strength to stand on his own, giving both Dorin and Werian a grateful nod. "He has claimed my sword."

"Who?" Maren drew her wand from her belt.

Kynan's gaze was steel. He bared his teeth, shadows rippling around him and the magic in his ethereal crown sparking wildly. "Tiergan. He is the only one strong enough to break my claim. King Tiergan is now the Master of Cynnwrf."

"But you claimed it..." Costel's brow furrowed.

"Only the fated master of the sword can draw it from the Moon Bog," Kynan said through gritted teeth. "Once that's done, any shadow lord may claim it if he performs the ritual properly."

Maren's blood frosted as her mind locked together the pieces of this new puzzle. "To save the realms, I must Bind to the most powerful shadow lord, the one with Cynnwrf. If he has the sword, then..." She didn't want to say it out loud.

"We have to get that sword back," Aury snapped. Maren hadn't seen her and Filip return, but they stood side by side near Werian and Rhianne. "You can't marry someone who makes you look like you're going to be sick," Aury said, eyeing Maren's face. "What do we know of this King Tiergan?"

Stomach rolling, Maren closed her eyes.

A darkly pleased laugh echoed through her mind.

Tiergan.

Come to me, my bride, he hissed, his words strangling her thoughts. *I am now the strongest of the shadow lords, and you must Bind yourself to me to save those you love.*

CHAPTER 31

Maren jerked back, heart sinking. "He's speaking to me."

Kynan's gaze snapped to her forehead. He knew what Tiergan could do, of course, because he too was a shadow lord and they had dealt with this once already at Hafwen's manor. "Push him from your mind before he sways you. If that's what you choose."

Her body shook. Aury, Rhianne, and Brielle gathered close, hands alighting on her gently as they whispered encouraging words.

"Do you need a cup of water?" Rhianne asked. "Sometimes thinking of a simple need and fulfilling it helps one find calm."

"Let's take her to our chambers at the fae court," Werian said to Rhianne. "She needs a dark room and some time to think."

"She needs an army." Aury crossed her arms and glared at Maren's head as if she could scowl Tiergan's voice away.

Filip whispered something in elvish to Dorin, who nodded.

Maren took a shuddering breath, wishing she could scrub her mind with the roughest of potions. She'd take pain over this any day. "He says...he says I must come to him and that now only a Binding with him can save us from the spreading poison."

Kynan swallowed and looked away, his grip on Maren's arm tightening.

"We can fight him, can't we?" she asked.

He turned toward her, concern softening his sharp features. Then his eyes gleamed that deep, deep red. The intent in his stare was clear: He would protect her above all else, above his own life, above the well-being of the realms. Her palms and forehead tingled with the truth of it, her witch's soul branding the reality into her very flesh.

She pulled him close.

"We will fight him together if that's your wish, my queen," he said quietly.

Oh, by the Source, she didn't want to go to battle again. One time was more than enough for a life. The blood. The horror of it. Fear like a second skin she couldn't shed.

But if she didn't go to war, she'd be trapped in the Underworld as wife and mate to King Tiergan. She shut her eyes against the truth for a moment. Then she looked around at Kynan, at her friends...

On tiptoe, she pressed a kiss to Kynan's cheek. "I choose you."

She stepped back to look at her found family. "I hate

to leave your lovely party, but I guess I'm once again going to war."

The celebration turned into a chaos of discussion on how to approach this and what the possibilities might be. None of them made a lick of sense to Maren, who had very little experience with warfare.

"We must find a way to go with you," Filip said.

"Definitely," Dorin agreed, his dragon wings stretching to reach behind Brielle.

Costel was tearing through the scrolls he'd brought in his bag. "Can we do it? Can we enter the Underworld with you?" he asked Kynan.

Kynan rubbed his chin, the red in his eyes still glittering brightly. "I don't think it's possible, but then again, I'm not the Awenydd."

All looked to Maren.

"I...this is a question for Lady Hafwen," Maren said, following her intuition.

A spirit approached Maren and curtseyed. "Awenydd." She was a tall woman who actually reminded Maren of Hafwen, although she had both natural eyes.

"Yes?" Maren felt the need to hurry back to the Underworld, but she couldn't ignore this spirit. The feel of her was too powerful and too kind.

"Is there a spirit speaking to you?" Costel asked.

Kynan nodded, answering for Maren as he gestured to her hands. But they weren't flickering with flame, of course. His brow furrowed as he took in this information that Maren's magic was different here.

"They don't do that in the Upperworld," Maren explained to him. She faced the spirit. "I'm listening,"

"If we escort your warriors," the spirit said, "they may enter the Underworld, but only for five days and five nights. Then they must leave with us or remain forever in the Shadow King's realm."

"How can you help them pass through?"

"It is the gift of the Awenydd," the spirit said. "Once you have claimed your shadow lord mate in word, if not yet in Binding, your burgeoning power allows you to arm yourself with a spirit force." Her eyes crinkled, and she grinned. "And we have our ways of getting you what you want, my lady queen."

"Did I claim Kynan?" Maren cracked her knuckles, her gaze skirting to Kynan and back.

"With your statement in front of those in your heart and with your kiss," the spirit answered.

"Does that mean we are Bound? Did we heal the Sacred Oak?"

"Sadly, no. The Binding ceremony must take place in full under the hands of the Underworld witch and at the Spirit Well where the Oak's taproot resides. This claiming by word spoken is a half step, for lack of a better term. It is not always done, but when it is, the Awenydd gains some power that speaks to what her future strength will be. The Sacred Oak still suffers. The decay has spread quickly and continues to do so. Only a true Binding ceremony will heal the realms. And you must Bind to the one who holds Cynnwrf. It is too late to Bind to one without it. You must help your mate regain his weapon or suffer the consequences."

Maren swallowed and studied Kynan, her mate. Her. Mate. He was the most dangerous-looking being she'd ever seen. But she knew his gentle touch, his loyal heart. The way love could break him and heal him in turn. She laughed suddenly, but the sound turned sad.

Everyone gave her questioning looks, but she ignored them.

"I suppose I did claim him," she said to the spirit. "How will moving everyone into the Underworld work, exactly? What do I need to do?"

"Assemble a force that doesn't exceed two hundred, including animals," the spirit said. "Do it quickly while we have the thinner veil of Samhain. It will be difficult enough to help them return five days hence. We can't waste our energy tonight. There's not so much to go around now."

Wincing, Maren asked about the damage and if any spirits were missing from the well.

"We don't keep track of one another in the way you suggest," the spirit answered. "I know that my hands are too cold and that my feet long to wander. It's not a good sign. I remember the last time the Sacred Oak was damaged, and it felt much like this."

"Thank you," Maren said. "We'll gather as soon as we're able."

"I'll muster what fellow spirits I can find as well. I would guess we can get around two hundred or so. No more than that, certainly. Not with so many weakened as they are from the poison at the Sacred Oak. See you soon, Awenydd."

They curtseyed to one another, then the spirit faded away.

Maren turned to face everyone. "If you are willing, gather a force that numbers up to two hundred including the animals. The spirits have agreed to escort our army through the veil tonight before sunup. We must hurry for this to work."

"But how..." Kynan frowned, his gaze on the place where the spirit had been.

"They said I had growing power because I claimed you in word." She felt her cheeks warm as she spoke. "I have come into some of my official powers. Not all. The Binding still must be done properly. She didn't put it like that, but that was what I took from it. She said I can call up a spirit force as the Awenydd who has sworn herself to a shadow lord."

Kynan's eyes widened a fraction, then his gaze grew heavy-lidded. He kissed her hand. "Never before has an Awenydd stirred so much loyalty from the spirits. Your kind and noble heart is obvious to all."

Aury and Werian raised their goblets. Filip, Dorin, and Rhianne each touched their weapons—hatchet, sword, and wand. Brielle stared, but Maren knew that was the look she had when she was plotting.

"Thank you," Maren said, trying to keep her voice from shaking. "Please assemble those you believe are best suited to the...to the job. Thank you." She was the worst leader, but she wasn't going to shy away from her fate. This was going to be chaos at its very best.

CHAPTER 32

O ver the next few hours, a multitude of spirits clustered beside the Sacred Oak. A host of servants, pages, knights, and royals assembled spears, halberds, and round wooden shields reinforced with bronze. Wearing metal plating on their snouts and front flanks, horses with bright ribbons of forest green, sky blue, and scarlet braided into their manes stomped the ground. Their breath clouded in the moonlight. Servants loaded lesser horses with sacks of bread, dried meats and fruit, and water skins.

Soon a veritable army stood at the mossy rocks of the ancient doors to the Underworld. Spirits glowing a bright white floated above elven, fae, and human warriors in shining armor.

Maren, with her wand at the ready, spoke in quiet tones to Kynan. "Will this be enough?"

Kynan's shadows whirled around them. Strange how she now felt them comforting and alluring rather than frightening. "It will have to be. We'll raise my shadow elf army as well." A wrinkle appeared between his black eyebrows. Was he worried about more than just the obvious—war and the possible loss of her to his rival? What else could they be going up against? What would he hide from her?

Maren shivered, and he wrapped her in his arms as well as his shadows. "Is there anything you need to tell me?"

"No. I'm borrowing worry," Kynan said.

"What does that mean?"

"I'm stealing worries from a day that may or may not happen in the future. It isn't a wise way to live, but as you know, those who lead must sometimes worry more than most in order to be prepared," he said.

Dorin glanced their way. His talons showed at his fingertips, and his wings were tucked tightly against his back. Brielle stood beside him with a confident stance despite being human and having no magic to speak of. Her throwing knives were strapped to her chest now, no longer hidden under her skirts as was her custom. She appeared more than prepared to slay anyone who looked at her wrong.

Filip rode over and gave Maren and Kynan a respectful nod. His gray eyes were pinched and he kept glancing at the sky. "I have unfortunate news."

"What's wrong? Where is Jewel?" Maren hadn't seen Filip's dragon familiar in a long while because it seemed the creature preferred the distant mountains to the lowlands here in Lore.

"That's just it." Looking exasperated, he ran a hand over his Balaur warrior braids. "I can't find her. She's run off again, most likely with that jade male Dorin and I saw her with in the spring."

"And there's no way to call her back from afar?" Kynan asked.

"I've tried. She doesn't communicate regularly with me. Rather independent."

Kynan's lip twitched. "I understand that."

Maren knew he was thinking of Ivar.

"Well, we can't wait any longer. At least we have one dragon," Maren said, jerking her chin in Dorin's direction.

Sighing, Filip nodded. "Big brother will have to do."

"What are you talking about over there?" Dorin shouted out.

Filip grinned, bowed his head, then urged his horse to trot back to his contingent of warriors.

Rhianne and Werian stepped forward, out of the array of mounted knights and foot soldiers.

Rhianne held out a black, high-necked military vest made of tough leather. Small stones sewn into the hide glittered like starlight. "I'd like you to have this, Lady Maren," she said, using her more courtly tone of voice.

Maren ran a hand over the cloak. Power fluttered up her fingers, into her arm, and filled her heart. Her palms and forehead warmed with magic. The stones were smooth and dark, but when she tipped the vest this way or that, their surfaces sparkled in hues of rose, indigo, bright yellow, and deep cerulean. "What *is* this?"

"Spirit agate," Werian said. "The stones are stitched in tightly so don't worry about losing them in battle. Even if you do, so be it."

Rhianne smiled. "It's yours to keep as long as you wish."

Werian tapped the largest of the stones, an oval one near the neckline. "Spirit agate increases one's power. It doesn't affect all types of magic..."

"But it gives me more power when its very near me," Rhianne said. "And I'm guessing from the flush in your face and that gleam in your eye, that you feel its effect as well."

"I do." She'd never heard of such a stone. Of course, the fae had many ancient secrets that they hoarded like greedy dragons. It astounded her that Werian and Rhianne were willing to give this up. "Are you sure about this?"

"Well, you are trying to save my life," Rhianne said, laughing lightly.

Kynan took Maren's weapons belt while she unlaced the side of the vest she'd donned earlier—a used one from Filip's contingent. With that one off and given to a nearby page, Rhianne slid the agate vest over Maren's head. Rhianne began to lace the side, but Kynan cleared his throat and she stepped aside, taking the hint.

"So possessive," Maren murmured, enjoying the tinge of pink at the tops of his pointed ears.

Werian chuckled and kissed Rhianne on the forehead.

"You will make a fine queen, Lady Maren," Rhianne said, giving her a curtsey. "I'm honored to go to battle with you."

Werian bowed to her, then to Kynan, and escorted Rhianne back to their mounts.

Maren buckled her weapons belt back into place and unsheathed her wand. The power from the agate made her feel as if she could run all the way to Balaur without stopping, like she could cast one thousand spells without breaking a sweat.

She set the tip of her wand against Kynan's forearm. He looked at her expectantly, curiosity making his eyes spark.

"Mark this man who lays claim to me,

Divine his nature for all to see,

A branch of darkness,

A leaf of light,

Trusted king, blessed be."

Her lips buzzed with the power of the spell, and her heart lifted. She'd never tried something like this. She wasn't very good with usual magic, her strength being in dealing with the spirits, but with the agate's boost, maybe it would work...

Inky darkness stretched from her wand and slid over his skin. He held very still and she wondered if perhaps this had been a bad idea. The darkness came together at varying angles, then twisted and rolled until it created an image on his flesh. It was a black tree with leaves that flickered like tiny flames. Roots formed two letters, *M* and *K*.

Maren gasped, delighted. "I did it." She looked up at him, hoping he didn't object.

He ran a finger over the letters, a slow smile stretching his lips. His eyes met hers and heat shot through her body.

"I love it," he said.

"Are you ready?" she asked, feeling so many emotions at once. Elation that he cared for her. Fear for the upcoming battle. Excitement at what magic she might create.

Kynan's gaze went black and she saw his rage against Tiergan there in the depths. "Definitely."

With the spirits hovering above and beside, Maren and Kynan led the army through the hill and into the Underworld.

At the end of the dark tunnel of earth, the runed doors shimmered. The spirits whispered to the doors, their voices a chaotic and rushing sound, and the runes lit up a bright yellow, a color she'd hadn't yet seen in them.

The doors swung wide, and Kynan preceded her into his realm.

A cold wind struck her across the face, and Kynan's shadows reached back to swathe her in warmth. He turned to look at her, saying something that was lost in the murmur of the spirits and the gasps of the oncoming army.

Beyond him, the Underworld was white.

"I thought we had five days!" Imaginary claws raked down Maren's back, and she gripped her wand in one hand and the reins of her borrowed destrier in the other.

"The poison spreads..." the spirits chorused as Maren's hands and wand sparkled with the fire of her magic. "Five days, Awenydd. You have five days."

"We only just left... How did it spread like this?" Kynan pulled his horse back and rode next Maren. His gaze darted from icicles like teeth hanging from a rocky outcropping by the roadside to a stubbled field covered in hoarfrost.

His panic made Maren panic.

Brielle and Aury rode up beside Maren. "Is it always like this?" Brielle asked as the wind pulled at her red braid.

"No," Maren said. "It was pleasant when we left. The same temperature as it was in Lore near the fae kingdom. The poison seems to have banished autumn completely."

"The power we used to help your army inside advanced the damage." The spirits' combined voices and varied accents poured over Maren's ears like cool water. "We are sorry, Awenydd. We didn't know. This poison is far more potent than any of us has ever experienced."

"It's certainly not your fault," she said to the spirits. "I'm grateful for your aid. Do we need to reevaluate our plan?"

"We believe you may keep your army for three days," the spirits said.

"All right." Maren bowed her head in thanks.

She told Kynan, Brielle, and Aury everything the spirits had said. "They've reassured me that we can move forward as planned. But this... Kynan, it's so..."

"Empty," he said. A shiver tremored through his large frame.

Maren pushed her fear down. She had to stay

focused and ready to fight. But to see him so afraid was incredibly unsettling. Empty was an accurate description, for the very air here felt lost and hollow. Her witch's intuition told her spells would be difficult to cast here. Not impossible, but far more draining. Perhaps not for her though. She felt stronger here, but Rhianne would struggle.

"Doesn't Tiergan care about his own possible demise?" she asked.

"I doubt it," Kynan said. "His soul is as gray and cold as the poison's damage. He only cares to ruin, and if he takes himself down in the process, so be it."

"That's the worst kind of enemy."

"It is." Kynan glanced her way, his eyebrows slightly lifted and respect in his dark eyes. "I am grateful for the time you spent with your royal friends. They have taught you much in the way of ruling."

"Yes, but they didn't teach me that," Maren said.

Kynan eyebrows lifted. "Your rough childhood on the docks did?"

"Definitely."

They rode hard to Hafwen's manor—well, as hard as a massive army could. Maren caught glimpses of Brielle and Dorin, their eyes wide as they took in the sites of the Underworld's towering distant hills and mountains, the ice-edged waterfalls, and the never-ending frost that had spread over it all. When Maren traded a look with Aury across the traveling mass of warriors and horses and carts, Aury was wearing that stoic warrior expression she had. Maren knew Aury was afraid, and it made Maren worry more. Would there be anything left to save by the time they did the Binding?

They arrived at Hafwen's to see not a manor house and stables but a pile of rubble. Maren's heart dropped into her knees.

She half slid, half fell from her horse and onto the crunching frost of the ground. "Hafwen..."

The roof was mostly gone, and the remains still smoked from what had to have been a large fire.

Kynan was as silent as the grave as he hurried inside. Maren stayed close behind.

Inside the hall, chairs and stools lay on the ground, and the doors were torn from their hinges. Someone had scattered Hafwen's dried herb bundles all over the floor, and wide scorch marks marred the walls. A heap of earth—now blanketed in snow and sparkling ice crystals—covered her fireplace, the place where they had eaten, shared their stories, and hidden Cynnwrf. The hiding place was no more, the entire area dislodged and torn open so that it was difficult to tell where it had even been. Mounds of dirt like graves sat around the room, moss and hoar frost cloaking the freshly turned earth and debris.

"Where is she?" Panic tightened Kynan's raised voice. "Lady Hafwen!"

He gave Maren a fierce look, then ran toward the back of the manor house, shouting for his friend.

Werian, Filip, and Aury rushed in and followed Maren as she trailed Kynan.

Outside, Dorin, Brielle, and Rhianne shouted

commands to the army, telling the elves, fae, and humans to halt and wait for instructions.

In Hafwen's private chambers, a bed frame made of birch saplings sat in three pieces, a straw mattress flung against the fire-marked plaster of the far wall.

A wand lay on the earth-and-snow-covered tiles.

"He's taken her." Kynan's words were careful, as though if he said them louder, he might not be able to keep from losing his controlled demeanor.

Maren covered his hand with hers. He was cold. Too cold. "We'll get her back."

She focused her thoughts on the spirit responsible for the army passing into this realm. Her fingers lit up with magical sparks, her elemental magic of air and fire helping her call the woman. The spirit materialized, looking exactly as she had in the Upperworld.

"They are traveling through the high moors," the spirit said. "Lady Hafwen is alive."

The urge to throw her arms around the spirit was nearly overwhelming. "Thank you so much."

The spirit nodded. "She called out as she was taken, naming one of her servants a spy to King Tiergan." The spirit wavered, then disappeared.

"Kynan," Maren said, "Hafwen lives. She had a spy in her household."

He spit out something quick and bladed in his language.

"They are on the high moors," Maren said. "I assume you can take us there."

He breathed out through his nose, and his jaw muscles tensed like he was trying not to lose his mind.

"Of course," he said. "But this is a trap, and we all know it."

"And still we will go. She is your friend and mine," Maren said.

His eyes flashed with passion, his intensity humming through his very presence. She gripped his fingers tightly, her heart surging with ten thousand warring emotions.

They returned to the hall, where Maren raised her wand. Suddenly, mending magic didn't seem as tangled as it once had felt. Magic blazed through her veins, warm and familiar. She drew the two pieces of the broken counter together, mending the area where Hafwen had worked up the concoction that allowed them to visit the Upperworld. She waved her wand in broad arcs to smooth the ground and uncover fallen pots, crockery, and a pair of bright green shoes with leather laces.

"Thank you," Kynan said from the doorway.

Werian and Aury stood behind him. Filip, hair braided tightly over his elven ears, was across the way, and he wore a grim look. Maren had seen the look once before—the day they'd fought those who had killed Maren's parents. It was in the past, but the loss of them and the fear she had felt in watching them die, as well as the terror experienced on the day of vengeance, would never leave her. All of it created a blade twisting in her stomach, so real that sometimes she grabbed for that imagined knife's hilt only to find her hand empty.

She shook her head to focus on the current problems. "What now?" she asked, leaving Hafwen's home as she walked behind Kynan, Aury, Werian, and Filip. The air outside was crisp but laced with the acrid scent of smoke. The horses stomped, the tension in those gathered making them nervous.

"First, I find Ivar."

Ivar. Of course. Surely he and the other wyverns had been able to escape. Tiergan must have shown some true power to evade Hafwen and the wyverns.

"Ivar!" Kynan shouted over and over into the bone-white sky as Filip, Aury, and Werian mounted up once more.

A screech sounded, and several dark shapes spun from the trees beyond Hafwen's orchards.

"Thank the Source and the goddess Nix," Maren whispered.

While the other wyverns rested on boulders, Ivar took a moment to alight on Kynan's arm. The two had a quick conversation as everyone except Maren looked on in confusion. Filip leaned over on his horse to whisper to Aury, and Maren could guess he had figured out that Ivar was to Kynan as Jewel the dragon was to Filip.

Ivar took flight, and the other wyverns joined him. They flew into the sky as if they knew where to go.

"It's time to go to Calon Dywyll to arrange further supplies now, yes?" Maren started toward the stables with Kynan at her side. She had little hope that their horses would be there, but it was worth a moment to look, and it seemed Kynan had the same idea.

"Agreed. Then we must visit the largest town in the Underworld and call up my warriors."

"How is that accomplished in this realm?" she asked.

Afal and Osian were in the stables, stomping and bumping against their half-open stalls but alive and well.

Kynan and Maren greeted their mounts, brought them to where the rest of the leaders waited, then saddled them, allowing a page to take the other two horses to join the rest of the forces.

It felt good to be back with Afal and riding beside Kynan, who was on Osian. They turned toward Brielle and the others.

Dorin shifted his horse so that he faced Kynan. "How can we aid you, High King Kynan?"

Kynan's gaze moved to Dorin, a flicker of surprise showing in Kynan's features. "I must call up my warriors myself. We don't send messengers when asking for a sacrifice of life."

Dorin nodded. "We follow your lead."

Glancing at her, Kynan asked, "Are you ready, my queen?"

Brielle smiled sadly at Maren as if she wished they were in a happier scenario and could properly celebrate Maren's new role.

"Will there be trouble considering we are Upperworlders?" Maren started down the road beside Kynan. The rest fell in behind them, reins and armor clinking and jangling lightly.

"Yes." Kynan glanced at the rise as if he were seeing something in the distance, but she wondered if he was simply avoiding eye contact and hoping she'd change the subject. He nudged his horse to trot ahead of her.

Aury rode up beside Maren. "Straightforward. I like

that." She took the reins in her teeth and knotted her silver hair high on her head. "He suits you."

"And he's wild about you," Brielle said, joining in, her voice loud as usual. The redhead never did speak at a normal volume; her enthusiasm for all things was catching.

"It's only the whole fate thing, princesses," Maren said. "I hate to disappoint you."

Brielle traded a look with Aury, then they both huffed. "You don't see it at all?" Brielle asked.

"See what?"

"The way he ignores everyone else like you're the only person in the entire world," Aury said.

Brielle nodded. "He undresses you with every glance."

"Brielle," Maren hissed, face burning. "Please."

"You teased me enough about Dorin at first. It's your turn now." Brielle grinned like a demon.

Aury chuckled and put her heels to her horse, heading to where Filip rode near Werian, their heads bent to what looked like a serious discussion.

Brielle adjusted the throwing knives strapped across her leather vest. "How did you manage to forgive him for taking you?"

"I haven't fully."

"Good girl."

"He harbors a great deal of anger for Upperworlders. I think that's why he acted as he did. He wanted to snatch me before someone else hurt me. The last Awenydd was killed by humans who thought she was a demon. She was a shadow elf."

Brielle's eyes widened.

"Also, the way I summoned him...it led to some problems," Maren added. "He wasn't best pleased with all of that."

"You're the..." Brielle started. "What was it again?"

"The Awenydd," Maren said.

"Yes, you're the Awenydd, not him. Who is he to have an opinion on how you carry out your fate?"

Maren shook her head. "It wasn't him. The spirits were frightened and angered by my summoning. He is their caretaker."

"You aren't?" Brielle's slim eyebrows bunched.

"With my access to the Between, I'm their voice," Maren said.

"So you and High King Kynan must work together not just to heal the Sacred Oak by Binding, but always."

Maren swallowed and watched Kynan's silhouette as he rode Osian over a hill and disappeared. She'd always thought affection was more of choice. This didn't feel like a choice. Her thoughts simply went to him more and more, and her stomach fluttered when he glanced her way or spoke a word. But to be with him meant leaving the others. How could she be happy if she had to give them up? Not that there was a choice in that either. Of course she would do what she had to do to save the realms and their lives. "I suppose."

"Since this King Tiergan fellow has claimed Cynnwrf," Brielle said, "he is now the dead's caretaker?"

"I don't think so," Maren said. "I think the crown is the key to that position. Perhaps Tiergan will eventually claim the crown if we lose to him and he keeps the sword. I do think Kynan is worried about that possibility as well."

Brielle nodded. "For now, Tiergan simply has the earth power because he holds the sword, and that power is what you must Bind with to heal the Magebane's damage."

Maren flinched at the word Magebane. That poison, inflicted on her in the Wylfen dungeon, had caused a pain that she would have welcomed death to stop. She hated that the spirits were being harmed by it now. "As far as I understand."

She sighed, wishing she were in a massive, hot bath with a goblet of wine.

Brielle frowned, her gaze studying Maren's face. Maren shifted in her saddle, longing for Brielle to look elsewhere.

"I'm so sorry you have to be the sacrifice, my friend," Brielle said quietly. "I wish I could take this for you."

Tears seared Maren's eyes, and she took a steadying breath. "Thank you. I'm glad you don't have the option, because your foolish arse would sign up for it."

Brielle laughed. "I do like to save people."

"Oh, I know. I'm the one who first pointed that out to you," Maren said. "A true heroine, you are, in every sense of the word. It's obnoxious."

Laughing and trading bits of spiced scones they'd nicked from the fae court's kitchens during the assembling of the forces, they rode side by side until they reached the area where the blue poppy fields of Kynan's grounds should have been.

Ice and frost cloaked the lost flowers. Even the river was mostly frozen over. Maren put a hand against her stomach, feeling ill. If the Magebane poison destroyed all the blue poppies, would the spirits forever lose the chance to bless their descendants? Even if they won this fight, would there be continued new challenges? She took a slow breath and touched Afal's neck to urge a slower pace as to stay in line with Kynan. She needed the comfort of his powerful presence, or she was going to lose her mind.

CHAPTER 33

"With all respect, my king, this cannot be. Absolutely not." Aeron, Kynan's general, bowed as he disagreed with the plans. The shadow elf had tied back his gray hair at the neck. His eyes were as narrow and sharp as a hawk's.

"I didn't ask your opinion, General Aeron," Kynan said even as he gripped the man's forearm and shoulder gently yet firmly like one would an old friend.

Standing in the inner bailey of Calon Dywyll, Maren shivered. The wind had grown teeth that bit at her cheeks, nose, and exposed fingertips. She wished they'd stop arguing and get moving. She wouldn't be able to do a single spell if her fingers froze together.

"We ride to Hywl."

"Hoo eel," Werian whispered to Rhianne, who tried likewise to pronounce the name of the Underworld's largest city.

"Do you think it would be wasteful to spell some warmth over my hands if I can manage it?" Maren asked

Rhianne. Rhianne was far more experienced and more powerful than her, and she gave solid advice.

"I'd save it if we are to fight anytime soon," Rhianne said. "This place drains one's energy."

Maren crossed her arms and tucked her hands into her armpits. She didn't want to say that she felt more powerful here. It would only rub salt in the wound.

Eefa, Ninian, and the rest of Kynan's staff stood at the doors to the keep, the courtyard's trees framing them in icy branches and the ground a glossy sheen at their feet. They'd gathered to see their master off, but Kynan had spent the last twenty minutes bickering with his general.

A contingent of shadow elf warriors were assembling in the outer bailey, and Brielle had told her that they were almost all mounted. It seemed the Underworld had no shortage of horses, and that was a good thing because it allowed faster travel.

Maren was more than ready to depart. "High King Kynan, we must go. If I stand here another moment, I'll become an ice sculpture in your fine courtyard."

Kynan waved his hand to the lads holding on to the various mounts in the courtyard. "Agreed. General Aeron, if you don't accompany us as I see fit, your inaction will be seen as treason." Kynan's gaze seemed to plead with Aeron.

"If you return," Aeron muttered. But Maren saw concern in the man's elven eyes. This wasn't simply a warrior rebelling against teaming up with Upperworlders. This was a fellow concerned for the safety of his friend.

"Aeron," Kynan said softly. Most likely only Aeron and Maren could hear due to how close they stood. Kynan continued to speak in the common tongue, and Maren had to guess it was to include her. She appreciated the gesture, feeling like more and more of a true partner to Kynan. "Please," Kynan whispered to Aeron. "This is the only chance we have against the sword's new master."

Aeron's eyes shuttered briefly, and he swallowed. When he opened his eyes again, a fire flickered in the gray depths. "Fine. It's a reckless plan, but I am yours to command, my lord." He bowed again, and Kynan's shoulders dropped with relief.

After Kynan made sure a contingent of warriors remained to watch over the castle, Maren and the army bid the staff farewell and left the ancient stone walls of Calon Dywyll.

MAREN FOUND HER GAZE PULLED TIME AND TIME again to Kynan and Ivar, who flew overhead as silent as one of Kynan's shadows. The site of Kynan and his familiar kept her breathing regular and held off her panic. He was just so formidable, he and his wyvern. To know they were on her side regardless of the outcome—it meant so much.

After a long ride through the strange daylight hours in the Underworld, Kynan called for a stop.

"This is Hywl," he said to those who rode close enough to hear. "As planned, the leaders of the forces and their chosen units will enter the city peacefully with all weapons sheathed. We will show my people that we are strong and we are here to defend them and fix what has been broken."

Maren rode beside Kynan through an archway of dark stone. The guards, armored in leathers and metal helmets, waved them through, bowing low to Kynan.

Inside the city walls, both slate-roofed and thatch-work homes—some four and five stories high—leaned precariously over the main thoroughfare, a cobblestoned street that had been meticulously cleared of ice and snow. The cursed gray ice was already returning though, its icy claws creeping in from the corners of the road and around the edges of the shutters.

Shadow elves of all ages emerged from their double doors. Some wore homespun woolen tunics and work boots, while others had fine fur-trimmed gowns and velvet cloaks with silver clasps similar to those seen at Brielle and Dorin's mountain court.

The shadow elves scowled at the party as Kynan led them farther inside the city. They'd obviously heard talk about the Upperworld army and weren't pleased.

As Afal clomped down the cobblestones, a mother tucked her twin boys behind her legs. The little ones trembled so much that their pointed ears shook.

Maren gave them a hopeful smile. Kynan needed to address these people and let them know that he trusted the Upperworlders.

The crowd increased in size, and as the leaders and units rode down the road, which was far too narrow for this size a force, Maren was separated from Kynan.

A man in a blacksmith's thick apron stood with arms crossed beside a couple who glared daggers at Dorin, their stares traveling over his dragon wings.

Granted, Dorin was the only one of his kind and was frightening to be sure, but if they knew his heart, they'd know how kind the elven prince was to his subjects. Dorin had held a grand festival in Balaur's capital during the summer, making certain that all had the access they needed to late summer root vegetables as well as time to trade with the wanderers who carted everything from rope to worked leather to pots across the kingdoms of Lore, Balaur, and Wylfenden.

A shout rose from the back of their army. Maren twisted in her saddle to see something small fly through the air and hit one of the elven warriors in the head.

"We will harbor no Upperworlders here!" a thickly accented voice shouted as the shadow elves lining the streets surged forward.

A battle was breaking out right here, right now.

CHAPTER 34

S words were drawn on both sides. "Balaur," Filip
called out, addressing his men. "Stand down!"

Maren kicked Afal's sides. "Get us through
this crowd, love. To Kynan and Osian."

Brielle and Aury both noticed what she was
attempting and moved to take her sides, clearing the
warriors, leaders, and shouting shadow elves from in
front of her.

Jostled and sweating with fear, Maren maneuvered
Afal through the chaos to the end of the road, where a
building crafted in a semi-circle shape stood. Amidst
the encroaching ice, a fountain bubbled in the front of
the stone structure, and jade-green tiles shone on the
roof, finer than tiles seen on some of the shops and
homes.

Kynan dismounted near the fountain and started
what looked like a heated discussion with a shadow elf
who wore all green and had a necklace made of hawk
feathers. They gestured dramatically, and both stood

with a wide stance like they were about to physically fight.

Leaving Afal on the far side of the fountain with Brielle, Maren hurried to Kynan's side.

Kynan was speaking in the Underworld tongue to the man in green. He glanced at Maren and switched to speaking the Lore tongue. "We have no choice, Mayor Symon."

Symon sneered at the change in language.

Kynan ignored the man's attempt to interrupt. "King Tiergan has the sword, and this will be the end of any kind of peace if he takes her to wife. You remember the uprising, don't you? The blood. The starvation."

"I fought in the uprising, my king," Symon said. "Please don't forget to whom you speak."

The elf's words sounded nigh on traitorous with their angry tone directed at a king. It was one thing to have a general disagreeing on strategy, but this was a public official of sorts.

"My king," Maren said, "take notice of what's happening in the street. A battle is breaking out. You need to address the city now."

He whirled, and his eyes moved quickly, taking in her face and body. "Are you hurt? Did anyone dare to lay a finger on you?" He was veritably bristling. "I'll end anyone who touches you."

"This isn't about me. I'm fine. Go, please. Prince Filip is trying to hold off his men, but they will break in this strange environment."

Kynan jerked his chin in a curt nod to Symon, then hurried to the fountain, where he jumped onto the icy water's enclosure. His shadows flowed from his palms and back, then the darkness lifted him while it also poured into the street like a river made of night.

The shadow elves and the Upperworlders went quiet, short gasps sounding as Kynan's shadows engulfed their bodies from the knees down. The horses reared and stomped, the whites around their eyes showing.

Maren rejoined Brielle and the others, taking Afal's reins. "Shh, Afal." She smoothed a hand down the horse's neck, then mounted slow and easy.

"My people," Kynan said, his deep voice thundering. "Please, listen!" He spoke the words in both his tongue and Lore's. "King Tiergan has taken Cynnwrf."

The shadow elves cried out, some in anger and others in what sounded like shock or fear.

"These Upperworlders are the Awenydd's chosen kin," Kynan said.

Chosen kin.

Yes, that was exactly right. A warmth passed through her heart. He understood.

"They are here with my permission," he said, "and by my request. They fight for us and for peace. We must regain the sword, and I must Bind myself to the Awenydd to save us all. I know you've heard the news. You are wise folk. Not ignorant. And you well know my feelings for those of the Upperworld. But we must put that aside in this fight. We have seen King Tiergan work his foul ways in small scenarios. The betrayal."

Voices murmured agreement. So they must all have known about the last Awenydd and what Hafwen had showed Maren in the crystal.

"This is a far larger development," he said. "If King Tiergan keeps the sword, if he Binds himself to our queen, he will rule here. Maybe not right away. The crown is mine and will be until I die because the magic of that calling remains, but it would only be a matter of time. He cares for no one and nothing but himself, and well you each know that truth. He will take and take and take until all the fields are dead and dying and the saving of this place made little difference. He only wishes to see it all go down in death and despair because his soul is hollow, empty, lost. Some of you remember the long war." His hands flexed. His chest moved in an erratic breath. "You recall how he treated the towns and villages he dominated, the torture, his sick games in the street."

Maren didn't even want to know. He should have told her this earlier. She might not have believed him, but he should have tried. Maybe it was difficult to recall and bring up, the memories too sharp and painful.

The crowd—both those dressed in wools against the increasing cold and those in thinner cloaks with not a piece of jewelry on them—spoke a phrase as one, but Maren couldn't make out the sounds or the meaning.

Kynan's cloak rippled inside the wisps of his shadows as he raised his hands. His presence was a hand on the back of her neck, a finger lifting her chin, a palm pressed to the heart.

He was just so much...more than anyone else.

"We will rise together," he said, "and reclaim what belongs to us all. I am your king, your shadow lord, and

you know well that my soul sings to do right by you."
But above all that, my soul sings for you, my Maren.

Her lips parted. He'd spoken into her mind.

His words felt like the softest caress, a completely different experience from Tiergan's hissed lies.

She swallowed, her mind spinning scenarios about Kynan that had no place here and during this alarming moment in time. She saw them tangled in the duvet in her chamber at his castle, his long leg exposed to the hip where the blankets wrapped them together. Her face flushed.

Shaking her head to clear it, she touched the warm wand tucked into her belt. A dream she'd forgotten, about a man with black eyes and shadow wings drawing her into his arms and the rush of a wind cooling the back of her neck as his fingers coiled into her hair, rushed into her mind.

Aury glanced at Maren. "Are you all right?" Aury asked.

"I am," Maren answered. "Do you speak their language?"

"No. Costel might know what the people said." Leave it to a master leader like Aury to know exactly what Maren, as potential queen here, needed to know. Aury called Costel over.

"What did the people say? Can you translate?" Maren asked him in a whisper as Kynan informed his people about the upcoming trek into the high moors to confront Tiergan.

Costel rubbed a hand through his wild red hair. "I

think, now don't hold me to it, but I think maybe... If the writings of Sir Niall are accurate—"

"Good goddess, Costel, spit it out." Aury shook her head like she was his annoyed older sister.

He smiled nervously, gaze going from Aury to Maren. "I think they said, '*Live as flame, free as air.*'"

"Oh, I like that," Brielle said, nudging her horse into their circle.

"You would." Maren rolled her eyes even though she was touched by the phrase as well. "Always wishing for a dramatic end."

"Adventure first. Safety second." Brielle smiled with all of her teeth.

"More like 'safety optional.'" Maren had to chuckle at her friend. When Brielle had met her husband, Dorin, she'd been more than ready to get close to the dragon shifter, while Maren had thought she was completely mad.

Kynan's voice grew quiet. "Who is with us?"

Would they turn on him because of her and the other Upperworlders?

CHAPTER 35

The entire crowd lifted their hands and shouted what appeared to be a positive reply.

"He made that seem easy," Maren said.

"Well, look at the fellow," Werian and his horse, Moon, had crept up behind Maren. Aury and Brielle stared at Kynan, nodding dumbly. "He's a force of nature, and I'll not hide that my previously unwed and lost young self would be quite envious of the drool he draws from the most formidable of women here."

"No drool from me, darling," Rhianne said, the witch's gaze all on her prince.

Werian's smile toward his wife was intensely private, and Maren turned away to look on the one she wanted to ride beside wherever he asked. But Kynan was gone.

"Where did he go?" Maren moved Afal to the edges of the crowd as Kynan's shadows dissipated and he appeared on Osian's back beside the fountain.

"I will do as you bid, my king," Symon was saying to

him. But the elven lord's face said he was less than pleased about the turn of events.

Kynan nodded. "See that you do, or there will be a payment your flesh doesn't wish to settle." He rode to her side and briefly gripped her arm as if to assure himself she was truly there.

"That was a bit rough, High King Kynan." Maren glanced at Symon, who stood by the semi-circle building beside two others who talked animatedly.

"You have befriended a variety of rulers. You know by now that many duties require a vicious blade. Mayor Symon must be reminded of his duty." He quickly turned Osian and looked over his shoulder to be sure Maren was following.

She had seen the ferocity with which her royal friends had to sometimes rule. "A confident hand on the horse works wonders, aye?"

"Exactly so, my queen."

The crowd parted, and they rode side by side through the street, everyone bowing their heads or curtseying, even Aury, Brielle, and the others. Chills ran down Maren's arms.

"I'm not sure I'm cut out for this role," she murmured.

"That's what makes you the perfect queen."

"It's not a false humility, Kynan."

He glanced at her, and she realized she'd called him by his first name with no title in front of his subjects and she hadn't been whispering. "Don't apologize," he said. "You call me what you please. I live to please you, and our subjects do as well if they know what is good for them."

The horses broke away from the village's low boundary walls and carried them down the road and into the low, rolling hills. A river gurgled beside the advancing army, barely audible over the rumble of horse hooves, murmuring voices, and the jangle of tack.

"I have had no training in leading a kingdom," Maren said. "You can handle everything in that regard, but what if you grow sick or die, and they're left with me?"

"Aren't you traveling a little far down the proverbial road?" Kynan said. "First, we must survive King Tiergan's foul plans and save the Sacred Oak."

"Of course, yes, but I'd rather not think about the upcoming battle until we are directly faced with it."

"Tonight, we will camp by Draig's Gorge and think very much about the battle, unfortunately. We must plan our attack."

"How many men will he have fighting with him?" Maren asked.

Kynan's jaw moved as he gritted his teeth. "In the last war, he had five hundred."

"Last war?"

"Yes, his sub-kingdom rose up in an attempt to overtake me," Kynan said. "This was before the last Awenydd. King Tiergan failed, but he retained his lands because I had no desire to lose the rest of my warriors. I made it possible for those in his kingdom who wanted to escape to slip into mine, but I stopped with that. I have no urge to rule every blade of grass in the

Underworld. But he still has a powerful military. Since that larger strike, he attacks every once in a while, but he doesn't seem to have the stones to try to overthrow me again. There is another shadow lord on his side of the Dark Sea, and if nothing has changed between them, he supports King Tiergan and lends his warriors when asked."

Setting a hand on her wand, she studied the banked rage in his eyes. "You've been enemies for a long time."

"Indeed we have. I should have killed him ages ago," Kynan said. "He always evades me somehow."

"How many warriors do we have now?" Maren asked.

"Around four hundred under my estimation. He trains children and forces all his subjects to fight."

Maren narrowed her eyes and tried to remember how tough she had been before she'd started living alongside royalty. "We need to fight dirty, like I learned dockside in Wylfenden."

His eyebrow lifted as if in invitation for her to go on.

"Usually," she said, "those of us on the seaside had enough to eat and sell. But every time King Raoul raised the taxes to go to war with High Prince Dorin's kingdom of Balaur, my life grew fangs."

"You are a survivor," Kynan said.

Maren shrugged. "I suppose so. One night, a reed-thin boy I'd seen further north, up the coast, slipped into our little house and stuck a knife into my mother's ribs."

"Coward," Kynan hissed.

"No," Maren said, "he was still a boy. He was starving. I was angry then, and incredibly scared, but he was hardly more than a child, and hunger can drive a person mad."

"I've seen it here, with the spirits."

"Ah." Maren pulled the edges of her cloak around her more tightly. "The boy stole our entire catch that day, he and his brothers, while my father and I cleaned Mother's wound and sewed her up again."

"It was wise for your parents to teach you the skills you needed to survive in your world. What did you mean by 'fight dirty?'" he asked.

"After that, the boy's cousin decided we were easy pickings and came at me in the alley between the boathouse and the sailmaker's shop." Maren remembered the day as clearly as if it had happened yesterday. "My father had instructed me on using the heel of my palms to break a nose and driving my shin between a man's legs to drop him where he stood. It worked rather well, and I only had to fight once to be rid of that foul lad, though there were, of course, more troublesome times after that day."

"Could you not use your magic?"

"This was before my wand appeared to me. Even after my wand appeared along the roots of an oak growing along the riverside, I had to hide my power in Wylfenden. At that time, King Raoul's Broyeurs killed anyone having to do with magic. They murdered my parents because of me." Saying it out loud twisted that imaginary blade in her stomach.

Kynan was looking at her hand, which was pressed against her ribs. "I am so sorry for your tragedy."

"Thank you." She hoped he wouldn't ask if she ever saw them as spirits. She never had, and the simultaneous hope and horror of the possibility wasn't something she cared to talk about. "What was the phrase the Hwyl villagers used during your address?"

"Live bright as flame and free as air. The motto helps us to remember to enjoy life in the face of fear during difficult times," Kynan said. "We often use the phrase before battle or during mourning ceremonies."

"It's beautiful. Your people are incredibly courageous."

The corner of his mouth lifted. "Thank you for noticing."

A strange thought flitted through Maren's head. Who were her people? Not the Wylfen, certainly. She'd never felt at home there even when her lovely parents had been alive. Magic wasn't a part of the culture, due mostly to King Raoul's doings. And she hadn't felt at home when she'd been in Balaur either. Not really. The mountain elves were a joyous folk, but they were harsh and loved the challenges of fighting and rough weather. Perhaps the kingdom Aury was set to inherit—the kingdom of Lore and the partially independent fae court tucked into its heart near the Sacred Oak—was where Maren felt most herself. She hadn't had the time to consider it, really.

Past a cluster of tattooed fae warriors with their bows and a unit of mountain elves armed with at least three weapons apiece, Aury, Filip, Dorin, Brielle,

Werian, and Rhianne rode side by side. Brielle was pointing at the surroundings and talking animatedly to Dorin, who looked down and grinned. Werian blew a kiss at Aury, his cousin by heart if not by blood, and then winked at Rhianne, his wife.

Aury locked gazes with Maren. The Magelord was frighteningly good at knowing when someone was looking her way. Maren waved casually, and Aury's shoulders relaxed as she waved back and returned to the conversation.

"They are your people," Kynan said, surprising Maren, "even though they come from three different regions, yes? I noticed you watching them, and the care in your expression pulls at me."

Maren glanced at them again, imprinting their faces in her mind so she'd never forget a single detail. Their voices echoed through recollections as she relived past events in a flash. She tried to imprint in her mind the way they spoke and laughed in her memories. "They are my people."

"I can't replace that, and well I know it," Kynan said. "But when we defeat King Tiergan and Bind ourselves together, I will endeavor to find a way for you to visit your adopted family regularly. I will never stop looking for the magic that can make that possible."

Maren coughed, trying incredibly hard not to cry. But goddess above and below, it wasn't working. Tears rolled down her cheeks in a way they hadn't since she'd lost Mother and Father. She felt like a child despite her twenty-two years of life.

Kynan stood in his stirrups and held up a fisted hand. "Halt! We break for camp now."

"No, please." She sniffed. He couldn't stop the entire army so she could have a festival of tears. This was foolish. "Let's keep going. This isn't where you wished to camp."

"It's where I wish to camp now." He took hold of Afal's reins and proceeded to lead the way into a small forest of red maples. Blue poppies grew at the base of a cave's opening.

Kynan dismounted and took Maren from Afal without saying a word.

She didn't fight him. She was crying too much to do anything worthwhile. "I hate this."

His jaw muscles tensing beneath his smooth skin, he carried her into the cave like she weighed no more than a wet kitten. He placed her on a cool, dry boulder, then rummaged around his pack in the dim light. A spark lit the cave, and then he was lighting a bundle of grass he'd apparently had in his supplies.

"What are your orders, my king?" General Aeron bowed low to Kynan and then to Maren.

"We remain here for the night," Kynan said. "We leave an hour before dawn."

"As you wish, my lord king." Aeron whirled and left, his red military sash whipping across his leg.

Within a few minutes, Kynan had a fire going. He swept her into his lap and wiped her tears from her cheeks. "You are the worthiest person I've ever encountered."

"What does that mean?" Maren said. "You can't know that about me already. We only just met."

"You fought for your blood family when they were alive and for yourself. When given the opportunity, you befriended and were loyal to a band of friends who span races and nations. You seem to harbor no prejudice at all." Awe tinged Kynan's voice. "Caring nothing for power, you seek to help at every turn even if your words pretend at attitudes opposite to such a heart."

"Now, don't knock my sarcasm." She smiled sadly. "It's how I show love."

He closed his eyes and shook his head. Then he pressed the gentlest kiss against her forehead and another at the side of her eye. "No Awenydd in history had the power you do, and the only way the Source saw fit to give you this power was for a purpose."

"Foul people often have great power," Maren said.

"True, but their purpose lies in spurring others to grow stronger in fighting them."

She'd never thought of life like that. "I've only fought in one real battle. I'll be pointless against Tiergan."

"King Tiergan," Kynan corrected.

"Good manners give you some odd kind of comfort, don't they?"

Kynan shrugged. "I like living within a framework, yes."

"Even when said framework gives a creature like Tiergan a title of respect?" she asked.

"Even then. Stop changing the subject."

She scowled, but there wasn't any heat behind it. "Don't boss me about."

"Oh, I shall never cease doing so," he said, his voice teasing.

She pinched his arm, then nestled her head against his chest.

"I will train you," Kynan said. "And your friend, the witch princess Rhianne, will aid us."

"Sounds like you're bossing me around once again."

Kynan frowned and scratched his stubbled chin. "Is it not a wise plan to enlist Princess Rhianne in this endeavor?"

"It is."

"And this is why I must order you about," Kynan said, looking pleased with himself. "I know what you need, my queen."

Maren's tears had dried, and now she was feeling pleasantly warm and rather happy about being in his lap. She shifted so that she straddled him. He inhaled sharply, his fingers tightening on her thighs.

"Careful, Maren."

CHAPTER 36

Her breath caught. The way his lips wrapped around her name warmed her from head to toe. She was quite glad he hadn't called her Awenydd, since there had been one in his life already. The feel of him against her was absolute bliss, a frightening whirl of what if...

Facing the cave's entrance, he called out, "Owen!"

A guard appeared at the mouth, the wan light silhouetting his large form. "My lord king?"

"See that we are not disturbed. Turn your back," Kynan ordered.

Kynan's hands wrapped around her waist, his fingers so long they nearly touched. He pulled her close and kissed her neck. "Is this all right?"

With his thumbs, he drew circles above her hipbones, and she wished she weren't wearing such a thick tunic. She pressed her lips against his temple in answer and moved her hips, relishing the sensation of his body flush with hers. His thumbs halted, and a groan rumbled through him.

"And I say again, Maren, careful."

"What will happen?" She moved again.

"You will push me to my limits. I plan to wait on taking you until after the Binding."

"If we are set on it, why worry about that?"

"The magic will be far stronger if we mate after the Binding."

She swallowed and drove her hands into his silky hair, undoing the knot at the crown of his head and loving the cascade of locks falling around his shoulders as well as the spicy scent of him. He kissed her throat softly at first, then with more teeth and less gentleness as he worked his way to her ear. Her body melted over his, her pulse pounding, skin sizzling with delight. She drew a finger across his collarbone, then slipped it beneath his woolen undershirt. The tightness of his leather vest kept her finger from moving further, but she savored the smooth feel of his skin. Rising up on his lap, she looped her hand around the back of his neck, under his heavy sheath of hair, then moved her palm between his undershirt and his back.

"I want this off of you. I want to feel your skin against mine. All of it."

"Ah, my pet. But of course." He released her and in a flurry of graceful movements had his cloak, vest, and undershirt off.

Taking in the sight of him, she sucked a quick breath. The firelight flickered over his lean muscle, scars, and the dips and curves of his battle-hewn body.

Shadows wrapped around his elbows, arced around his temples and his powerful shoulders, and collected with golden sparks at his head. His shadow crown flickered, the magic in the chaotic diadem shuddering and blinking brightly as she stared, like perhaps her presence affected him strongly.

He exhaled roughly as she placed her palms on his chest and ran her hands down the rippling muscles of his stomach all the way to his narrow waist, where his hipbones showed just a bit over his trousers. His hips rolled, and his body pressed against her warmth. She swallowed and took a shuddering breath as desire pulsated down her torso and gathered low.

Kynan uttered something sharp in his native tongue, grabbed her roughly, and lay her on the ground. He hovered above her, his chest moving quickly and his eyes dark and wild. A strand of ebony hair fell over his face and dragged against her neck. His shadow and spark crown flashed and danced in the flames' light, and she sensed the tenuous hold he had on his incredible power.

"With one word, I am yours in every way, my queen."

"But it's better if we wait..." She licked her dry lips and tried to remember why. "Better for the Binding, for saving the realms."

He nodded once, curtly.

Yes, they needed to stop. It was the best move. The only move.

She pulled him to her, and his skin was slightly damp beneath her hands. His weight fell on her, and his hand raced up her thigh and tugged at her clothing while she bit his lip.

"Maren," he uttered, his voice a growl.

The crush of him made her delirious, and she arched her back to get closer, closer. His kisses traveled down the column of her throat as his fingers and shadows drew circles along her sides.

With a groan, he shifted away, and the chill of the cave swept in where his heat had been.

She sat up alongside him, panting. "And here you thought I was selfless. I almost said '*eh*' to the welfare of every living being for a tumble by the fire."

He laughed, bending his head and draping his arms over his bent knees. "You nearly broke my control. Even after I've had centuries to practice patience."

"I don't want to hear about all of your conquests," she said, chuckling and straightening her clothing. "I'm definitely too selfish to sit through those stories."

He twisted and took her face between his hands. Grit from the cave floor roughened his touch, but Maren didn't mind at all. His look was fire. "You are nothing like any of them. This is nothing like anything I've ever experienced. You are my heart, Maren. Know that."

Footsteps sounded at the mouth of the cave, then Owen shouted.

Werian leaned against the entrance to the stone room. "Easy, shadowy guard fellow. While I'm so glad our Lady Maren has at last found someone worthy to wet her whistle—"

"I don't think that's how that saying goes," Maren said. She was going to punch his fancy fae face in.

"Details, lovely. Details."

"I tried to stop him, my lord king." Owen was nearly stuttering with rage, his eyes trying to pop from his head.

Kynan held up a hand, then flicked his fingers. Owen bowed curtly, muttered something in the Underworld tongue, and left. "What is it, Prince Werian?" Kynan asked.

Maren knew Kynan was as incensed as Owen that Werian had intruded, but instead of shouting and glaring, Kynan showed his anger through the slip of a sharper shadow over his weapon hand and the glint of certainty in his gaze.

"I was innocently walking by on my way to the river when I heard what I can only describe as my favorite type of activity happening here in this rather conveniently private cave, and I suddenly had an idea."

"Do get on with it, Prince Werian." Kynan's hands fisted. He tugged on his shirt.

"If we manage to seize the amazingly incredibly and altogether legendary sword, how does it work?"

"What do you mean?" Maren asked.

Kynan draped his cloak over Maren even though she was fully clothed. He was so protective. She couldn't help but smile.

"Once we physically have the weapon," Kynan said, "I must give my blood and speak the oath and be accepted. It's not something one can accomplish in the wilds of a battle. It takes focus and time. Something I'm certain Lord Tiergan is working on while we speak." His voice had gone dark and deadly. "If the claiming of Cynnwrf is done improperly, the sword will take the shadow lord's life instead of giving itself over."

"So you're telling me I can't hold Tiergan's arms behind his back while you relieve him of his legendary and problem-causing steel, then boom, war is over and Maren gets the happy ending she deserves?" Werian pouted.

"Well, yes, but you'll have to hold him for a good while," Kynan said. "The claiming takes time and focus, as I have said." His hands fisted, but he took a breath and relaxed his fingers. "When we defeat King Tiergan—"

Werian smiled. "*When*? Fabulous word choice." He looked to Maren. "Is he always this positive?" He strolled farther into the cave, nodding approvingly. "I like this cave, by the way. Very barbaric." He wiggled his eyebrows.

"As I was saying..." Kynan appeared more than prepared to give Werian a tutor's lashing for his bad manners. "After our win, we will need to take the sword to a place of quiet where I can request its magic once again. It is not easily done."

A riot of terrible thoughts flashed through Maren's mind as she imagined how Tiergan could have seized the sword with Hafwen and Ivar there. How Hafwen must have fought back and what Tiergan must have done to put a stop to it.

"Lady Maren?" Kynan's hand was on her shoulder, and she hadn't noticed the men had stopped talking.

"Did Ivar mentally tell you any details about how Tiergan stole the sword and claimed it?"

"No, he tried to explain the nature of the fight, but I insisted he stick with where Lady Hafwen had been taken and in what condition she was in when he last saw her."

They walked out of the cave and faced the sky.

"Ivar?" Kynan called the wyvern's name three times, then a dark silhouette flitted from the distance.

The wyvern looped around and landed on Kynan's outstretched arm. Kynan nodded and narrowed his eyes, listening to Ivar's mind-to-mind communication. Then Kynan looked at Maren.

"King Tiergan had difficulty in claiming the sword." Pride shone in his eyes. "It seems Cynnwrf didn't think him worthy until he shed quite a bit of blood. He repeated the oath three times before the sword permitted him to access its earth magic."

Werian grinned. "He doesn't have the shadow lord stones that you have, eh, High King Kynan?"

"I guess not," Kynan said, raising an eyebrow as if he didn't approve of Werian's use of the word *stones*.

After eating and resting, everyone ran training practice in varying groups with generals and leaders ordering units of warriors here and there.

"Why do they need practice? They're mostly experienced warriors in each army, right?" Maren asked Werian as he and Rhianne joined her and Kynan in a meadow beyond the rockier outcroppings of the area. Dorin, Filip, and Aury were there too, discussing the upcoming battle and which units should be in what location.

"If warriors are left to their own devices for too long, they grow..." Werian rubbed his chin like he was searching for the right word.

Rhianne unsheathed her wand and stared into the distance, appearing deep in thought—but not about the current topic if Maren had to guess.

"They gamble and fight," Kynan said. "Their nerves fray. One must keep one's forces busy or properly resting and only give short breaks for pleasure and entertainment."

"It's true, sadly," Werian said. "I wish there could be more fun and less training, but I've seen both fae forces and elven grow dangerously frantic when given too much free time leading up to battle."

Rhianne edged her way between Werian and Kynan and came close. "Maren, are you ready? I want you to visualize air magic converging."

Eyes closed, Maren lifted her wand.

CHAPTER 37

Maren imagined the air crashing together at the point. Her hand shook, and she didn't want to open her eyes yet. She feared there would be nothing there except some sad smoke issuing from her wand.

"Yes, exactly like that, Maren. You have a strong affinity for air and fire," Rhianne said, her voice calmer and more measured than Maren's would ever be. The woman's ability to take things as they came was incredibly admirable. "I saw your fire during our fight with the Wylfen, but you haven't used even half of your power. It's obvious now."

"It is?" Maren peeked. The end of her wand flickered like a small torch, the dark orange flames mixing with pale blue sparks. "Ah!"

The fire died and left a trail of smoke that circled Kynan. He took a seat on a mossy rock and said something quiet to Aury.

"Try again. Stop gaping at the king," Rhianne whispered and elbowed Maren. "Focus."

Maren snorted, laughing at herself, and did as she was told. She pulled magic from her blood, sizzling and quick, and drew the air and fire elements from around them. A subtle hint of charcoal, citrus, and the minerals in deep well water touched her tongue. She opened her eyes to see the flame at her wand had reappeared, this time stronger.

Dorin glanced her way, his head lifted. "I scent your fire magic."

"It's the dragon in you, perhaps?" Maren suggested.

Flexing his hands on his knees, Kynan narrowed his eyes and looked from Dorin to Maren. "And I sense the air magic. I can feel the weight of your power on my skin." He touched his cheek with his palm, then rubbed his hands together.

Rhianne nodded like a proud tutor. "She is incredible. Her witch's will begs me to join her in this unspoken spell, and Werian can tell you my own witch's will is no easy thing to sway."

"You can say that again," Werian murmured.

"What is your goal with this witch's wand fire?" Dorin asked Maren.

"Striking the enemy, of course." She looked to Rhianne. Wasn't that obvious? What was he getting at?

Dorin waved a dismissive hand. "I'm sure High King Kynan would agree that your air power mixed with your fire element could work far greater magic. What do you think, Princess Rhianne?"

Although their magics were quite different, Rhianne

was an incredibly powerful witch, and Maren thrilled to have her as a tutor.

"I'm venturing into the unknown here," Rhianne said. "High King Kynan, what power did the last Awenydd possess?"

"She wasn't a witch," Kynan said. "She had the ability to speak for the spirits as Lady Maren does, and her power was rooted in fire, but her magic only manifested when we were Bound and set to healing the Sacred Oak." Sadness flickered through his eyes, and Maren hoped they wouldn't press him for further information regarding his last wife.

"Truly the unknown, then." Rhianne gestured to Maren's wand. "Feel your blood sparking with magic. Let the breeze pass through you. Bring the air into your presence and ignite that fire."

Maren relaxed and let her mind go where it wanted, allowed what felt like her soul to wander the paths of her body and the space just outside her flesh. Fire leapt from her wand like a whip, and everyone shouted, jumping away.

"Nicely done," Rhianne said, the rope of fire reflecting in her brown eyes. "The Underworld feeds your power, doesn't it?"

"I think so. I never could have accomplished this above."

"Agreed," Kynan said.

"It drains me," Rhianne said. "I hope we Upperworlders don't weaken further the longer we are here."

"I feel that drain as well," Dorin said, "but proximity to Lady Maren seems to strengthen me."

"Maybe it's the fire element in your dragon magic," Kynan said.

"Perhaps?" Rhianne tapped her wand against her lips. "It would make sense. My power is more earth related, and this is not my earth."

Dorin nodded. "If I remain somewhat close to Lady Maren, I believe I can shift into my full dragon form for the battle."

"That would be tremendous," Kynan said. "I wonder if King Tiergan's shadow magic will be less effective against your dragon flesh."

"You should have a sparring match to determine the strengths and weaknesses between your magics," Maren said. "We don't have that information yet, do we? Can someone ask Sir Costel?"

"We don't," Filip answered.

Maren nodded, then looked to Dorin. "Transform, and High King Kynan can attack with his shadows."

"I'm willing if you are, High King Kynan," Dorin said.

Kynan tipped his head. "As soon as my lady decides she is finished with her training session."

The fire whip sizzled against the frosted clovers and wildflowers, not burning through the ice, but making them spark with magic.

"Why isn't the fire doing any damage?" Maren asked.

"Because you don't will it to do so. Your witch's will is tied to everything you do. You control your power fully," Rhianne said.

"Step back. I'm going to see what I can manage."

The group moved away, Dorin calling out a warning to the warriors nearby.

Maren drew a large circle over her head, the fire of her magic spinning like a great wheel. The heat of it warmed her, but even when the whip crossed her shoulder, it didn't burn her cloak or her skin beneath. She imagined the fire growing and reaching... Voices echoed in her ears, and the scent of dragonfire poured through the air.

She heard Dorin say something, but she ignored him and stared into the twilight of the cloud-cloaked sky. A shape glowed brighter and brighter above her circle of fire. She continued spinning the wand over her head. What was it? The shape grew distinct boundaries and sharper edges until it revealed itself to her.

The spirit of a dragon.

"It's about time," the dragon said.

Maren nearly dropped her wand, and though the fire circle disappeared, the dragon spirit remained. "Greetings, Goddess Nix."

"What?" Dorin and Rhianne said in unison.

Kynan's powerful presence hummed at Maren's elbow, though she wasn't sure when he'd moved. Everyone looked around. They obviously couldn't see Nix.

"She is there," Maren said, pointing and willing them to see what she could. It might be important for the battle. She pushed her will into her wish and pointed her wand.

Everyone gasped.

"The dragon goddess." Kynan's eyes were wider than she'd ever seen them.

"Greetings, Awenydd," Goddess Nix said. "I've been waiting for your summons. I'm more than ready to fight that little snake, Tiergan."

A thrill went through Maren. "How can you fight him? How does it work?"

She heard Rhianne shushing those nearby.

"You have more fire magic than any previous Awenydd, and so you give me the ability to affect the living. Including sniveling shadow lords who think themselves more important than they are. I can break his shadows as one does a brittle branch. They won't contain me, and I can work to keep your army moving freely and without his intervention."

Aury and Rhianne cocked their heads as if they couldn't quite hear Nix's words, like they were catching some of the words but not all. Maren would have to explain this.

"May I ask something?" Kynan said, his gaze flying from Maren to Nix and back again.

"Of course," Maren said.

"Can you do anything about the sword's power?" he asked Nix.

The dragon tilted her head and regarded Kynan. "I can do nothing against the sword. That is an untouchable power, forged in the most ancient of magic, far beyond my reach and even Vahly's reach."

"Not even the goddess of earth can help with that?" Maren asked.

"No, Vahly desires to help, I'm certain, but she has

no power over the Underworld sword."

It sounded so strange to hear her refer to the goddess Vahly by a first name, but with goddess to goddess, Maren supposed, there was plenty of room for casual reference. Kynan would disapprove of the informality, she knew, which caused a smile to tug at her mouth.

Nix began to fade from view. "I must go now. Do just as you did to call me up for the fighting."

"Thank you."

The dragon goddess bowed her large scaled head briefly before she was nothing but mist and then gone completely.

Everyone stared.

"It turns out my magic can harness a sliver of the power that the goddess Nix's spirit wields and make use of it in the world of the living, here in the Underworld." She went on to explain how they would have a formidable weapon against Tiergan's shadows, but it would have no bearing on Cynnwrf and what damage it would rend upon them.

Kynan's eyes shone as he listened. "You are such a miracle, my queen."

She gave him a smile. Her body longed to leave off battle practice and find another cave.

But she knew what she had to do, and so throughout the day, they trained with blade, wand, and shadow, Filip's men joining them in the meadow.

And finally, it was time for Dorin and Kynan to spar.

Now they would see how this exciting little situation played out.

CHAPTER 38

"If Maren's work with the goddess Nix can combine with your ability in order to break the shadow magic, we would have a better chance at surrounding King Tiergan," Aury said to Dorin.

Filip blocked Costel's strike with his hatchet's handle, then whirled to feign a hit to his knight, Sir Drago. Drago's eye patch slipped to show old scars as he lunged to avoid the spot where the hatchet would have landed in a real fight. Sliding the patch into place, Drago spun and reached forward with the stick serving as his practice weapon and nearly stuck Filip in the stomach. Filip laughed and leapt backward, moving incredibly fast.

"Nearly speared you like a campfire roast, my lord!" Drago chuckled.

Filip narrowed his eyes. "If you'd succeeded, I'd have forced you stand in my place at Dorin's next address to the royal family."

Drago's eye widened. "Gods, just stab me back. Anything but that."

Filip barked a laugh.

"Enough, you two," Aury said. "Take mental notes on this little show."

Werian walked up with Rhianne on his arm. "I'm quite excited to see how this turns out," he said, brushing red maple leaves from a log and motioning for his wife to sit.

Maren approached Kynan. "Umm, good luck?"

He glanced at her. "Thank you. How does the transformation work?" His breath tickled the top of her head.

She looked up at him, enjoying the simple pleasure of regarding a tall, handsome elven lord who found her alluring. "I have no idea. I've only seen him do it once, and all I recall is a bright light that gave me a headache for an hour afterward."

Dorin stood in the small clearing, naked and with his head bowed. In the deepening blue of the evening, sparks snapped around him like fish scales catching sunlight under the water. A wave of power issued from the dragon prince. A thin layer of Kynan's shadows slipped over Maren's eyes so that the flash of Dorin's transformation only made her wince slightly. It was such a little kindness, but so thoughtful. She was surprised he hadn't blocked her view of Dorin's naked form.

She moved closer, her hand brushing his. He wrapped his fingers in hers, squeezed them gently, then left her to join a fully formed golden dragon in the clearing.

Dorin lashed his spiked tail at Kynan, who extended his arms, shadows snaking from his palms. The shadows wrapped Dorin's tail and pressed it to the ground. Dorin stumbled backward on his four legs. He roared, shaking more maple leaves from the surrounding trees and creating a flurry of bright red.

The scent of dragonfire rose in the air, smelling of Khem oranges and woodsmoke, then a stream of fire rippled over Kynan's head.

Maren ducked just in case.

Kynan's crown of shadows and sparks reached higher above his head, and his shadows flung themselves forward. Dorin's wings caught the wind, and he lifted himself into the air. His scales glittered behind Kynan's wall of magic-infused darkness. Dorin blew another blast of dragonfire, and the shadows in the fire's path melted away.

The dark fingers that slipped past the fire grabbed Dorin's wings and pinned him in the air as he roared again. Kynan spread his fingers, and the shadows eased Dorin to the ground before releasing him.

Dorin shook, and magic flashed again.

Maren shut her eyes, and the white light of dragon transformation showed behind her eyelids. When she looked again, Kynan was gone and Dorin was slipping on his trousers while Brielle brushed out his cloak and tunic and a knight held out Dorin's belt and sword.

"I look forward to the day you gaze on my body as you did the dragon prince's," Kynan said.

Maren flushed hotly. "I…"

Kynan stood very close behind her, his warmth

spreading through her clothing to touch her skin. His hand slid up her body, and his fingers brushed her hip. His lips moved against her ear. "I do think you'll find pleasure with me, my queen."

Maren melted like the shadows had under the fire. She'd heard Werian joke with Rhianne using similar phrases, but hearing such a thing from the stoic shadow elf king was an entirely different experience. With a dry mouth, she tried to choke out some sort of snappy answer or quip, but she couldn't think of a word to say.

His shadows slid up her calves, under the heavy wool of her split dress, stopping at her knees to drag cool fingers of magic back down to her ankles. The shadows caressed the back of her neck and smoothed the curve of her jaw as waves of desire crashed over her. Her stomach tightened, and warmth bloomed across her belly and lower. She pulled in a ragged breath.

The cool air of night replaced Kynan's warmth, and she turned to see him walking away, striding purposefully toward a few others who had gathered near General Aeron, presumably to discuss what they had learned from the sparring match. Kynan glanced at her, a mischievous glint in his eyes.

"I've never seen you speechless," Aury said.

"Please leave off teasing me. I don't think my confidence can take it. Kynan has turned me into a simpering fool."

Aury grinned widely and spun her mage staff. "It's called love."

"Lust, more like," Maren said. "I'm not above it."

"No, if you only lusted for him, you wouldn't have

watched him deal with Dorin's dragonfire with a look of utter fear. It's obvious you truly care for him even if a part of you still wishes to stab him for the way he took you."

Maren narrowed her eyes and touched her wand. "I do feel a bit like stabbing."

Aury tilted her head and nodded. "And kissing."

"Sadly, yes." Maren sighed.

"Well, maybe stick him where he won't suffer much," Aury said, cleaning a speck of dirt from the top of her mage staff. "Then you'll be satisfied and have the chance to indulge your lusty side."

Maren cracked her knuckles. "I like that plan."

Aury smirked. "Glad I could be of assistance to the queen of the Underworld."

"I'm not the queen yet."

"Your king seems to think otherwise," Aury said. "He calls you queen at every chance. He's as smitten with you as you are with him. You are in for a lovely life, my friend."

Maren's heart lurched and sagged. "But I won't be able to live with you and the others. I can't even think about never seeing you again."

"You'll see us at Samhain, right?" Aury asked. "Can't you work that magic each year?"

"Not if Hafwen doesn't make it through this," Maren said.

Aury's light eyes sparked with an anger that echoed Maren's own rage. "That's the woman that Tiergan took, yes?"

"Yes. And I don't know how difficult it was for her

to create the potion she used to help us through the division between the realms. It might be impossible to make twice." Some spells were like that. She'd read about them in some of Costel's scrolls, spells so powerful that they refused to be worked by the same person more than once. Some spells hid like frightened deer, keeping just out of sight for generations before showing themselves again to the world of witches. "Besides, I can't handle the thought of not having you all. Although I'll do it for the sake of everyone, I'm afraid of how lonely I'll be here."

"You'll befriend the shadow elves," Aury said as she looked toward the group talking about spells and magic. "We will miss you terribly. Make no mistake."

Maren linked her arm in Aury's, and the Magelord Princess jerked in surprise but covered Maren's hand with her own.

They stayed like that for a time, listening to the plans and simply enjoying the solidity of a friend at one's side. Maren treasured the moment more than a dragon cherished gold.

She would need the memory of that moment if she was going to survive what was to come far, far too soon.

CHAPTER 39

After a night filled with leaders of every unit explaining plans and discussing preparations tweaked for what they'd learned from Maren's interaction with the goddess Nix and from Kynan and Dorin sparring, the army set a quick march into the hills. Misty peaks, forlorn but achingly beautiful, loomed in the distance. This land seemed like an extension of Kynan himself with its dark beauty, foreboding atmosphere, and alluring mystery.

Kynan whistled, and Ivar flew from a copse of oak trees beside the road. His black wings partially blocked the purple and gold hues of the Underworld sky as Kynan stretched out his arm and laced shadows into the air in the echoing shape of the wyvern's wings. Ivar landed on Kynan's arm, then hopped up to his shoulder.

"Your new fellow is rather dramatic." Werian trotted up beside Maren, smoothing his hair around his large ram horns.

"You're the expert." Maren gave him a wry smile.

"That I am." He winked, then looked toward Kynan. "How can I get my own wyvern, High King Kynan?"

Kynan glared over his other shoulder, and Ivar shuffled his wings as if he were insulted. "He is my familiar. You do not *get* a wyvern."

Werian leaned closer to Maren. "His attitude needs work."

"You've done wonders with Prince Dorin, so perhaps you can work your particular brand of magic on him."

"Dorin still has a very large stick up his—"

"Prince Werian?" Dorin's words carried on the wind from where he rode behind Rhianne and Brielle. "Don't forget that dragons have very good hearing."

Werian smirked. "I'd pretend to be frightened of you, mighty dragon prince, but your wife and mine will keep you from torching my naughty tongue from my mouth. They adore me."

"You're terrible." Maren almost laughed despite her grating fear for Hafwen and what they were riding into.

Hours passed, and they rode higher and higher, making it onto the frosty moors that braced the mountains' lower reaches. A tingle of apprehension crawled down the back of Maren's neck. The army pulled together, riding closer and those at the edges turning their heads, constantly scanning for threats.

Ivar and his fellow wyverns flew above the group, studying the landscape with their keen eyes and calling out to Ivar every few moments.

"They're reporting to you, aren't they?" Maren asked.

Kynan nodded and turned Osian toward a rockier expanse of the highlands. "He is near."

"Tiergan?"

"Yes. Very close now. Look." He tipped his head toward the horizon.

Maren squinted, trying to see more than a blur of low growth and scant and spindly trees.

A column of black shadow spun into view, then spread wide like hands. The shadows churned and disappeared again.

You've come to me, my queen.

Maren shivered at the sound of Tiergan's voice.

How lovely, he said into her mind. *I have the witch Hafwen here to do her duty by us.*

Maren mentally pushed back at him and silently shouted, *Stop playing games and fight us!*

A laugh slammed into her thoughts like a punch, and she dropped her reins and gasped.

Kynan drew close. "Maren?" His voice was gentle and quick.

"It's him. He's in my head again."

In the tensest silence Maren had ever lived through, they led the army over the rise and onto a flat expanse. The wind tore across the frosted heather and tugged at Maren's braid and cloak. A dark haze lingered above the cold ground. She felt as though a sword's edge was poised just at the back of her neck, ready to fall and end her life in one fatal blow.

In front of a row of ice-tipped pines, Tiergan sat atop a gray horse beside lines of shadow elf warriors in pale white leather armor, their blades unsheathed and ready for blood.

The sound of Ivar's warning growl filled Maren's ears as the wyverns flew beneath Dorin, who was now in his full dragon form. Dorin echoed their growl, and Maren looked up to see his scaled stomach. Wind snapped at the edges of his wings.

Maren drew her wand, and magic surged to life inside her, pressing through her veins and rising into her hand, prepared to bring fire and Nix's spirit to the battle. Her heart pounded so hard she was certain it was visible through her thick vest and at the side of her neck. How did anyone go into war with a clear head? Every plan they'd made fled her mind like last year's mediocre recipes, forgotten and seemingly unimportant. How could they possibly survive this?

"Steady, Queen Maren," Kynan said.

"You keep calling me that, but I'm simply Maren."

Kynan stared straight ahead. Danger emanated from him, and his shadows branched out like searching roots. He was so darkly beautiful that the sight of him oddly pained her. "Not in my hearts, and those are the only ones, aside from yours, that truly matter."

She closed her eyes briefly and shook her head. "If I'm a queen, then I'm the ruler of all sweating palms and heart palpitations. How are you so calm?"

"I'm not."

"You look as cool as a mountain cat's gaze," she said.

Kynan shook his head. "It's a facade, and one I intend to hide behind safely until this battle is won and King Tiergan is dead and scattered to the winds."

"I should have asked for a mask to go with this fancy spirit agate vest. I'm going to give Tiergan so much confidence when he sees my face pale with more fear than any one person has ever held in their body in the history of time." She was being silly, but she truly was deathly scared. If they lost, Tiergan would take her. In every way there was. A shudder wrapped cold arms around her and didn't let go.

Kynan's shadows slipped across her shoulders, warming her with his magic and chasing away the shiver. "I will not lose you. You chose me, and you will not regret it. We will be feasting and making love by tomorrow."

"Sign me up for that, please. I'm quite done with being brave and adaptable."

His lips twitched, but then his features went as smooth as stone again. "It's time. Are you ready?"

"No, but I'll pretend I am."

"That's what every warrior does, my queen. You are one of us, a fighter, a leader, a courageous heart in the face of death." He nodded and raised his fist to signal the rest of the army, and they nudged their horses into a canter.

"I'm a baker, a sleeper-inner, a fearful soul that would rather chat with ghosts than become one," she murmured, catching up, wand ready.

In the distance, shadows leapt from Tiergan's side. Black fingers snatched Maren's wand and tried to pry it from her fingers. She clung to it, swearing. Kynan's warmer shadows sifted across her skin and peeled back Tiergan's bit by bit as they galloped onward. Holding her wand so tightly that her fingers throbbed, she glanced toward Kynan.

His crown sparked and swirled, and shadow wings unfurled from his back, the ends fading to invisibility as he rode faster and faster. "Stay by my side!"

Maren pushed her power into the wand, and fire erupted from the tip to draw a line of bright light around her head. Raising her magical weapon high, she made circles with the wand's tip and begged the Source for help.

CHAPTER 40

The dragon goddess appeared, wings like starlight, eyes like moons, flying so quickly that Maren feared she'd fall behind and the spell would break.

"Go, Afal! Faster!" Maren dug in her heels.

They were galloping full out now. Afal wouldn't be able to keep up this pace for long, not after the climb she'd had to this altitude.

Shadows rose in the shapes of hands and blades over the stretch of land as Kynan shouted in his tongue and Tiergan raised Cynnwrf.

Afal would have Maren in the thick of the already wild fight in seconds.

Aury was there—how had she slipped past?—whirling her mage staff. Her ice shot across the battlefield and encased a swathe of Tiergan's warriors, whose screams went silent. She pointed her staff toward Filip, who was cutting down an enemy shadow elf with his famed hatchet, his hair in long, tight braids and his teeth showing as he snarled in rage. Aury's magicked water solidified as it flew through the air. A spear of ice pierced two of the fighters headed for Filip's back.

Maren wanted to search the melee for the others, but Tiergan was suddenly riding at her, eyes alight with the red glow of a powerful shadow lord. Fear froze her to the spot, and everything she knew dissolved in her scattered thoughts.

Kynan shouted, and Osian reared and twisted before galloping toward Maren. "Maren, wake!" he called out, his voice a tattered flag.

Shadows shaped like Ivar left Kynan to fling themselves at Tiergan. The wyvern shadows joined Ivar and the rest in diving at Tiergan's face and sword hand, drawing blood that ran down Tiergan's cheeks and dripped from his elbows in thick drops. But his shadows fought back, fists of black rising from Tiergan's body. Tiergan's shadows cut through the wyvern-shaped shadows, then hammered Ivar from the sky, folding the wyvern nearly in half.

Maren's stomach dropped as Ivar disappeared from sight, surely landing far too quickly. He had to be injured. Or worse.

Kynan threw a dagger at Tiergan's back as he drove Osian to catch up. Tiergan's shadow hands caught the weapon and dashed it under his horse's pounding hooves.

Maren shook herself and moved her wand in a wide circle. Nix grew more visible, and her light blasted across the field. Tiergan drew his mount back.

Shaking, Maren grinned and pointed her wand. "Tear him apart, Nix."

Nix's ghostly roar reverberated in Maren's ears as Tiergan's horse kicked. The spirit of the dragon goddess flew at Tiergan and ripped his shadows apart with tooth and rippling white-blue flame. Tiergan lashed out at Nix with his sword, but the weapon's edge passed through her dragon form without affecting her. Rage contorted Tiergan's features, and he jammed his heels into his mount and rode hard again toward Maren, his gaze on the whip of fire she hurled from her wand. She flung her fire whip in his direction, and as Nix kept his shadows from stealing her wand, her whip of magicked flame stung his cheek and chest. Nix disappeared.

Tiergan gasped and faltered, his shadows disappearing. Smoke rose from his leather vest, and his skin blistered badly enough that she could see it easily even in the dim and chaos.

Shouting something unintelligible, he drove his horse at her.

Where was Nix? Maren thrust her wand upward, and flames exploded from the end. Nix leapt from the blast of fire and air magic and raced toward Tiergan again. With her ghostly talons, Nix dragged his shadows away from his body and stripped him of that magic.

Dorin roared in what sounded like terrible pain. Maren glanced skyward to see him veering sharply west with a spear jutting from his side. Blood rained down.

Kynan rode toward Tiergan, then leapt from Osian's back. Maren's heart hung lifeless in her chest. Wyvern-and-root-shaped shadows lifted Kynan as he launched himself at Tiergan, landing on Tiergan's mount in front of his enemy, barely hanging on. With a feral shout, Kynan plunged another dagger into Tiergan's chest, and his shadows enveloped them both until nothing was visible except Tiergan's wild-eyed and rearing mount.

Tiergan's head appeared above the shadow magic, then the flash of Cynnwrf showed and Kynan flew through the air. Shadows caught him and kept him from cracking his skull on a boulder. He shot to his feet and ran at Tiergan, who faced Maren and rode on. Speeding toward her on horseback, Tiergan leaned low to drag the sword's tip in the ground.

"I don't like that look, Nix," Maren said, raising her voice over the cacophony of the battle. "Can we try something a bit more evil?" Maren poured fire into the magical bond between them, feeling the bump of heat in her heart and wand hand.

Nix laughed—deep, throaty, and altogether frightening—and whirled through the night sky. She flattened her ears, tucked her wings, and shot straight for the foul shadow lord.

Below her, the highly trained humans, shadow elves, mountain elves, and fae fought like wildfire, so fast and deadly, their strikes landing with precision at neck and thigh where the armor left a warrior vulnerable.

Tiergan drew Cynnwrf through the frosted ground. The earth between Kynan and Maren buckled. The scent of wet ground rose, and Afal was tossed left as the earth leapt up to roll toward the others.

Dropping her wand, Maren fell from the horse's

back and landed hard, the breath leaving her lungs in a painful rush. Nix vanished.

Panting and trying to breathe, Maren struggled to her feet.

Where was her wand? She searched the ripped-up ground desperately.

The Underworld's crust had risen to form hills between Kynan's forces. Tiergan's men pushed Maren and Kynan's forces back and sliced them down, one after another. Maren couldn't see who was where in the swirl of Kynan's and Tiergan's battling shadows.

It was so dark.

Was that a glimpse of Kynan's loaned sword and the indigo hue of Rhianne's magic? She thought she saw a flash of horned Werian leaping over a mound to attack but couldn't be sure.

Then the ground swallowed Maren whole.

Mud and roots churned over her body and smothered her completely. She coughed, dirt choking her. Her lungs burned, and she tried to move, but her limbs were trapped in wet earth, and she couldn't do more than pointlessly struggle.

Tiergan had buried her alive.

Pulling all her power in tightly, she then tried to push it out through her palms in an attempt to shift the cold earth. It didn't work.

A hand worked through the dark ground, and she fought to grab it, her heart pounding painfully and her head dizzy. The earth gave way, and she breathed deeply, so relieved to at least be alive for now. Her hand gripped warm fingers and she was pulled free.

"Kynan, I—"

Tiergan's grin drove iron through her soul. "Greetings, lady wife."

She stumbled backward, and he caught her.

"Oh. Apologies," he said. "You aren't yet my wife. I shouldn't put the cart before the horse, as you Upperworlders say." He held out an arm. "Shall we?"

Five warriors stood around him, their own gray shadows like lost specters at their backs. Tiergan gestured to his horse and Afal where they stood beside the eerily silent battlefield. Where was everyone? Only Tiergan's warriors in their pale leathers were visible in the wreck of ice and mounded earth.

The familiar grain of her wand peeked from an icy puddle of mud.

CHAPTER 41

S he launched herself forward, snatched up the wand, and raised it high. Fire leapt from the end, and Nix shimmered into form above them. Tiergan drew back, holding Cynnwrf, his glances going left and right as if he wasn't sure what to do next.

Kynan's voice shot across the torn earth, and then he appeared, face speckled with dirt and blood as he climbed over a mound. With a unit of his elves behind him and Ivar flying overhead, he rushed over new hills and crevices, heading her way. His dark magic snapped and swirled around him before reaching toward Tiergan. The peaks of Kynan's crown flickered high above his head, and he shouted, his face twisted in rage. Tiergan called out his name, and a dozen shadow elves in bone-white leathers rode Kynan down.

"No!" Maren's throat was on fire.

Kynan's shadows swelled high like a wave, then crashed over Tiergan's warriors. All dropped, lifeless, except two of the elves, one of whom raised his sword. Kynan cut the man down with a wide root of shadow magic, but something flashed in the dim.

Kynan fell.

A sob crawled from Maren's burning throat, and she went to one knee, unable to stand. No, he couldn't be...

Nix gnashed long teeth at Tiergan's head. His shadows peeled away, and Maren flicked her wand and let out a bright slash of crackling fire. Tiergan snarled, his leathers charred and his eyes wide. Lunging at him, Nix exhaled spirit-blue fire at his head, the magic tugging at Maren's bones and pulling at her heart. The pale flames rippled across his face, and if those flames had been live dragonfire, Tiergan would have been undone.

He shuddered and dropped Cynnwrf, and his skin went as light as scraped parchment.

Maren drew her wand back, then flung her hand forward, and her witchfire snaked across his exposed throat.

He staggered, gasping.

"Now, Maren!" Aury called out as she fought. "Finish him!" She spun her mage staff in a wide arc and sent icicles flying at a behemoth of a shadow elf. Moving faster than any creature that size should, the elf dodged the icicles and threw a boulder.

Maren ripped her gaze from the flying rock and pointed her wand at Tiergan.

His lip curled, showing his sharp incisor, then he launched forward, seized his sword, and hissed a phrase over the blade as he jabbed it into the mound beside him.

A shriek split the night.

Whirling, Maren screamed as the ground at Aury's feet turned into writhing roots. Pine bark grew over Aury's boots and legs. The earth magic sparked its way up her body, dark wood flying down her arms, covering them and every last finger. Her staff dropped to the mud as her neck became part of the new tree's trunk. The battle raged all around, Dorin fighting in his elven form, still bleeding.

Maren stood frozen as the bark grew over Aury cheeks, the wood almost black against her fair skin.

And then Aury was gone.

Tiergan had turned her into a tree.

Maren shivered hard, teeth clacking together, trying to gather her wits and call up Nix who had faded away once more.

Where was Brielle? Rhianne?

Rhianne climbed on a riderless horse as the ground beside her undulated. A pine sprouted beside her. Branches snatched her by the arms, and bark spread over her flesh and clothing. Werian cut down a shadow elf and ran toward her, shouting her name. The sound tore at Maren's already bleeding heart.

Maren spotted Brielle, who threw a short sword. The blade flew through the shadow-strewn battlefield and pinned one of Tiergan's fighters to the ground.

The earth trembled, and before Maren could throw her magic into the air to call Nix, Brielle's red hair disappeared, and only a slender pine stood in her place, bending in the frigid wind.

Pines grew all over the battlefield.

Only a tiny remnant of warriors fought on, and Maren couldn't see who still remained.

"Hafwen! Filip!" Maren was overwhelmed. She hadn't even seen Hafwen yet. Was she even alive?

Maren bent and vomited.

Where were they? She wasn't trained for this. What could she do? Nothing was working. She had failed them all.

Tiergan pointed Cynnwrf at Maren and uttered a phrase.

Vines erupted from the ground and stole her wand. She leapt for it, but the vines lashed her ankles. She ended up face-first in the frosty mud of the battlefield. His magical vines bound her wrists tightly at her back, and shadows lifted her, carrying her to him through the air.

Regret wrapped her more tightly than the vines and shadows.

If she had accepted Kynan, none of this would be happening.

The warriors walking on foot away from the pines that had once been the Upperworld army and toward their lord, Tiergan, dragged something behind them.

Kynan.

Her heart shuddered violently. He was alive.

His eyes were shut, and blood ran freely down his forehead and chin. No shadow magic flickered around him. His shadow crown remained with its black curls of power and golden sparks, but it was incredibly faint, fading in and out of view as they dropped him at Tiergan's feet.

"Will you kill him?" Maren hadn't meant to ask that question, but her mind was so scattered... Fear was a taste on her tongue, the color of her world, the filter through which everything flowed.

"That is up to you, darling," Tiergan said.

A whirling coil of shadows spun from the forest at the far end of the field and came to rest beside Tiergan. The coil frayed slightly, and there was Hafwen. Her eyes were wide open—one gray, the other golden metal—and her hair flew around her face and body, blown by the shadows encircling her.

"Is he alive?" Hafwen asked.

Maren knew she meant Kynan. "Yes." Shadows laced her throat and tightened like a grip.

Hafwen's head dropped in what Maren supposed was relief.

Glaring at Tiergan, Maren said very quietly, "If you don't return the Upperworlders to their original form, I will refuse the Binding in any and every way I can."

Tiergan tilted his head and studied her. "So you agree not to fight this as long as I restore your loved ones and free High King Kynan?" He said the last two words like they made him sick.

What choice was there? "Yes."

With Cynnwrf's tip, Tiergan drew a runic shape in the iced mud. The ground rolled under everyone's feet, further spooking the horses and sending the remaining wyverns scattering into the sky. Was Ivar alive?

Maren squinted, straining to see who stood and what the magic would do. Would Tiergan trick them? Or hold to this one agreement?

The new pines disappeared in great clouds of yellow pollen, bits of swirling rock, and dust. Aury, Brielle, and Rhianne—no longer trees, but themselves once more—stood along with the Upperworlder army and the princes who were like brothers to Maren. Some warriors looked side to side in confusion as their fellows exclaimed in relief or rage, others embraced or took up arms, readying to fight again.

"Behave, Upperworlders, or you'll never see your princesses and princes again. And I might just decide to tighten the Awenydd's restraints and watch her struggle to breathe for a while. A half-dead Awenydd might be enough to save our realms. I'm not completely certain." Tiergan tapped his chin like he was considering it.

"You're a madman," Maren hissed.

A crack sounded, and even Tiergan appeared shocked as ice suddenly sped over the rise and crossed the newly turned earth. The needles on every pine in sight glistened with fresh ice. The horses stomped, their hooves clattering against the hard ground.

All was gray.

All was ice.

A nauseating calm flooded Maren's senses, her ears buzzing, wand hand humming with unspent power, eyes dry as ash. If only Kynan would wake and she could see his gaze...it would give her strength. She knew it.

"Release me, King Tiergan," she uttered past the

tight vines and shadows at her neck. "It is past time we end this."

A howling pealed through the moors, and Maren fisted her hands, knowing immediately what that sound meant.

Hungry spirits.

CHAPTER 42

"**I** need my wand. Now." Yes, she'd driven back a hungry spirit without a wand once while in the woods with Kynan, but this didn't sound like one spirit.

Proving her right, a veritable horde of empty-eyed, gaping-mouthed spirits poured out of the forest.

General Aeron called out in the shadow elf language, and his forces—Kynan's army—echoed him. They swarmed around Maren.

Tiergan nodded his approval at the army protecting her, his movements stiff with what she guessed was fright. The vines and shadows around her loosened completely.

But beyond him, a slender shadow slid under Brielle's pale chin, lingering at her neck.

Tiergan glanced at Maren, making certain she understood. She inclined her head. Yes, she knew. If she did something Tiergan didn't like, that shadow would slice through Brielle's throat and end her life.

The earth cracked and churned at Maren's feet, and her wand appeared in the dirt. She grabbed its cold length and readied herself as best she could, allowing that sickening calm to press back her fear.

Rolling shadows—with none of the deep and heavy power of Kynan's or Tiergan's—flowed from the surrounding shadow elves and created an undulating wall around Maren. Pinpricks of energy lit along her arms and face.

"You're feeding me power?" she asked them, just now noticing the mayor of Hwyl in the gathering.

Hafwen almost smiled inside her prison of shadow, and guilt hit Maren's heart. She should have demanded Hafwen's freedom and—

The hungry spirits reached the small barrier the shadow elves had created.

Maren lifted her wand. She called up fire and air and spun her wand high above her head. The spirits began to draw life from everyone present. Aeron clutched his chest and tumbled as Tiergan shuddered and Brielle called Dorin's name. Dorin sat at her feet, his side wet with blood as he shuddered. Even if Kynan didn't survive, Maren thought, her heart clenching, she would save his people. She could do this.

"Goddess Nix!" she shouted into the bitterly cold air.

The spirits pulled energy from her as well, their howling crashing against her eardrums and their presence sucking her dry. The fingers clasping her wand weakened, and she dropped the magical weapon.

Gasping, dots swimming in front of her eyes, she bent to retrieve it and thrust it into the air again.

"Nix! I call upon you as the Awenydd!"

Magic seared its way from Maren's heart and forehead and flowed into her wand hand. Fire lit the oaken wand and illuminated the faces of those around her, those being drained to death by the hungry spirits. Cheeks devoid of any color, Kynan lay still on the ground at Tiergan's feet. Brielle's lips were blue as she rasped an unintelligible word. Hafwen shuddered inside her prison, and the shadows flickered in and out like Kynan's crown.

The spirits were killing them all. Good and bad. Wrong and right. It didn't matter. The hunger dealt out by the poison affecting the Sacred Oak had possessed the spirits, and they would not be turned away. Maren didn't have enough magic. Sweat beaded on her upper lip and trickled down her back as she held her flaming wand high and whispered Nix's name over and over. It wasn't enough power to bring the dragon goddess. It was over. Maren was going to lose consciousness and die beside them all.

A snapping sounded at the tip of the wand, and the air cracked. Above the horde, Nix's glittering, spirit-bright scales sparkled into life, and her pearly wings unfurled. Hope lit Maren up, and she urged more of her struggling magic into the spellwork. She should have been speaking a spell, giving voice to her wish, but no words rose to her cold lips.

Nix roared. The spirits bent their heads as one, then they all turned to face the spirit dragon. Magic tugged at Maren's chest, and she fought to stay on her feet. Nix unleashed spirit dragonfire onto the horde. The fire rippled in ghostly rivulets from Nix's toothed maw. Grief pressed into Maren's magic, making the fire sputter, but the spirits had to be put down. It was the only way; she'd seen that in the forest with Kynan, and he'd said as much. But there were so many, so many souls who could have lived in peace and goodwill…

The dragonfire intensified, and the power of it blew cool magic over Maren's face, tossing her mussed and knotted hair away from her forehead. The fire washed the spirits in a deep blue, and they shimmered like fish scales as their mouths closed in unison, the howling cut off, leaving only the whoosh of the wind and the snapping sound of Nix's fire. The dark holes where their eyes had been lightened and faded until the spirits looked like themselves again.

Maren tried to speak, awe stealing her shout of hope.

"Awenydd." A small boy spirit looked at her. "Your call to the goddess has saved us."

"Thank you, Awenydd," another spirit said. "And thanks to the goddess Nix!"

The spirits collectively sighed and began streaming back the way they'd come.

"You did it," a deep voice said.

Maren's breath caught. It was Kynan, standing, eyes open. Thank the Source and all the stars. He was smiling at her, smiling like they weren't facing probable death by some evil ice and trapped by a madman who wielded a legendary, unbeatable sword.

She grinned back, snagging this moment for them because what had been blooming between them would end now.

Tiergan drew a quick rune in the earth, and stones crawled from the ground, joined like rope, and encircled Kynan's wrists.

Kynan grimaced as if he were in great pain. Perhaps the earth magic manacles were hurting his power. The idea turned her stomach because she could easily imagine what that felt like after her experience with Magebane, the poison that a past enemy had wielded and the same foul stuff that had created this entire problem. She recalled the wrongness of the absence of her magic, the feeling of being scraped clean like a melon at the market.

Swallowing, she forced that terrible calm over herself. "Let's crack on then, Tiergan."

Kynan winced, a confused and terribly sad smile stretching his bloodied lips as if he appreciated her blunt approach.

Tiergan's gaze went flat. He lifted his arms, and shadows turned Maren's world to black.

CHAPTER 43

The air was as sharp as a well-honed knife, and it cut at Maren's skin. She and Tiergan stood at the Spirit Well. Maren guessed Tiergan had either thrown her on a horse and magically kept her sleeping as they rode hard to this place or that he had used shadow magic to shift their position.

A few steps away, Hafwen looked down into the half-frozen well, her body mostly cloaked in Tiergan's dark hands of power. "It will be gone soon, King Tiergan," Hafwen said, likely speaking of the well's imminent destruction. "You must act in haste, or those hungry spirits will rise again. I don't think any kind of magic will save us then. The air is so empty of power..."

No one else was nearby.

What had Tiergan done with everyone?

Shiver after shiver rattled Maren's bones, a blend of fear, dread, and magic shattering her thoughts even as she formed them. Two of Tiergan's men approached, boots crunching over the frozen ground, and they held

Kynan between them. Tiergan grinned cruelly at Kynan and then at her. She hated him so very, very much. She refused to look up at him again; she couldn't stand the light of victory in his eyes.

Would the Binding even work with this soul-eating hatred surrounding her heart?

There was no way to push the hatred away. It was too powerful, a veritable part of her like her wand hand or the color of her eyes. The Binding would either work or they'd all die, and Maren simply tried to hold on to the one image that gave her a reason to keep on breathing.

She imagined Brielle, Aury, and the others around the fire at Balaur Castle.

Someone is rolling dice, and Filip's deep laugh echoes across the stone walls. Brielle shows Dorin something half-covered in dirt, an artifact she dug up in one of her regular trips to the far reaches of the mountains. Her elven tongue is so fast now that Maren can't even grasp a word of their conversation.

The image shifted. *There is Kynan walking in the woods beside Hafwen. Ivar flies overhead, and Hafwen discusses the new orchards she has planned for her rebuild of her estate. Kynan's frown and downcast eyes show the way he misses Maren, but he still walks easily and smiles occasionally at something Hafwen says.*

It was for them that Maren continued to breathe, to live, to be the hope of the world.

Focusing on what was actually happening now, she turned her gaze to Kynan.

He shifted his stance so that he was looking only at

her with his body angled away from Tiergan as if to pretend he wasn't there.

Tears filled Kynan's black eyes, not falling but making the ruby depths glisten like gems dropped into a spring river. "You know what I will do while you survive for me." His voice was deep and sharp.

"I do." Maren's chest was hollow. The pain was similar to the agony of losing her parents.

Kynan would search for the Calon y Dderwen, the great crystal that could release her from Tiergan without destroying the realms, the realms that would take a long while to finish healing after such damage. But that venture involved little more than a legend and a prayer. All they knew was that the crystal had been thrown into the Dark Sea and that it could balance the magics in the world.

She set a hand on Kynan's stubbled jaw, her fingertips lying on the smooth, angled planes of his high cheekbone. He gave her the best of smiles, a rare Kynan smile. A wave of desire and love swept through her. It was darkly funny to think that in another life, their biggest obstacle might have been their cultures—her humanness and his elven blood. Despite it all, a feathery sensation tickled her stomach, and she smiled back. He cared for her. Deeply. And she cared for him. Even if their love was fully doomed, it was still a beautiful feeling to experience. Perhaps more so because it was a path they wouldn't have the chance to explore. Though she would always hope...

"Enough." Tiergan's voice cut the sweet sadness and

turned everything bitter. "I'm growing ill watching this inane display."

Rage sparked to life inside Maren's wand hand, surging into her wand, and anger heated the spot between her eyes. She glared at Tiergan. "Someday, I will find a way to silence you."

"By placing your mouth on mine, dearest wife-to-be?" Tiergan fluttered his honey eyelashes and flashed his elven incisors.

The guards grunted as Kynan jerked toward Tiergan, but Maren pressed Kynan back, her hands on his broad chest. Under his leathers, his chest moved as if he were about to explode.

"Let me end him," Kynan said. "Damn the realms."

Hafwen made a choking sound of shock. "The Spirit Well is icing over."

"Someday, you'll get your chance, High King Kynan," Maren said, hoping the use of his crowned title would irritate Tiergan. Kynan had said once a person was crowned, it was permanent, another type of magical binding. Tiergan might do his best to rule, and he would definitely ruin the land, but he'd never be its true king.

Tiergan growled, low in the back of his throat.

Success, she thought, as petty as it was. "Someday," Maren continued, "we will sort this out properly, but for now," she tried to keep on speaking like she was as confident as Aury, but her voice trembled, "for now, we must do what we must do."

Keeping his gaze on Tiergan, Kynan broke one of his stone manacles with a flash of shadow and snaked a hand around the back of Maren's neck. His fingers drew shivers to the surface of her skin, and her body thrummed with desire and love and fear for him.

"Don't give up," he whispered before he crushed his lips to hers.

He kissed her with the desperation of the moment. Maren's eyes tried to well with tears, and her heart made a good show of clawing its way out of her chest and into his. Every fiber of her being wanted to be as close to Kynan as a person could be. She wanted to be Bound to him. To be forever wedded to him. Not because of any magic, but because she loved him and he loved her.

The guards pulled him back.

"I love you, Kynan," she said softly. "It might be a bit late for that, but I do."

A half sob, half chuckle rumbled from him. "And I love you, Maren, witch and queen and hope of the realms. Find a way to stay bright in the darkness, for you are the only light in my life."

Tiergan began to drag Maren even closer to the Spirit Well, but she went willingly and made his struggles look foolish. They knelt together, Maren glancing toward Kynan. Her stomach rolled, and she bit back a plea for help. There was no help coming. She was the savior here, and it wasn't a joyous place to be, that was certain.

The icy ground cracked under her knees as she joined hands with Tiergan. His gray eyes sparkled with triumph. She started to pull away.

"No, no, no. You may be his queen, but you are mine now, and this Binding demands complete devotion. You can either be my wife in every way or reside in my dungeon."

She was going to be sick. "I choose the dungeon. I'd rather sleep beside a thousand rats than beside a monster like you." She closed her eyes and breathed through her nose until the nausea abated.

"We'll see how you feel after a year or two."

Bile rose in her throat. She opened her eyes and locked gazes with Kynan. The determination in his eyes fed her strength. He hadn't given up.

One of Tiergan's men drove Cynnwrf between the circle of their joined hands. Though she knew she wouldn't be able to claim the sword because she wasn't a shadow lord. A shadow snaked along Kynan's neck, threatening and poised to kill. If she grabbed the sword and threw it to Kynan, could they possibly change this outcome?

He glanced at Cynnwrf, then at her. "Think not on that, Awenydd," he whispered.

Maren gritted her teeth and tried to think around her fear and anger.

Hafwen began to recite a spell. She spoke in the shadow elf tongue, but Maren felt the power of the magic dust her skin and seep into her very bones.

The sword glowed bright blue, and a sad song echoed from the spirits undulating in the well's shimmering water.

The Underworld faded, and then Maren was standing alone in a place of melting heat.

CHAPTER 44

Maren gasped, unable to take a good breath because of the intense heat. Orange stars shot through this strange place's sky so quickly that they trailed light in long lines. This was the place Kynan had spoken of, the realm she would only survive if she followed the voice of the shadow lord to whom she was now Bound.

Come, Awenydd, Tiergan's voice boomed through the weighty air. *Don't delay. Don't give up, or your Upperworlders will die before the perishing realms have their chance to kill them off. I told Lady Hafwen we wouldn't be long. If we tarry here, my guards will slowly end the lives of each of your loved ones. That mouthy redhead might already be silenced. You don't want that same fate for each of them, now do you?*

Brielle! No! The heat fogged Maren's eyes, and she stumbled on the sharp rocks of the ground. Falling to her hands and knees, she coughed. Her mind shattered like a dropped vase. Why was she here? She couldn't breathe. The flying stars made her sick. Bile rose in the back of her scorched throat. Perhaps if she just closed her eyes and stopped trying to stand, maybe some of the agony would leave her. Yes, she could lie down here and simply take a moment's rest. She couldn't be expected to live through this.

Suddenly, the heat abated and she was falling.

Dropping from an impossible height.

Swallowing, gulping air, she plummeted so quickly that the very force of the air threatened to peel her skin away.

Awenydd? Did you reach the place of the air element yet? Tiergan's voice warbled and grew almost too distorted for her to understand. And she was still falling, falling, falling. *You truly are taking your time, Awenydd. Hurry on, now.*

Hours or moments passed. She had no idea. Everything was horror.

Time is up, I'm afraid. Come to me now or die with the rest of the realms.

A spark of clarity melded the pieces of Maren's mind back together. "How?" She shouted the question into the abyss, the air snatching her word before it could fly. "How do I find you?"

She envisioned his horrible face, cruel eyes, and foul mouth. She pushed her will into seeing him. Magic surged through her blood like a lightning strike, and she gasped.

The fall ceased.

Dizzy, she blinked, coughed again, and realized she was kneeling with Tiergan beside the Spirit Well, their hands still linked. Her soul was firmly back in her body. Tiergan's power flowed from his hands to hers, his shadow magic allowing her to see into the areas of lower light near the base of the Sacred Oak's roots and into the woods beyond. She felt stronger, as if she could leap over ten men and climb the highest mountain.

Tiergan smiled like a satisfied cat.

"Stay, Awenydd," Hafwen said, her voice careful and grave.

The magic passed between their joined hands faster and faster until it became a continuous hum of power. The sword flashed a bright white.

Hafwen raised her wand. "And so the Binding lives!"

Magic blasted from inside Maren's body, and the air and earth shook. The well sparkled, and the gray ice on the Sacred Oak's roots melted into nothing. Deep green spread from the well's edges and coursed across the ground. Flowers in a riot of colors, thick clover, glowing mushrooms, small insects, birds—life itself rose from the healed realm. The air held the properly crisp feel of autumn's breath, and Maren took it in and was grateful, but still grieved.

"It is done," Kynan whispered, and the blend of pain and joy in his words cut Maren in two.

She glared at Tiergan, then looked from Hafwen to Kynan. Tiergan would take her to his castle on the far side of the Dark Sea. She knew that. And no doubt, she'd be treated like a prisoner or worse. But death wouldn't find her there. She would escape and make things right.

The wind stirred in her ears, the sounds turning into words as the scent of magic drifted past Maren's face.

"We aren't going anywhere," the wind said in Rhianne's magicked voice.

Heart pounding, Maren looked into the near distance and saw them all—Brielle and Dorin, Filip and Aury, Rhianne, Werian, and Costel—held fast by Tiergan's men but alive and standing on their own. They weren't leaving. They'd keep fighting for her.

Kynan glanced at them, then at her. He nodded. *We will come for you. Have no doubt,* he said into her mind.

Maren stared Tiergan down. She would never, ever surrender. "It is done when I say it is done."

Readers,

I hope you enjoyed Stolen by the Shadow King! Order book two, Rise of the Fire Queen today! My family and I thank you for your support. I had such a great time writing this Hades and Persephone inspired book. I felt a little bit like Kynan was a Darcy version of Hades. haha

If you'd like a sneak peek at book two as well as a prequel scene (March 2022), sign up for my newsletter at https://www.alishaklapheke.com/free-prequel-1 The second book in this duology will be out as soon as I can write it. I'm doing my best. I promise. :)

. . .

IN THE MEANTIME, IF YOU'D LIKE TO CHECK OUT THE other books in the Kingdoms of Lore world, start with *Enchanting the Elven Mage*. It's Aury and Filip's story. I put a sample below for you.

THANK YOU FOR READING!

LOVE,
   Alisha

ENCHANTING THE ELVEN MAGE
   Kingdoms of Lore Book One

THERE WERE ONLY TWO GOOD THINGS ABOUT THE winter solstice celebration at the fae court. Wine and wine.

Aury didn't long for the drink overmuch herself, but it was definitely her ally. Wine turned watchful eyes blurry and slowed cruel, pinching fingers.

Wishing she were still in the barn with the horses, she gripped a rough crystal goblet of spiced red and forced a smile as her aunt, the Fae Queen, strolled through the great hall in a trailing gown the color of pine needles. The queen's hair had been braided artfully around her twisting amethyst-and-ink-hued horns.

Though she was a nightmare crafted of snide remarks and cold looks, Aury had to admit the lady was gorgeous.

The queen's gaze flicked away, focusing on her glittering court, and Aury slid out of the hall and into the corridor.

Her fine slippers were nearly silent on the mosaic tiles, but pureblood fae had far better hearing than her half-fae, half-human ears, so she kept the wine as some sort of excuse to be wandering. She crept onward, stealing down the passageway on the sides of her feet and holding her breath. She only needed a peek at the queen's court itinerary to see why in the world she was to be sent on a mysterious journey in the morning.

Nearly to the doors now...

A mewling sounded, and Aury's heart jumped. She turned to see a calico ball of fluff climbing the curtains.

"Oh, no. You can't be here, little love." She set her wine on the floor, then detached the kitten from the silken drapes. It was the runt from the barn cat's last litter. "The servants will beat you with a broom if they see these claw marks."

Doing her best to keep quiet and silently praying to the Source the kitten's mews weren't heard, she hurried to the nearest window on the outer wall of the palace. Unlatching the locks, she gently deposited the kitten on the pebble path that led to the stables and the gardens beyond.

"Go find your mother, little love. Hurry now!"

The kitten mewed once more, then ran clumsily toward the barn.

Aury exhaled, closing the window and going back to her wine and her mission to discover where the queen was sending her tomorrow.

In the near dark of the corridor, her foot caught on something. Knee hitting the floor, she lost hold of the goblet and the wine flew, splattering red like blood over the stone walls.

"Oh, sorry!" Bathilda said, even though she was never sorry. "I didn't mean to trip you like that." Her lip curled as she looked down her nose at Aury. "Let me help you up, half-breed."

Ducking out of Bathilda's reach and away from her sharp nails, Aury grabbed her slightly cracked goblet, then shot to her feet. "I'm fine, but thanks ever so much."

But the pureblood wasn't to be thwarted. Bathilda snatched her arm roughly and pulled her toward the great hall. "Your presence is required, Aurora."

Bathilda thrust Aury into the great hall, then grabbed a servant. "Take that hideous necklace off of the half-breed," she said to the servant.

The servant tore Aury's necklace, sending the tiny, flame-colored pearls of the dragon goddess Nix rolling across the tiles. Tears burned Aury's eyes, and her neck throbbed where the broken chain had bit into her skin. Nix was the goddess of fire and festivity, and Aury had always loved the hilarious tales her cousin told of the long-ago dragon shifter.

Bathilda pointed a finger at Aury's face. "Don't even start to tell me that your dear cousin Werian bought you that necklace. I don't believe he cares for a half-breed like you. You lie and lie, a deceit only those with human blood can manage. You're disgusting, and you're a thief."

Werian had indeed given Aury the necklace, and she'd treasured it as a symbol of the one individual who actually seemed to care for her. "I've never stolen a thing in my entire life," she said, meeting Bathilda's glare with one of her own.

"Save your breath. I don't believe you. I'll make certain you're punished for stealing tomorrow."

"But tomorrow, I'm leaving. The queen told me so herself."

Bathilda shrugged. "You'll be back. And I'll be waiting in the shadows." Her cruel smile sent chills down Aury's back. Bathilda crooked a finger at the servant, who had quietly stepped away. "Fetch a washing bowl. Aurora has stable mud under her fingernails."

Aury glared. "Better than the blood of innocents."

Bathilda laughed coldly. "What do you know of innocence? I saw you sneaking toward the queen's rooms."

"At least I don't sneak toward her consort."

Bathilda raised a hand to slap her. Aury fought the urge to flinch, and somehow, she managed it. Bathilda noticed the queen's wandering gaze and relaxed her arm.

The servant took Aury's goblet, then shoved a bowl of water into her hands as Bathilda sauntered away to join in the festivities.

A buzz traveled through Aury as she shook off her encounter with Bathilda, a blend of curiosity and joy. Tomorrow, she was leaving the fae court for the second time in her entire life. Finally, she'd have a break from this place and see more of the human regions of Lore.

As she pulled her hands out of the wash bowl, a deep, golden light passed through the uneven lines of the water's reflection. She paused, lingering over the basin. A cool tingling spread over her body, down her arms, then into the tips of her fingers as a quiet, rushing sound echoed in her ears. It was a sound like the waves she'd heard at the Sea's Claw during her only visit to the ocean. The reflection in the bowl of water showed her face—that of a nineteen-year-old with pointed ears, blue eyes, and silver hair.

But her features faded away. Another face appeared.

Her stomach lifted like she'd jumped from the balcony of the Agate Palace. "What in the name of Nix's Fire..."

It was a man—handsome, with a slightly crooked nose, as if he'd been in a few fights. She couldn't see his ears. He could have been human, fae, or elf. His storm-gray eyes flashed below jet-black eyebrows. Wind Aury couldn't feel or hear tousled the man's dark hair. His image tugged at her, demanding attention. The vision in the ripples was hazy, but stubble showed on his strong chin, and his lips were surprisingly soft-looking and full for such a man.

The vision expanded to reveal that he was holding an axe and pacing around a much larger fellow. Through the inconsistent haze of the golden light on the water, the black-haired man's mouth curved into a grin shaped like his opponent's mountain saber—sharp, dangerous.

The handsome man lifted an eyebrow. The axe slashed through the image.

Aury gasped, heart drumming in her ears alongside that strange rushing sound. The Fae Queen glanced her way, her cold eyes filled with a level of disdain only pureblood fae could manage.

The servants took the bowl away and left Aury standing with her refilled wine goblet, frozen and panicked. Did the queen sense the puzzling inside her head? Was she going mad? It was certainly within the realm of possible outcomes.

Horns sounded, and Aury jumped, nearly spilling her wine on Werian, who had just approached.

"Do we truly need to bring down the skies for every announcement?" she asked him, tugging a length of silver tinsel from his black horns and hoping he didn't notice the absence of the dragon goddess necklace. She didn't want to make him angry on her behalf. Not tonight.

His eyes held mischief, the same look he used to have when he sketched human villages and ships for her when they were young. The Fae Queen had never approved. "You know how my mother loves her drama."

"The king and queen of Lore!" the herald shouted.

Aury looked to Werian in question, but he just shrugged, his gaze skirting away. "This should be interesting," she murmured.

The Fae Queen approached the royal retinue with open arms, as though the king and queen of Lore were friends, but everyone knew the Fae Queen had no friends. She had allies. Entertainers. Kin. The human

329

rulers weren't the last two, so they must have been the first. Allies to the fae court.

"What do they do to make her smile like that?" Aury asked Werian.

"They control the farmland and vineyards. My mother may like rubies and intrigue most," Werian said, "but she also enjoys a nice braid of light bread and spiced red wine. You two have that in common at least." He raised an eyebrow at her empty goblet.

She elbowed him. "I can't put up with you pure types without proper intoxication."

He placed a hand on his chest and shut his eyes briefly. "I understand." His gaze flicked to where the king and two queens were chatting it up. "If it weren't for the human army of Lore, we fae would've been ground into dust by our enemies."

"Why are the human rulers here?" This was the first she'd seen of them. They didn't come around here, supposedly because of an old grievance with the Matchweaver Witch that had happened around the time when Aury was born.

In his youth, the human king had probably been a fine-looking man with flaxen hair, but now his beard looked stained, as if he smoked a pipe a little too often. He held a water mage staff that was covered in runes.

The human queen's eyes were soft, but her mouth had the hard lines of someone who did more frowning than smiling.

"I don't like them," Aury said.

Werian's gaze landed hard on her face.

"Do I have something in my teeth?" She looked around for a pitcher to fill her goblet.

Werian didn't answer; he only crossed his arms and watched his mother talk with the human rulers. "I have loved you, Aury," he finally said, his voice a whisper. "You are my dearest cousin. And a friend. Remember that."

A cold finger of dread dragged across Aury's neck. "Are you drunk?" Of course she knew he cared for her. She loved him too. But to say it like that, with that sadness... Her stomach clenched. "What are you not telling me?" she hissed.

"I was bound to keep the secret, Aury. Remember that, as well."

"What?"

Werian stepped back as the human rulers approached. She hadn't realized they were walking toward her, and now, here they were, and she felt unsteady, for once wishing she hadn't had all that wine.

She bowed clumsily. The Fae Queen, standing behind the retinue, looked skyward and sighed as if Aury's manners were the worst sort of torture.

The king took Aury's chin between his thumb and finger and studied her face. The urge to whinny like a bought horse nearly overcame her good sense. "You are a lovely woman, Aurora Rose."

Rose? She'd never been called Rose. That was...

The human queen smiled, her perfume rolling in like fog. "You have my second name, my dear."

"Why would I be named for you?" Aury asked. "With respect, of course."

The human king and queen traded a look and laughed like only royal people can. Aury forced a smile. What was happening? She looked for Werian. He stood beside his mother, his head lowered as he spoke to a servant.

The king took Aury's arm and looped it through his. "Let's take a walk through the gardens, Aurora Rose. We have much to discuss."

She let him fairly drag her across the great hall with the two queens trailing. Unless this king fellow had something to say about horses, pain-in-the-arse fae, fig tarts, or wine, they had absolutely nothing to discuss. "I'm sorry, but what are we talking about?"

"The two greatest forces, my dear. Magic and marriage. Specifically...yours."

And suddenly, the emptiness of Aury's goblet became the least of her worries.

Get Enchanting the Elven Mage to continue reading Aury and Filip's story!

ACKNOWLEDGMENTS

Thank you to Myra, Erica, Paige, Rachel, Megan, Ali, Laura, Melissa, Melissa Frain, and many, many more who helped me turn this idea into a book. Thank you to my Denners, the Turtles (Babs ftw), and my MT mushrooms for all the brainstorming and emotional support. Thank you to my amazing Typo Hunters including Andra, Cheryl, Emily, Liz, Gale, and many more. Thank you to my Welsh translation team—any errors are my own. Thank you to all the kind folks in the indie publishing world for the advice and assistance. I love my job. Thank YOU, for reading. I hope I could give you a little escape from the crazy world.

Milton Keynes UK
Ingram Content Group UK Ltd.
UKHW040121140224
437791UK00005B/400

9 798985 276428